HIGH BEAM

HIGH BEAM

A D.I. Mahoney Mystery

SJ Brown

Printed in the United States of America by BookMasters, Inc
Ashland OH
December 2014

Rev. date: 11/21/2014

To order additional copies of this book, contact:
Xlibris
1-800-455-039
www.Xlibris.com.au
Orders@Xlibris.com.au
663072

PROLOGUE

Wednesday 3rd March 11am

It was rare these days for Max Watson to have any time to himself. As a builder he found his services were called upon even more than ever, as home owners organized kitchen and bathroom renovations to make their properties more appealing to prospective vendors. Although he preferred to construct a dwelling from scratch, he was never going to knock back the avalanche of jobs that came his way to spruce up the interiors of suburban houses: it was money for jam. The property boom that had gripped Hobart for much of the 'noughties' had shown little sign of abating, despite the effects of the GFC. If anything, it spurred it on as people put their faith in property as an investment. They were shying away from the share market as they looked on in dismay at their superannuation funds careering backwards.

After the gloom of the previous decade, Tasmania was no longer an economic 'basket case' and, to put it mildly, good tradesmen had been coining it for quite a while. Mates who were electricians and plumbers down at Margate had work coming out their ears. Blokes with philosophy degrees were driving cabs while anyone with half a clue in the building sector was doing really, really well. How he would love to run into his old careers teacher now.

Life was good. His three kids were finished school and all had decent jobs. The wife seemed pretty happy though it was hard to tell sometimes. She'd taken to doing an interior design course and had come up with plenty of useful suggestions for the nearly completed 'Ponderosa' they were building for themselves on ten acres at Acton. Handy for the beach and close to the Royal Hobart Golf Club, it was still only twenty minutes from town. And there was easily sufficient room out the back for his pet project: a lap pool.

Today he was going to spend some 'me-time' on the bobcat shifting the soil to create the hole where the twenty meter in-ground pool would soon be. As always, it was an early start for him. Thanks to Tassie's benign summer, the swarthy six-footer only needed to wear boots, King Gee shorts and his blue work singlet. After an hour, he had already shifted a fair old quantity of dirt and rocks but now he had to hop off the machine to work away at a huge stone that was stubbornly lodged in the soil strata. By jimmying away with the crowbar, he intended to loosen it just enough so the excavator's shovel could get under it and heave it up and away.

Impatient to get it done, Max had neglected to put on gloves. Out here in the semi-rural countryside it was a measure he should normally have taken. He was one of a small segment of the population that was critically allergic to the sting of jack jumpers. These centimeter long earthbound insects delivered a nasty sting to everybody but to some the poison could be fatal if not treated quickly. Another of the perils of the Australian terrain.

Having loosened the soil around the boulder, Max turfed the crowbar aside and leant over to prise the stone away from its spot. Just as he braced himself to pull with his arms, he was struck with a sharp and very intense jabbing pain. Leaping back, he saw several of his enemies on his right forearm. He brushed them quickly away but they had already got him good and proper. He had known this pain before. When he was six he'd inadvertently trodden on a nest of 'jackies' which had hurt like hell and had generated this lifelong allergy. He quickly checked the rest of his limbs for the little buggers and was glad to see none.

There was no need to panic; he knew he was severely allergic and therefore prone to anaphylactic shock if bitten. As an essential precaution last month, he had already put an epi-pen in the electricity meter box for just this eventuality. Administered correctly, this device shot a dose of adrenalin into the body's system thereby alleviating the otherwise inevitable swelling of the frontal air passages leading to suffocation.

Max breathed steadily and walked in a measured way around to the side of the house. Was he imagining a slight constriction in his throat? If he stayed calm and jabbed the needle correctly into his thigh he would survive: there was a foolproof solution. As he opened the latch on the meter box, his stolid approach took an extreme jolt. The epi-pen wasn't there.

Oh, Christ almighty, where was it? Only put it there last week. Now was the time to panic. He couldn't shout for help…his throat really was tightening. His mobile! He ran over to his van…stuff worrying about his pulse rate now. Opening the passenger door, he found it in the usual spot by the gear shift. Pressing the green button, he couldn't believe his eyes for the second time that morning. No charge. No recharger. Nothing. Dead. As he rasped his penultimate breath he thought of his old man. On his last he simply keeled over. Gone.

CHAPTER 1

Thursday 4ᵗʰ March 10am

It would have been practically impossible for James Cartwright to be feeling anything other than buoyant as he strode along the walkway from the Morris Miller Library to the lecture theatre. The planets were aligning themselves. By mid-morning a bright day had developed: the sort of Hobart day that encouraged shirtsleeves but did not quite justify a trip to the beach. A visiting Sydneysider would recognize the sort of weather enjoyed by that metropolis in May and be grateful for the lack of humidity. Cartwright felt alive: his New Year's exercise regimen was still in place (remarkably so, given the track record of previous attempts) and the flat stomach and more upright posture were testimony to regular attendance at Pilates classes. They were not cheap but the feeling of well-being they helped to generate made it money well spent. An investment in the temple.

And all the kit for his freshly developed enthusiasm for bike riding had stretched his credit card as well but the general benefits were certain…fat loss, stronger legs and the acquisition of a completely new group of mates. The intestinal broom of a detox diet for all of January had also helped him tidy up his body. He felt sharper, slept better and was more confident in himself. *Mens sana in corpore sano*: his body had caught up to his mind.

As he neared the Stanley Burbury Building, he noticed a lone female sitting at one of the refectory's outdoor tables. Recalled she was a regular participant at some of his Pilates classes. Having surreptitiously ogled her figure through the summer, this was an opportunity to exchange more than a quick greeting. He paused by her table. "Hello there, how are you?"

She looked up from the newspaper and, he was pleased to note, recognized him straight away. "Oh, hi. You're a hard-core man, aren't you?"

Cartwright was gratified she acknowledged him and delighted the conversation was already skirting the edges of innuendo. "Yes. I thought I knew you from our attempts to cultivate inner strength." Take a cerebral approach. "I'm Jim, by the way. May I join you?"

"Sure. I'm stuck on a clue so a diversion would be good. I'm Amanda." She offered her hand. "Nice to meet you."

Cartwright shook hands with what he hoped was a firm, but not a macho pressure. Her skin felt smooth. This was going well already. He sat down. "So cryptic or straight?" In support of this witticism was a quick rising of the eyebrows and a half-smile.

Amanda wondered why he was smirking. Figuring the attempted quip to be a clumsy effort to camouflage his eagerness, she decided to play him along. Why not? She was a bit bored anyway and her lecture was still thirty minutes away. "Cryptic. I prefer complexity. Don't want to take the path most travelled, do we?"

"Absolutely not. Thinking outside the square is definitely the way to go." This conversation could get very interesting. Get the minds to meet and the bodies would follow. "That's one of the things I love about Inspector Morse. Perfect mix. Crosswords, beers and an open mind." And an intangible appeal to willing females, he could have added but managed to contain himself.

She had no idea to whom he was referring but understood exactly what he was talking about. Subtle as a sledgehammer. Why not ask her straight out to screw him? It was obviously what he wanted but not what he was going to get. Still, there was no need for him to know that…just yet. "Definitely. Flexibility is the key, isn't it? That's what opens doors. Not much use sticking to the tried and true." A Greek bearing gifts. She leaned forward in her chair. "You've really toned up in the last few weeks. Looking good."

Cartwright was certain this had tipped over into fully-fledged flirtation. "Why, thank you ma'am." Rhett Butler had come to town. "You look as if you should be the instructor." She smiled straight at him. Nothing ventured, nothing gained. "Would you fancy a drink one evening soon?"

"OK, that would be good." She could easily stretch that out to a nice dinner somewhere. Let his presumptuousness foot the bill. "Give me your mobile number and I'll call you."

Cartwright nodded. "Oh, good, here you go." He scribbled it on a slip of paper and handed it to her. "Right then, I'd better be off. See you sometime quite soon." He stood, collected his satchel and strode off with a spring in his step. Amanda turned her attention back to the newspaper and waited for her friend.

Cartwright went up the stairwell and entered the James Macaulay Auditorium. The 11.10 lecture in Australian Political Systems for an audience of approximately one hundred first year political science students would be starting in half an hour, to be delivered by his good self. His style was to arrive early, set up his notes at the lectern, check that the PowerPoint display functioned correctly and then sit quietly on the stage reading the opinion columns in *The Age* newspaper. Students filing in for the first lectures of the new academic year were supposed to witness a reliable professional who, despite his various external responsibilities, accorded them the respect they deserved as undergraduates by giving the task of lecturing to them his full attention.

In truth most barely registered his presence while a few thought him to be a poseur. Such a reaction would have perturbed Cartwright, had he the capacity to notice such indifference, as he had assiduously cultivated the persona of a dedicated educator who loyally remained in the tertiary system for reasons of altruism when he could be garnering very healthy consultancy fees in the wider world. Or so he thought.

In practice, the think tanks and companies which might provide such an income stream were a bit light on the ground in his native state so the forty-eight year old should have been a mite more grateful for the work commissions he received from the local media. As it was, he carried on as if he was the only expert worth consulting on matters of Tasmanian politics.

The journalists from *The Mercury* and the television stations regarded him amicably enough but sometimes wondered why their editors insisted on using Cartwright: it was not as if his insights were all that incisive. Still, it did mean that certain subjective positions could be justified because the spokesman for such claims was an academic and therefore theoretically independent of the media outlet. And, they grudgingly admitted, he was an academic capable of communicating the complexity of the local political scene in a manner which did not confuse the average consumer of the media.

His article in the most recent edition of *The Sunday Tasmanian*, 'Not so Hare-Brained', was a lucid and accessible explanation of the historical background and contemporary repercussions of the extraordinary Hare-Clark voting system that determined which politicians represented the electorate. Although he loved language and displaying his dexterity with it Cartwright had learned long ago that, if he attempted to use the same linguistic exuberance in the mainstream media as he did in research papers, he would experience a very short tenure as a pundit on the machinations of state government. The public exposure more than compensated for having to curb his linguistic skill.

Time to begin the lecture. Smoothing the broadsheet, Dr. James Cartwright stepped up to the lectern – up to the plate as an American colleague described it – and began the fifty minute performance. For him it was another chance to demonstrate that on this subject his was the voice worth listening to. He took in his audience with a measured glance and launched into the task at hand; a more carefully documented and more rigorously argued examination of the same topic he had considered in the latest newspaper article. And it went well, very well. The hands of the busy bees in front were almost a blur, the grumpy greens were taking down some notes and even the languid lopers up the back were paying attention.

Apart from one well-built young man who, having arrived late, spent the greater part of the lecture texting on his mobile phone and occasionally showing it to the attractive girl sitting next to him; the very girl with whom Cartwright had so recently had that very pleasant little chat. He finished his presentation but before signaling the conclusion of the lecture he decided to make a point. The lecture had gone particularly well and he felt in command of the room so an admonishment of the tall blond texter would not be altogether unsuitable.

"Before I formally conclude, may I just say this. The reason I do not provide copies of my notes is partly environmental – too much paper would be expended – but mainly because I believe the skills of listening carefully and compiling thoughtful summaries are abilities you should acquire. Many of you do this well so there is no problem. Obviously, then, it is unlikely it would be possible to download the lecture from hyperspace so I am at a loss to comprehend why the young gentleman attired in a yellow shirt in the second back row should have spent the bulk of my presentation on his mobile phone." The man blushed while his female companion giggled into her hand. "At the very least, it constitutes a significant breach of etiquette. I trust it will not occur again. Ladies and gentlemen, thank you for your attention."

Cartwright closed his folder and turned away from the students as they began filing out. As he slid the folder into his satchel, a voice clearly called out. "The reason you're at a loss, mate, is that you're a loser." Cartwright wheeled around. It was the object of his censure who then flipped him the finger and exited through the rear door. The postscript soured Cartwright's ebullience.

CHAPTER 2

Thursday 4ᵗʰ March 10pm

John Mahoney rarely took risks. The deeply ingrained professional habits of checking information, scrutinizing actions and reviewing conversations usually led to him being as predictable as he could be. Inspiration was for artists not police detectives. But tonight he did something spontaneous. As he drove his Toyota wagon along Narrows Beach Road, he flicked off the headlights and continued driving at the same speed for as long as he judged reasonably safe. The cloud cover and absence of any street lights rendered his surroundings almost pitch black. Suddenly he felt enveloped by darkness and the immediate response was a small surge of exhilaration.

He was physically removed from not just the minor metropolis of Hobart but also the increasingly popular area of the Huon Valley. It might not exactly be wilderness but on this dirt road to his shack he began to feel well away from the routines and cares of his job in the CIB. The long days and endless jostling with departmental bureaucracy would soon be shunted from his mind as he could bunker down at his little getaway and start moseying about for a week or two.

After a few hundred meters he reactivated the lights – not too big a risk really given his knowledge of the road – and cruised the remaining kilometer to the property's rusty gate. The simple process of stopping, shoving the gate open, idling through the gap, halting again, easing the gate back into place and driving the remaining hundred or so meters to the back door made him fleetingly wish he had invited someone. But the thought passed as quickly. He was aware he would not feel alone over the next few days: solitary yes, but not really bemoaning the absence of another.

He parked by the water tank. He picked up the large sandstone brick at its base and felt for the Yale key. And felt and cursed and felt some more. No sign of it: obviously Kirkwood, his colleague up in town, had not listened to the carefully given instructions he had pretended to acknowledge when visiting the shack over New Year. Bugger! Mahoney went back to his car and fossicked around in the glove box for a torch. He shone it around the hiding place and the light caught a glint of metal. The key had been pressed into the soil, probably because someone had dropped the large sandstone paver right on top of it instead of placing it. He smiled to himself. Again he realized that not everybody was going to do things exactly his way and that was probably a good thing. He was becoming increasingly fastidious now he was in his mid-forties. Only last week he had caught himself putting credit card receipts in chronological order instead of just dumping them in his tax folder. An alphabetized personal fiction library made sense: the other was just anal.

Finally, he let himself into his shack; shack being something of a misnomer as the building had been purpose built as a passive solar home. It was a beach shack in the sense it was near sand, on tank water, had few 'mod cons' and possessed an uncomplicated layout. But there was no fibro sheeting, drop toilet, cracked linoleum, plastic strips in doorways or spring wire doors in sight so most traditionalists would argue it was not a shack at all. Stuff them. To keep their places at basic warmth required tons of firewood whereas his heating bill was zero: the thermal concrete slab took care of that. Tradition could easily be a byword for bloody-mindedness.

*   *   *

The following morning was clear and bright. Mahoney was feeling rather pleased with himself, having successfully renegotiated the well-being program he intended to start with each day of his autumn break. Half an hour of fairly vigorous cross-fit exercises and stretching had warmed him sufficiently for a swim off the postage stamp strip of sand at the bottom of his block. Not so much a swim as a darting sprint into the bracing water with a showboat dive before he could have a second thought. It made him feel alive: as long as the cold current did not induce a heart attack, that is.

Now he was perched on his deck with coffee and sourdough toast as he read *The Mercury* newspaper. Of a work day a quick read-through of the main stories was all he allowed himself time for but holidays were a different matter altogether. With no deadlines to concern him, he could linger over every news item, story, piece of trivia and so could make the provincial paper last an hour at least.

So it was that Mahoney started reading an item about a forty-two year old builder who had been found dead in the backyard of his Acton property. The deceased had suffered a severe allergic reaction to a series of jack jumper stings and the resulting anaphylactic shock had killed him. It was obvious what had caused the man's demise but what set the detective thinking was how such a calamity could have been allowed to happen. To be at risk you had to have been previously bitten and suffered a smaller reaction which would alert someone to a problem. Surely this person, named as Max Watson, must have been aware of his medical condition – it was noted he had first aid qualifications – and taken sensible precautions such as gardening with gloves and having the correct medication nearby. Yet this chap had been found collapsed at his own building site sprawled next to his work van.

He continued his leisurely perusal. The Tasmanian election campaign was in full swing and Mahoney read with interest a good article on the heritage of the state's unique voting system. The prose was clear and there was some witty anecdotal material: the writer would be an interesting man to meet.

The morning rolled by and he settled into the easy rhythm of the day. At times such as these he was most glad he had returned to his home state after spending almost a decade in England. He had made a hasty departure in the late '80s to put as much distance between him and a failed engagement. A colleague from their days at the Training Academy had maneuvered himself into his fiancée's affections and ultimately into Lisa's bed. Perhaps he should have been more attuned to what was going on but he had been absorbed in part-time study for a law degree, his new position in the Criminal Investigation Branch and helping to lift his soccer club up the ladder. But he never felt the betrayal to be his fault. Yes, he should have given more time to his partner, but so could just about everybody, and he was only eighteen months short of completing the tertiary course that would lead to a rewarding career as a public prosecutor and financial security for them both and any children they might have. Why didn't she talk to him if she felt she was being left on the sideline?

Mahoney went into the kitchen, boiled some water and refreshed the coffee pot. Sitting down again, he gazed across the dazzle of the bay to the lithe eucalyptus trees on the far side. You could almost feel the reflected warmth off the water as the sun bored into the cool depths. In the Old Dart he had yearned for moments like these, especially during the interminably long winters. Without the drama and freshness of Nordic snow they were merely monotonous sagas of drab greyness. And the rain never really seemed to pelt down but drizzled from the skies or degenerated to an annoying mizzle. Still, London had given him a career of which he could be justifiably proud. Nonetheless, he had never been gladder that he had returned home. Especially now as he faced the prospect of a complete fortnight without the rigors of his position as the head of Serious Crimes.

CHAPTER 3

Friday 5ᵗʰ March 9am

Another working week in the 'lucky country' was drawing to a close. The roads through central Hobart were congested with work commuters and parents ferrying children to school. Visitors from larger cities tended to find local radio traffic reports of logjams laughingly alarmist compared to the serious gridlocks that beset Sydney and Melbourne. Hold ups and delays were indeed small beer down here. Nevertheless, some days it could be particularly painful getting through Sandy Bay. It was here that some of the state's more prestigious private schools were located as was the University of Tasmania. The campus had been constructed on the former site of a rifle range in the 1950s hence its long rectangular shape and the unprepossessing nature of the architecture. There were no dreaming spires to speak of amid the functional blocks housing the various faculties.

Amanda Pattison was seated in the alfresco area of the university coffee bar. Each morning as she walked the kilometer from her rented flat on Churchill Avenue, she never ceased to be amazed by the number of SUBs prowling the streets. Sure, this was the most prosperous suburb in a city that was still on the up, but did these people *need* Super Urban Bulldozers? If even a quarter of these 4WD vehicles had genuinely been off-road she would be surprised. In supposedly democratic Australia, the grotesque bully bars were the current status symbol to indicate you were a cut above the riff-raff. That a full tank of petrol in these days of inflated fuel prices cost about as much as the weekly rent on a small flat did not seem to deter this demographic. Nor the indisputable evidence that they were practically certifiable people-pulpers. It was the modern equivalent of the British gentry mounted on their steeds riding to hounds among the village peasants.

She did not suffer fools gladly: that she thought this about herself suggested she was not quite as self-aware as she imagined. Nonetheless she was quick-witted and could usually run rings around most of her peers in tutorials. So she naturally enough bridled at the comments, admittedly infrequent, that she was interested in Brad Finch merely for his body. The most banal hinted that she was a football groupie. The simple truth was that their relationship was completely platonic. They just got along well together. He was personable and consistently capable of making her laugh. What principally endeared him to her was his ability to genuinely listen to her and engage in conversation: a rare quality in 49% of the population.

Although there was one aspect of their friendship that ever so slightly narked her; his lackadaisical approach to punctuality. He managed to get to training on time but in most other facets of his life a text saying "c u in 30" usually suggested a ballpark estimate. Part of the mess in the lecture hall yesterday had been his tardiness. Mind you, the lecturer had taken a hammer to a nut with his response. Cartwright was definitely a good lecturer but he could not expect each and every student to pay rapt attention right throughout his presentations. Lord only knows what would happen if his reputation as academia's gift to the great unwashed was ever tarnished.

Turning her attention to the crossword, she mulled over 4 across. 'Richard the Lionheart unfaithful in love (10 letters)'. Why some people got married was beyond her knowing. Did they truly believe the fairy tale? Were they fully aware of their true selves, let alone the essential natures of their partners? Did the old pressure to conform to the social norm still exert itself that strongly? Amanda, for all her pretensions to wisdom, did not know the answers but was adamant, if pressed, that she had a career to pursue that would never be subordinate to the demands of any male partner. No matter how much of a SNAG he may be.

"Arsehole." Brad had arrived. And not happy by the sound of it. No steam coming out of his ears but by the way he thumped into the spare plastic seat you could tell something seismic must have happened to dent his normally happy demeanor. "Fucking arsehole. He is insane. What a prick." A couple of heads turned. Any display of raw emotion stood out in this domain of uber-cool and disinterestedness.

"Hey, settle for a second." Amanda had never seen him this agitated and was temporarily taken aback. "Sit tight, drink some water and breathe for a bit." Brad acquiesced and his shoulders dropped slightly. "Right. Now in a calm voice tell me what's going on. Without the expletives, if you can manage."

"Bloody Cartwheel." Amanda frowned. "You know. That dickhead Pol Sci bloke. Cartwright."

"Oh, right. What about him?"

"He's only gone and whinged to the Devils' board. Reckons I'm bludging on the scholarship system. I could lose my money. Bastard."

"Brad, stop. Go back. Who did he talk to, exactly, and what was said? And go slow and quietly. The whole café doesn't have to hear."

He breathed slowly and deliberately. "OK. Cartwright called Doc Randall yesterday. Told him about the 'incident'." Accompanied by an exaggerated finger gesture in mid-air. "Said my behavior 'was not in accordance with the standards expected of a sports scholarship holder' to quote the snitch. He's an old friend of the Doc. Doc Randall's on the board at the club and also here at uni. He believes the snake and so gets stuck into me with a long lecture about privileges and responsibilities. You know, the old 'role model in the community' stuff. Really gave it to me. Said my scholarship would be re-examined if it ever occurs again. I can't afford not to be here. Footy's a good earner but you're one injury from forced retirement. I have to graduate. And all hell would break loose at home if I stuffed up."

Amanda allowed for a pause. Gears started very quickly clicking into place. "Right. Well we can safely assume you'll do that. You're one of that club's best ambassadors and as for here, you'll pass without hassle. Just keep your head down for a while. Skip you-know-who's lectures for a bit. I'll get you the notes. Attend every tutorial. It'll be fine. You'll see."

"What about Cartwright?"

"I think I know how that can be fixed."

CHAPTER 4

Friday 5th March 8pm

"Like bees to honey, mate," Roger Sproule enthused as his gaze took in the room.

Bruce Randall didn't get the reference at first. "Do you mean the players at the bar?"

"Nah, Brucie. The female players, the girlies. All over our blokes. Reckon a fair few of the squad will need sticks soon to beat 'em off. Not that they will."

The penny dropped for the board member of the fledgling Tassie Devils Football Club. The inaugural President had a point: the room swarmed with what, in his day, were called 'sweet young things'. The talent of Hobart was out in full force. "I see what you mean. We've certainly got good numbers in tonight."

"Bloody masterstroke. Rang a few modelling agencies and booked all their decent talent. Told the agencies we needed as many good-looking girls as they had for the Season Launch. Tell 'em to dress up and we'll provide the transport and refreshments. Your agency will get a good mention in the media. No booking fees. Practically a 100% take-up."

"It certainly appears to have worked."

"Too right. Couple of coachloads from the pick-up point in town and they get dropped back in there to hit the nightclubs. Properly fired up. Bit of red carpet out the front and the prospect of the cameras. Not many of the local lookers are going to pass that up. Good incentive for our boys to show up in decent clobber too." Sproule's appreciative scan of the room took in some of the more senior figures. "See, all the politicians and business guys are here too. Can't get enough of us, Brucie. How good is that? Flavor of the month."

Randall conceded as much. "Yes, great publicity. Good chance for you to press the flesh. I think the Premier could do with a greeting."

If Sproule felt at all chastened by the reminder of protocol he didn't show it. "Yeah, better get over. After all they have coughed up a fair whack of dough for us. Thanks to Fothers. He gets his way." With that he was off to the bar to pretend to be grateful for the presence of various dignitaries.

Randall remained standing by the huge plate glass windows of the Elwick Racecourse Function Centre. Sproule was right. All and sundry were in attendance: all and sundry from the well-heeled end of town, that is. Without fail, various business owners, department heads from the public service and parliamentarians had accepted invitations to the gala event. The middle-aged men and women who believed they exerted influence hovered together or simply threw their noses into the trough. The Sports Minister looked as if he'd already enjoyed a long lunch before arriving for the 6pm function.

Aside from this group were the players, laughing and drinking with the bevy of local beauties. Cocktail dresses seemed to have gotten a lot shorter since Randall was last out. Admittedly that was a while ago but these little numbers looked less sophisticated and more, well, obvious really. So much healthy flesh on show. And the promise of more revelation later in the evening if the champagne kept flowing at this rate. And it would, as well as the beer and the top-shelf stuff. Everyone wanted in on the act so any company associated with hospitality was donating product and services. The whole Bacchanalian frenzy would not cost the club a cent. Rental on the function center waived. Good publicity. Waiting and bar staff provided gratis by government trainees. Good experience. All the food and drink supplied free by various local businesses vying for contracts with the club or the government. Good exposure.

Great deal for the club. Randall could not fault the acumen of Rory Fotheringham. He may have concerns about the man's scruples but he sure knew how to get things done…to people's advantage. Principally his own, of course, but the flow-on effect to the club was beneficial.

In front of him the lurid face of modern sport was playing out. The prosperous identities who had already booked the corporate boxes for every home game this season. The second tier supporters who would pay through the nose to attend the match day functions and lap up the trite commentaries provided by guest speakers. The media which helped fuel the frenzy of attention that came with local participation in the big league. The players with their lucrative contracts that ensured they needn't be distracted by everyday jobs. Their days could be easily filled with training, preparation and meeting media commitments for sponsors. Some studied part-time. For most it was the time of their lives. Living the dream. Playing footy. Papers reported their mundane utterances. Beautiful women along for the ride. Who wouldn't be seduced by the package?

It was a stark contrast to his playing days. Modest didn't come close to describing the conditions in the 1960s at the local football clubs. The money was such that it really only covered expenses. No such thing as a season launch. The only comparable gathering being held on the Thursday prior to the start of the season in April. A jumper presentation attended by the team, training staff, committee and the publican of the hotel where the players drank. Woolen jumpers, muddy grounds and boots with stops that you nailed in yourself. How antiquated was that?

Yet Randall still would not swap any of the current advantages for the days of yore. Even allowing for misty-eyed nostalgia they were glorious days. In 1958 he had debuted as a 19 year old with North Hobart under the tutelage of the legendary coach, Len Hibberd. Hibberd had fought on the Kokoda Trail in World War 2 so he knew a thing or two about sacrifice and commitment. Players were drilled as if a Sergeant-Major was running proceedings. The training was brutal: pure and simple. But the message wasn't fire and brimstone. Unusually for the era, the coach cajoled and inspired his players. The addresses had volume but never vitriol. An ethos of selflessness and bravery pervaded the senior players. Youngsters learned from the example of those already in the club.

Premierships followed. Back-to-back pennants in 1961 and '62. Randall played in those premierships and later in the decade captained the club to two more pennants before retiring in 1970. His total player payments over a dozen years would easily be eclipsed by what a rookie player now earned in a season. He did not begrudge that. Time moves on. But he couldn't help feeling something had been lost. The passion. Players moved clubs on the offer of better conditions and prospects, i.e. money. For his contemporaries, to be a one-club player was the norm. You played for the jumper, literally and figuratively. And the chance of glory.

Now a player could enjoy a financially rewarding career, and the motivation of being part of team success had ebbed. The nationwide football competition was a behemoth. Professional sportsmen entertained the large crowds. The old ways were retreating into the past and many saw it as a cause for regret. Particularly as some of the traditional football clubs were facing extinction. North Hobart was being threatened by a forced amalgamation with a neighboring club. Why? Not because it was struggling but because it suited the master plan of the corporate planners in Melbourne who wanted to maximize their control of all football leagues. It was intolerable and it wasn't even progress.

Randall was part of that process. AFL money from the sale of TV rights had been injected into the Tassie Devils to help establish the club and so it could compete reasonably well in its first season. Nobody wished to repeat the debacle of the second team launched in Sydney the year before. They had been lambs to the slaughter. Against his own better judgment he had agreed to serve as a board member for the year: his standing in the local football community as a past player and administrator lent credibility to the new venture. And, by and large, it was proving to be a good thing. The city of Hobart needed a boost and this club would provide that. It wasn't all bread and circuses.

The singular element that ensured his tenure would be brief was his reluctance to associate with Rory Fotheringham. He had come to witness the brute that was the man. An iron fist in a velvet glove barely described his methodology. To almost all he was either efficient or ruthless depending on their allegiance to him. Randall had glimpsed enough to realize he was a complete and utter sod. Pity help anyone who stood in his way.

He could see Fotheringham now on the far side of the room. Unusually for him he was looking very relaxed. Possibly half-cut; hard to tell. What was obvious was the discomfort of Felicity Sproule as Fotheringham monopolized her personal space. There was a leer on his face as he whispered something to her. She half turned from him and Randall followed her gaze to where a small knot of footballers were standing.

Even the most obtuse dullard would have had no difficulty interpreting the glance she shared directly with one of the taller players.

No difficulty at all.

CHAPTER 5

Saturday 6th March 11am

It was indeed a vision splendid. And James Cartwright was in the right frame of mind to enjoy it. His bike ride this morning had been an arduous test of his summer regimen of fitness. Rising early he'd saddled up around 8am for a long ride. The first half hour from his South Hobart home down through the city and along the boulevard of Sandy Bay Road was not very taxing at all. A gentle warm-up. The already strong sun was bouncing warmth across the Derwent River as he rode past a string of substantial residences with one of the best views in the country. With a bit of imagination you might think you were living on Sydney Harbor. Then though the winding bends of Taroona to the start of the Channel Highway and the stretch that got his thighs working. Bonnet Hill was a favored section of road for his cycle club members to practice time trials and Cartwright had savored the burn as he climbed. Then down into Kingston to the Southern Outlet and the long slow ascent to Mount Nelson.

Hard work. But well worth it if his current sense of satisfaction was any indicator. He may be a touch saddle sore but the well-being in his mind overrode any discomfort. He had conquered his lethargy. Getting out of his chair and exerting himself was now a fully-fledged habit. He was in a good place. Literally, here at the Signal Station Café with its panoramic view of Greater Hobart and its surrounds. And figuratively too as he patted his flat stomach and sucked on his water bottle.

Cycling for recreation was slightly odd. There was no practical purpose to it like commuting to work or going to the local grocery. It was simply for exercise. And the requisite attire was a bit weird. Shoes that clipped onto the pedals allowed for a smooth action as you rode but off the bike it felt like you were walking in something about as well-equipped for the task as flippers. The padded shorts he understood: they were a pragmatic necessity. The skin-tight top had initially been a cause for self-consciousness as it exacerbated the swell of his belly. But now, three months after taking up the sport he had gone down two sizes and the zip-up Lycra clung to a torso that was bordering on the athletic. The helmet was a worry. No matter how you tricked it up it still looked extra-terrestrial. Pity. He thought one of those little caps worn last century by the French riders would look pretty nifty.

If he kept this form in place he could seriously consider using part of his sabbatical to joining some of the club riders on their annual trip to France for Le Tour. Not to compete of course. Nobody was within eons of that league. But it was possible to ride some sections of the course prior to the peloton coming through. What a great experience that would be. And just to be there for the whole carnival atmosphere.

"Good workout, mate?" The question came from a burly man who was walking on to the terrace carrying a bottle of water.

Cartwright's reverie was broken. He looked at his inquisitor. Short brown hair, ruddy complexion and a body you would charitably assess as stocky. A roll of fat protruded over a pair of football shorts. A pair of Nike trainers and a tatty Russell Athletic singlet completed the workout ensemble. The sweat patch on his front resembled the silhouette of a small panda's head. Beneath the top was a mat of curly chest hair saturated with perspiration.

"Yes, so far. Beautiful morning for it."

"Wouldn't be dead for quids, eh? Great part of the world." The man was taking in the view as if seeing it again after a long time away.

"Definitely. Get up this way much?"

"Nah. Live down the hill in the Bay. First time up here in years." He took a swig of water. "Yeah, years. Last time would be when I was with some visitors 'bout a decade ago. Had a tourist guide with us. Nice old biddy. Explained how the station master used a whole series of flags to signal messages to ships coming up the estuary to port. She went on a bit but everyone seemed to find it interesting." He sat down at the table next to Cartwright and extended his hand. "Roger."

"Jim. Nice to meet you." A brief shake.

"Same. Reckon I need to do a fair bit more to get as trim as you. Still, it's only Day One. Only way is up, eh."

"First fortnight is the tricky bit. If you can crack that then you find the exercise becomes part of your schedule."

Roger nodded. "So I've heard. I'm a bit time poor. But I'd better do something. Not keen on the gut for a start. That's gotta go. Too much sitting down. Desk at work. Restaurant tables. You get the drift." A wave of his hand to signify the whole cycle he seemed locked into.

"Sedentary lifestyle. We're not evolved for it. Too much sitting, not enough walking. Way too much processed food. Carbs are the killer." Cartwright knew it all. He was trying to pitch it at a level this man would understand.

"Yep, you're right there. And the booze. An occupational hazard I'll need to ease up on." He half turned. "And don't forget the sugar. It's bloody everywhere. Cookies, soft drinks, the works. Half the kids are addicted to the stuff. No wonder they get irritable and can't concentrate. Worse than smack."

Cartwright couldn't help but feel the brushstrokes were a bit broad but the general thrust was right. A colleague at the university had engineered a similar weight loss to his own by simply eliminating sugar and processed carbohydrates from his diet. And by walking a few kilometers each day. It was as if his paunch had literally fallen off.

"The good news is the exercise becomes a bit addictive. Endorphins and all that. You stop prevaricating and look forward to sessions on the bike or whatever. What have you done today?"

"Walked along from my place in Churchill Avenue and up the track. Beaut views for the last kilometer or so. Definitely going to make the time to do it regularly." He slapped his stomach. "Need to, eh?"

"Can't hurt."

"Don't reckon I'll do your thing though. Not that it isn't good, mind you. Just the drivers round here are pig ignorant. People get in a car and they go into some sort of daze. Miss everything. Don't indicate. And don't get me started on the stupid pricks who text while they're behind the wheel. Worse than the hooligans out in the 'burbs."

Cartwright merely nodded. It seemed this chap was an unbroken series of diatribes.

"Some of the cyclists don't help themselves either. Last week a bunch had spread 'emselves to block a whole lane of the Huon Highway. Traffic backed up. Idiots. Thought they were in the Alps on the friggin' tour." He smiled at Cartwright. "No offence." A pause for another mouthful from the plastic bottle. "Not that they could be. Wrong shape."

"How do you mean?"

"Too big. Not like me as in porky. But muscular. Real road riders have to be built like whippets. Otherwise they're too heavy. That Armstrong bloke was only any good once ball cancer had wasted a lot of his bulk away. Most pro sportspeople include bike training as part of the pre-season but as tour riders they'd be useless. Muscles too big. And the wrong sort of drugs. They must give that EPO a belting."

Feeling he should stick up for his new pastime, Cartwright said, "But you have to admit those riders are some of the fittest people on the planet."

"Fit for what? Life? Don't kid me. They're not even healthy. And it's not just the drugs I'm talking about. There is that, of course. They're juicing up all the bloody time. Including Armstrong. He's never going to admit it and nobody who runs the sport really wants to find out. Too much riding on his success, pardon the pun. Anyway, they're only fit for riding huge distances. As normal human beings they're fucked. Their shape is all out of whack. No energy for regular stuff. But on the bike, bloody marvels. Once warmed up they thrive on the endurance stuff. Get off on the pain. It's more than those brain hormones. They love the pain. Masochists. I mean you've got to be doolally to put yourself through all that."

Cartwright found himself nodding in agreement. On television the riders in the peloton looked fine. Only when seen against the background of regular folk did they look like emaciated old men. Gaunt, bent over, wheezy.

"Don't get me wrong. I like that sort of determination. Beat the odds. But the cost. Ever heard of Tyler Hamilton?"

"Ah, no." Cartwright never liked to admit ignorance of any sort but Roger looked like he was a good bullshit detector.

"Cyclist. Good one. Rode on Armstrong's US Postal team. Big league. Great money. Living the dream." Another swig. "Except it wasn't.

Apart from when he was competing at his peak, courtesy of the blood transfusions etc., he felt like a crock. Pissed off his wife coz he didn't have the energy to walk to the shops."

"That's not good".

"Nah. Can't afford to upset your missus." No smile. "Just kidding." He tapped Cartwright's shoulder who managed not to flinch. "Determined bugger. In one of the tours he fractured his collarbone in a crash. Kept going. Won a mountain stage and came fourth overall. Mighty effort." He tapped his front teeth. "The pain of all that was so bad that while he was at it he ended up grinding his teeth down to stumps."

Cartwright felt his insides turn. "It hurts just hearing about it."

"Too right. It's admirable but it's mad. Crazy bugger. You want a coffee?"

"Yes, OK. Thanks." His new companion trudged inside to order. Having a good old blokey chat was almost as satisfying as the sense of physical wellbeing he was enjoying. Feeling good in the morning sun.

Roger returned. "They'll be out in a sec. Ordered you a skinny latte. OK?"

"Perfect."

"What do you do for a crust?" The inevitable question, a means of placing someone in Australia's 'classless' society. In Britain those of a certain ilk would ask where does your family hail from: in the 'lucky country' your job and suburb were the crucial indicators. Indicators of your personal wealth and therefore your social standing. Cartwright was in an interesting position. In real terms his salary had been overtaken by countless others but a university lecturer retained considerable social cache.

"I lecture in politics at the university." He didn't proffer any information about his media sideline. He hoped whenever he met someone new he might be known already. Just then a middle-aged woman with huge glasses and her hair in a bun delivered their coffees. "Are you sure I can't tempt you gentlemen with some goodies. Raisin toast?" She bore an uncanny resemblance to one of the eccentric TV cooks that used to gallivant around on a motorbike and sidecar.

"No thanks, luv. Me and Cadel are in training. Thanks anyway."

"Well, if you do change your mind just let me know." And with that she was back into her counter.

"Nice old stick. Funnily enough she's probably our age but she's not doing herself any favors with all that garb."

Cartwright silently agreed. The flower print dress and the embossed apron were just a bit chintzy. "And yourself, Roger?"

"Run my own business. Hardware stores. Bit of development here and there. Not that the charlies you're interested in are much help."

The typical cynicism of the public towards government at every level. Australians, in the main, were a law-abiding bunch. They just bitched about it every chance they got. Faced with an abundance of regulations in their everyday life, they adopted a low-key strategy. Whinge about those that governed them at every opportunity and then quietly sidestep those strictures that didn't suit them. Even real estate agents, car salesmen and journalists were held in higher regard than politicians. There existed a strange dichotomy: everyone expressed dissatisfaction with their elected representatives but continued to vote them in. The proportion that got themselves directly involved in grass roots political activity was surprisingly small. And those outside the traditional parties who protested or did something to stir things up a bit were promptly labelled as troublemakers. So the populace got the politicians they deserved.

"Well, I'm more interested in the theory and processes of government. More how things should be than how they are, so to speak. That's what I endeavor to teach my students."

"Students." It was practically spat out. "About as productive as the clowns in parliament. What do they do? Learn to read and write better? Haven't they got enough of that by the end of high school?"

Cartwright breathed slowly. Should he let go? Or joust with this brute? "A university helps guide a student to be a deeper thinker about the world. There are many professions where the analytical skills required can only be gained through a tertiary education. The school of life needs a certain structure. Do you expect an eighteen year old to argue a case in court?"

"Jesus, don't get me started on lawyers. Or those damned scientists. Is the world getting warmer or not?"

Cartwright ignored that old chestnut and brought the conversation back to his specialty. "Yes, there are too many layers of government in this country. Yes, the constitution adopted at Federation does hamstring certain reforms. And yes, some of our elected representatives leave much to be desired in their behavior. But that hardly means we shouldn't learn the theories of good governance in order to ensure the practice of politics improves." This bundle of sweat and bluster deserved to be needled. "What would you propose in its place?"

Rather than bridle, Roger decided to engage. He was not a wit but enjoyed a battle. "Sack the lot of 'em." He held up a hand. "Before you start up, hear me out. Seriously, sack 'em. Replace them with a select group of proven achievers to make the vital decisions. Where to put the hospitals and services etc. Delegate loads of the admin stuff to a pared down public service. Free up the bureaucracy. The money saved, the tons of money saved, would go to development projects that would get the go-ahead with all the red tape slashed. We're engulfed with rules. Each of the twenty-three local councils in this little state of 500,000 people has its own planning and approval process. Everything takes so long. I'd amalgamate those twenty-three councils into three administrative areas for a start. Streamline the whole system."

Cartwright nodded. The last point was sound but it was the first idea that demanded a response. "So we dismantle the Westminster system and replace it with an oligarchy?"

"A what?"

"Oligarchy. A committee of powerbrokers who run the show. Bit like China, say."

"Works for them. This is going to be their century. US is gone. Well, not quite gone but it's so bound up with dealing with sectional interests that the President can't even get a halfway decent healthcare program going."

Cartwright felt the ground shifting again. This man was proving very hard to pigeonhole. "So you're not totally *laissez-faire*?"

Roger snorted. "God, no. Decent wages for decent work. Proper services for everyone provided by the public system. Keep the shysters out. Reasonable taxes, reasonable mind, to give people the basics of housing, transport, schooling and health services. That's government work. Keep government out of business and business out of government." He polished off his coffee. "And get the idiots and the time-servers out of government."

This was a reasonably compelling argument if put a little baldly. Still the academic decided to push a few quibbles. "What about the democratic rights we currently enjoy?"

"Wasted on most people." He looked directly at Cartwright. "Look, I know I'm sounding a bit like the Tea Party. That's coz this is just a basic chat. You'd need to put some meat on the bones of what I'm saying for it to make sense. The guts of it is that while democracy is a good system in theory it just doesn't go well with capitalism which is the most efficient system of running the economy to give the best for everyone."

"And people should sacrifice freedom to escape poverty?"

"There you go again. Wrong end of the stick, son. I know you're being provocative but you're the one making this simplistic with your Socratic stuff."

Cartwright was chastened, not least because his technique had been rumbled. He knew from close observation that the body politic was in a mess. Knew there must be a better way. Having made an assumption about Mister Stocky, he'd begun to make an ass of himself. He lifted his hands in mock surrender. "You've got me. What you're essentially saying is very much out there provocative but there's a lot to it. Civil libertarians would have a field day with you but our current system isn't fulfilling the electorate's needs. Maybe a bulldozer approach is the way to go. Tweaking the formula doesn't seem to do much good." He thought a bit more positive reinforcement would help. "I'm pleasantly surprised you seem to believe in redistributive taxation."

"As in those doing OK should help a bit with those doing it tough?"

A nod. "I guess that's a good way of putting it."

"Yeah well, despite the fact there will always be scroungers, a lot of people start life on Struggle Street and it's not that easy to move out." After a pause there was an edge to his voice. "And the squattocracy don't like them so I do."

A bemused Cartwright asked, "Taxes or strugglers?"

"Both. Once a month I'm in a lunch group at the Colonial Club. Just about all the men that go would call themselves successful. And in most cases where does that so-called success originate? In daddy's testicles, that's where. You get a good start in life then it's not too hard to maintain it. Start behind the eight-ball and it's much, much harder to get going. Simple logic and history proves it time and again. Yet these numpties in their suits all pat themselves on the back and bray about their attainments as if they're 100% self-made. Idiots. And then they dump on the poor buggers who are stuck on the other side of the tracks. So they're hypocritical idiots."

Cartwright thought 'Thomas Paine' but said nothing.

"And whinge and moan about taxes. Lordy! The graziers take thousands in subsidies yet do everything they can to minimize their tax bill. The doctors manipulate every possible deduction yet they've gotten their exorbitant degree courtesy of the public healthcare system. One bloke, an accountant, said to me at one lunch we should have really low income tax levels like Hong Kong. 15% or whatever. I told him if he wanted to only pay that he should fuck off to Honkers then. Get crutch rot in the 90% humidity of their summer. Clown. And it's not as if they'd all become great philanthropists either. Just want bigger boats at the Marina." Most of the steam was spent. He smiled at Cartwright. "So you could say I'm in favor of paying my fair share of tax, yes."

"Am I right in guessing you're not too keen on the plethora of taxes government still places on business?"

"Too right. A reasonable company tax is fair enough. The Goods and Services Tax was needed as a consumption tax. But the bastards promised to get rid of rubbish ones like payroll tax. If that's not a disincentive to employ people I don't know what is. Kinda proves my point that the politicians are liars and idiots, doesn't it?"

Some more soulful nodding from Cartwright. "Yes, yes it does." Both men looked at the view for a time. Then Cartwright stood. "I'd better be off then. It was good to talk to you."

"Yeah mate, same. Much planned for the rest of the day?"

"Oh, you know, some stuff around the house than off to dinner this evening."

A twinkle in his voice alerted Roger to the possible nature of the meal. He laughed briefly without humor. "Good luck with that. All I'd say is don't take everything at face value. You with me?" The tone was melancholic.

"Yeah, know what you mean." Cartwright hadn't a clue what had abruptly turned his new mate into a morose contemplative. He wasn't sure what the last bit of advice meant so he said his farewell and walked back to his bike. The evening promised much for him no matter what old sad sack felt about romance.

CHAPTER 6

Saturday 6ᵗʰ March 9pm

James Cartwright had pushed the boat out. No doubt about it, he intended to make sure his date for the evening was suitably impressed. He had agonized over the choice of location. He thought she would be the sort of girl who would drink, eat and party at Metz, the Sandy Bay venue that was enjoying a burst of popularity with svelte twenty-somethings. Trouble is he might stand out as an old-stager in that crowd and he did not want Amanda to be distracted from his charms by her peers. The same proviso applied to the ever more crowded bars down on Salamanca Place. For his purposes he required somewhere classy, contemporary and intimate.

As they perused the menu at Vue d'Amour in Battery Point, he assessed that his selection had been spot on. One of the best restaurants in the state yet not snootily pretentious. And, thanks to a late cancellation, they were seated at the prized window table on a Saturday night. Someone was looking benignly upon him. And Amanda was definitely regarding him favorably at this early stage. She was dressed in a black satin cocktail dress that showed plenty of her toned legs, hugged her hips and revealed a sufficiently tantalizing view of her breasts. It was enough to make a dead man sit upright and pay attention.

Cartwright was pleased to note that she sat her curved derriere back in her chair and leaned forward on her elbows to converse. It had a marvelous effect of opening more of her breasts to his surreptitious gaze. And when she leant back slightly to run her fingers through expensively cut blonde hair Cartwright was tremendously grateful he was seated at the table.

As the evening steadily progressed and they moved through the delicacies of the degustation menu, Cartwright was becoming more relaxed and increasingly confident of his chances. The food was adventurous yet remarkably delicious and the service was solicitous and professional. The conversation was not unlike the excellent Shiraz: pleasantly spicy. By the second bottle they had even ventured onto the topic of favorite sexual positions. When she told him hers resembled a certain canine maneuver it wasn't just his heart that leapt. To defray his eagerness to kidnap her there and then, he rolled out a droll aphorism he had heard the writer Kathy Lette use. "What, I sit up and beg while you roll over and play dead?"

This was greeted with genuine throaty laughter. Amanda had really loosened up and just dessert to go. She ventured off on a bit of a tangent. Ever so slightly slurring, she said in a low voice, "Thank you for this beautiful meal, James. My last boyfriend seemed to think I found Ching food a treat. I don't like dogs that much. To be honest, I'm not all that keen on your Asians per se. Funny bunch. Slopping and slurping their food in the refectory. And the nose-tunneling. One guy in your lecture was up to his middle knuckle. Gross!"

The normally circumspect Cartwright, courtesy of plenty of vino, blundered in. "I know. They come down here and make stuff-all effort to fit in. At least the Indians can talk about cricket but your yellow peril make no connection. Just jabber away in their native tongue and have the gall to complain that I speak too quickly in lectures. I mean, get with the program. At least learn the fucking language." As he spoke he felt slightly uneasy. Knew he wasn't thinking with his brain but if this was getting him closer to bedding her then what was the harm.

"Yeah. And they spend all day on their mobiles rabbiting on or playing games. They've all got the flashiest phones."

"That's because they're all so bloody well off. That's why they're here. Not because they're bright or hardworking or anything. Ma & Pa Wong in Honkers have forked out big bucks to get them in here as private students and the uni gets to put more in the coffers. It's a cash cow. It's just the poor bloody academic staff who have to deal with all the collateral damage. They don't understand the set texts, can't decipher the lectures. And the essays! It's like alphabet soup. But they expect to pass with flying colors. They've paid, after all. It's criminal, a bloody joke. And the Board hasn't got the balls to do anything about it."

Amanda had been listening particularly attentively, nodding all through the diatribe. Just then her own mobile caught her attention. "Sorry. Didn't realize it was on. I'll just get this text. It's from Mum."

Cartwright magnanimously agreed with a wave of his hand as she got up and walked to the foyer. He could easily afford to appear relaxed. His chances were looking good. No doubt about that. The train to Pleasureville was boarding: he was not intending to give up his seat.

Amanda's return promptly put the brakes on. "James, I'm so sorry. Bit of a crisis with the olds." She waved her phone. "Dad's been picked up at a random breath test and Mum's in pieces. I'll have to head home and try to be a phone counsellor."

Cartwright managed to hide his disappointment rather well he thought. "No, no, of course. That's fine. Needs must. Do what you have to and we'll catch up soon." It was a struggle but the words were delivered in just the right tone of genuine sympathy. Not a bad little performance really.

"Oh, James, thank you. It's been a lovely evening. First of many, I hope." With her brightest smile she blew away any chagrin Cartwright felt. She got up to leave. "I'll grab that taxi outside the pub and call you tomorrow. Thanks again." A delectable kiss on his right cheek and she was gone. Onwards and upwards, thought the ever so slightly frustrated academic.

CHAPTER 7

Monday 8*th* March 8pm

As the March long weekend drew to a close, Cartwright sat quietly in his lounge room. If anything, he felt content. His article on Tasmanian politics had been syndicated over the weekend through the Murdoch press nationwide, with a commensurate lifting of his profile. The producer of the ABC's *7.30 Report* had called proposing an appearance on the program during the coming week. If this momentum was maintained, he could feasibly be offered a regular opinion column in *The Australian*, the national broadsheet. His fifteen minutes may be drawn out. Ego was not a dirty word.

Also pleasing, perhaps even more so than professional developments, had been Amanda's response to their dinner. Although their evening had been truncated by the distress call, she had phoned, not texted, the next day: waxing lyrical about the date, apologizing for having to dash off and then accepting Cartwright's offer of a home cooked meal that Tuesday evening.

So his weekend had been very fulfilling and augured very well for the coming weeks and months. That day he had even genuinely enjoyed the company at his sister's birthday barbecue at her Lindisfarne home. Given she was a secondary humanities teacher, he had expected a bunch of light green lefties but was pleased to discover a disparate assembly of people whose opinions covered much of the spectrum.

Even the old stallion of the local political scene, Hodgman QC, was present. Ill health had prompted recent retirement from Parliament but he maintained his devilish humor as he regaled one group with anecdotes of racing appeals and legal cases. One particularly entertaining yarn centered on how a magnifying glass was used to examine documents in court to convince the jury it was vital material. He brought a touch of Rumpolian theatricality to a fairly staid Supreme Court.

Cartwright was now sitting placidly in his lounge room. He had not needed to worry about an evening meal: grazing on the plethora of offerings cooked up on the barbecue had filled him and all the guests rather well. Listening to the book show on Radio National, he reflected on the nature of Australia's public holidays. People enthusiastically enjoyed them but they seemed to have become increasingly divorced from their original intention. Australia Day was a jingoistic booze-up that alienated the indigenous population who could see little point in supporting what was, after all in their opinion, a commemoration of the European invasion of their land. Anzac Day had drifted into a celebration of militarization instead of a somber remembering of the grievous losses caused by war.

Good Friday, in his youth the quietest day of the year, now saw cafés open and bursting at the seams. Sports fixtures were scheduled in the afternoon and it was mooted that a priest would deliver an Easter homily at half time in a local football match. Cartwright's view was that if such a parody should occur and the day went forward like a normal Saturday then the holiday should simply be abandoned. Too much had been commercialized. As for the very holiday they had just been celebrating, he doubted very much if many people would know the significance of the declaration of the eight-hour day. The land of the long weekend. Bread and circuses.

He switched from the radio to the television. The psychic detective was on one of the commercial channels: a guilty pleasure. Part way in during the ad break, there was the nightly live switch to *The Mercury* newsroom to provide a taster of notable items in the next day's edition. It would probably have been a quiet news day so he wondered what would be the lead item. The young reporter concluded, "And in a sensational development, evidence that Tasmania's political pundit, Dr. James Cartwright, has made a racist attack on overseas students at UTAS. More in *The Mercury* tomorrow."

Cartwright was too stunned to move. He sat still, merely blinking a few times. How? Where did that come from? What to do now? He breathed deeply and reached for his phone. It had been switched off all day: he had wanted a break from being contacted. He ignored the messages and speed-dialed the one man who could possibly help.

CHAPTER 8

Tuesday 9ᵗʰ March 10am

Rory Fotheringham was a fixer. Standing comfortably over six foot with broad shoulders, large hands and a swarthy block head, he had the look of a woodchopper. If dressed in a shirt, jeans and boots, he would merge into a public bar easily. However, that was unlikely.

The middle son of prosperous Midlands graziers, he had seen the rougher side of country life in his teenage years. During the long summer break from boarding school in Launceston, the Man O' Ross Hotel of a Saturday night was a good place for him and a few of the lads to go on the tear. Following his final year of school and toughened by weeks of fence building on the property, he had got into his first decent brawl. It had been a stinking hot day on the back of a bloody warm week and Rory was necking quite a few Boag's stubbies with his Dad's farmhands.

About 8pm a trio of blow-ins sauntered into the front bar. They were obviously three sheets to the wind and looking for some action. Tatts, moeys, loud voices; the works. The locals tolerated them for about an hour: boofheads wanting to take over the jukebox and feeling free to ark up the bar staff was par for the course on a Saturday night. But there was a limit. The shortest one of the threesome with his rat's tail hair and gap-toothed grin was calling the shots. After a period of leering at the pert barmaid, Alison, he suddenly wanted to know if the "stuck-up bitch was on heat tonight". Brian Turner tolerated much in his hotel but this was just a bit much. Service was refused and the 'gang of ratbags' was told to clear off.

Next thing, a steel toe boot went straight into the front of the jukebox and fists were flying. Rory had reigned supreme in the odd dust up at school but this was something else. In the space of seconds it was like the brawl at the start of every episode of the classic TV comedy series *F-Troop* but the crashing chairs were genuine wood and the thwack of knuckles on bone was all too real. The young fella tore in. Already his full adult size and bloody tough, he was more than a match for all three. All it took for the first to fall was a savage right cross while the bigger bloke took all four punches before keeling over. The rat slid out the door before his caning. For the rest of the night it was open bar for Fothers and the Bundaberg Rum flowed freely.

From then on Rory walked just that little bit taller, not just in the Ross Hotel but any room he walked into. He discovered that by simply holding himself in a certain way when he strode in a room drew people's attention: there was a sense of latent power to his stature. Rarely did he ever need to actually assert his authority in a physical manner. Those who knew him respected his potential and those who did not sensed that this was a man not to be messed with. He progressed through his tertiary studies because he was intelligent and knowledgeable but he instinctively knew that people increasingly used him professionally because they regarded him as shrewd and ruthless.

Having qualified with a Bachelor of Business from Charles Sturt University in NSW, he returned to Hobart to work as a property valuer. By the age of thirty he was a partner. The established rural families, ex-students of private schools in business and all the contacts he made through sport turned to him for advice and his reputation as a straight-down-the-line broker grew. The logical step into property development beckoned and he took it. Southern Tasmania may have been slower to follow the trends of the populous mainland regions but it surely would.

Rory saw his chance in the property recession of the mid-1990s. Urban and rural land was available. He swooped. He bought up a few grazing and timber properties on the East Coast that were no longer operating profitably and were grossly devalued. Prices for wool and wood may have fallen but the essential worth of the land was still high if someone with vision could see it. He could, and by subdividing the land for future holiday homebuilders, made the sort of money his male forebears would not have thought possible.

He then turned his attention to the Hobart waterfront. Although Salamanca Market had partly rejuvenated the area since it started in the late '70s, no one had clearly seen the potential of the area for development. Behind the fine stone buildings fronting Salamanca Place was a slightly decrepit area. Demand for inner city living was growing so Fotheringham's project development of eighty townhouses with accompanying car park and retail space was in the black even before planning approval had been granted. It was 2002 and easy finance was bringing investors out in droves.

Rory was persuasive. He had cultivated people in all the right places. Lunches at the Colonial Club, afternoons in his corporate tent at race meetings, afternoon cruises on his yacht, all helped decision makers to believe that Rory Fotheringham was a safe pair of hands. And so it had proved. He was thought to be, by those who knew about such things, one of the most influential men in the state.

From his offices atop one of the original warehouses on Salamanca Place, he looked straight across to Parliament House. Not only was he far, far wealthier than any of the incumbents in the political chambers, he quietly knew that he held greater sway than those who had to endure the vagaries of public office. At the age of forty-five he had fingers in all the best pies in town. Not that it was all plain sailing. Others in his sphere of influence regularly needed his capable assistance. By sorting out their difficulties he incrementally solidified their loyalty to him and ensured he could call favors in when he needed to. Now was such a case in point. Another poor sap who couldn't keep his nose clean.

He turned away from the expansive view of the waterfront precinct and sat down to his teak desk to read the offending article on his laptop. James Cartwright had been careless, very careless. He was facing public opprobrium and potentially a career-damaging inquiry. But it was not a situation that couldn't be fixed. The trick was to assess the problem quickly and move straight onto a pragmatic search for a solution. Just as he was doodling a few points on his writing pad, his secretary rang through to announce the victim's arrival. Cartwright was sent through to the sparsely furnished inner sanctum.

"Rory, thanks for seeing me."

"Jim, no problem. Pity about the circumstances."

He looked terrible. Bags under bloodshot eyes, like he'd been on a bender. "Yes. It's bad news. In fact, it's about the worst news I can imagine at the moment."

Worse than cancer, thought Rory. He stood to shake hands with the academic and guided him to the leather chairs next to the window. As they sat he noticed Cartwright had taken to wearing, like himself, R.M. Williams leather boots. Smart, comfortable and suggestive of a no-frills approach, unlike those poncey brogues most suits got about in.

"So, the story is under wraps for a while. Can't help the rumors but you're going to have to wear that. Damaging but not fatal if handled right."

Cartwright bridled at the assessment. "Great. So I get smeared and at my expense she gets to laugh along with the half of Hobart that hears the gossip. I'm meant to sit quietly and wear it. Is that it? And as for that bloody paper, you'd think they'd at least get my version. Pricks."

The fixer crossed his legs and spoke calmly and directly. "Settle down. If you want my help, and I'm quite sure you really do, then you need to breathe and listen. First, I need a few details. Did you say anything remotely like what was written?"

"Yes, no, sort of. I was semi-inebriated on Saturday evening and a couple of injudicious comments slipped out. But the context wasn't given. It was a private conversation, for Christ's sake." Exasperation raised the decibels.

Injudicious! Private! Rory wondered how anybody could be so naive and arrogant at once. He held a flat palm to Cartwright. "Again. Stop, breathe. Getting angry won't help you. Getting even might but you've got to get some equilibrium and help the man trying to help you. Now, as I see it, you did say something like it and it was obviously recorded by this girl. What's her name?"

"Amanda Pattison, little vixen."

"Right. This Amanda records it and relays some gold plated material to a journalist. The journalist wants to spice up a quiet news day with some muck. From their point of view all good."

"But not for me, obviously."

"Obviously. So you're up a very smelly creek and I'm your paddle. But that's not going to bother the journo, or the other girl for that matter. We can exert a bit of downward pressure. Already have in getting it temporarily pulled. Further to that, a defamation threat to the individual journalist to open negotiations. I'll chat to the commercial manager about my advertising budget and how money could be drawn from print into radio. Then a quick talk to the editor and we'll have got the damage limitation up and rolling. This story is never going to see the light of day. Trust me."

"And what do I say? The local radio wants me on at 11.15 this morning."

"Nothing. Don't go on today. Claim a prior commitment or something. Give this time to fade away. There'll be some other election issue emerge. Trust me."

"That's it? Nothing? Oh right, that'll work! It's not your academic reputation on the line here."

"That's right. Zip. And before you let rip with anymore sarcastic incredulity here's why. You can't go with an 'out of context' defense. You must know from politicians' efforts it makes you sound smarmy and deceptive. You don't deny it...they'll dig deeper. You simply shut up and let me make the whole thing disappear."

"What, gone... altogether? How?"

"Well, simple really. It's only her word that it's you on the recording. But by the very clandestine nature of the act, it's only her who can confirm it's your voice saying those unfortunate things. Once I've talked to O'Brien he'll see it could be pretty much anybody and that is no basis to defend a colossal defamation writ. I can trust him to take care of the recording and then in all the brouhaha of the election the story will slide away into oblivion."

Cartwright was somewhat relieved. "But what about Miss Pattison? What about her?"

"Oh that's easy. We gut the bitch."

CHAPTER 9

Tuesday 9ᵗʰ March 11am

Amanda felt seriously pissed off. She had gone through the paper from cover to cover. Nothing. Nyet. Not a smidgeon about Cartwright. She had been certain of a damning article. It would be a slow news day after the long weekend she had been told. Well, that was certainly right if the offerings in that day's *Mercury* were anything to go by. But no sign of any newsbreak about a racist hypocrite who lectured at the local university.

Her subterfuge had gone so smoothly: the gadfly lured into the Venus flytrap. Her contact at the paper, a journalism student on work placement, had assured her it would make it to press. After all, it was a big break for Grace so obviously she would do her absolute best to push the scoop. But someone must have nobbled her article.

So she called Grace who turned out to be equally aggrieved by the omission. "I'm so sorry Amanda but one of the higher-ups canned it. Oh, they've said it's just a temporary postponement but I detect a distinct whiff of 'rattus rattus'. They advertised it and then in the wee hours it transpires there's no room for it today. Can you believe that? No room in a Tuesday edition?"

"You're right, it beggars belief. I've read it and that's just nonsense. So when's it going ahead?"

"Well, that's where it really starts to wreak. I'm onto the duty editor first thing to ask what's going on. Get some gobbledygook about legal obligations. Reckons it's too much of a risk to print a potentially defamatory article by someone who is technically a freelancer. They'd called Cartwright who denied everything."

"What a crock. Filthy liar. I was there, Grace. He said it, all of it."

"I know. I believe you. But I don't print the paper. So it's your word against his and they won't publish on that basis. It reeks of the boys' club."

"Sure does." Amanda looked out of the kitchen window over the parched lawn. Where to now? "We could release it online. You know, YouTube it or something."

There was an overdue by several days pregnant pause. "Well, if we still had the recording we could." Grace's voice no longer contained the same zeal.

"Are you telling me you didn't download a version on your laptop or a USB? And that the editor has the only recording? Please, Grace, don't tell me that."

A forlorn voice confirmed the worst. "Then I've nothing to tell you. I am so very sorry, Amanda."

"What happened to it?"

"I was so keen to get the story in I overlooked doing any back-up. I left your phone with the subeditor so he could liaise with his boss and when I got it back it was wiped clean. There's no trace of my original story in the system either. Some elephant has squashed it."

There was very little else to say on the subject so Amanda did not bother. Having thanked Grace, she hung up. Where to now? Disconsolate was not the word. She mooched over to the kitchen table and sat down heavily. The man was going to get off scot-free. Her scheme had seemed foolproof.

Cartwright was not unintelligent – his academic record was genuinely strong – but he definitely had the fatal flaw generic to so many males. Insecurity. Insecurity that could manifest itself as vanity. What spurned that lack of real confidence could be down to any number of things. He was not a sportsman and that was an issue for many men in a society that continually lauded the bravado and skill that was exhibited on the playing arena. Being a player in the professional football codes lent charisma to non-entities who would otherwise be buffoons in the everyday world. It also gave some of them unimaginable financial rewards out of all proportion to their contribution to society. So what if the odd few squandered this windfall on stupid investments or gambled it away? They were all good blokes who were pandered to by the media and celebrated by the man in the street. What full-time carers or teachers' aides made of this topsy-turvy system of remuneration was anybody's guess.

Amanda thought it bizarre. A lecturer such as Cartwright with years of experience probably earned one-tenth of the more famous footballers. No wonder he was so keen to work in the media. Not only did it provide helpful income, it gave him a public profile. He may not be sporty, nor a man who could do useful work with his hands, but he was an identifiable face in the community. It may only be Hobart but it was fame, of sorts. She had discerned in him a desire to be respected and an even stronger yearning to be liked.

Sipping a strong coffee, she wryly reflected that their evening had been quite enjoyable. He was still a presumptuous fool for assuming she might genuinely be interested in him. He was the instigator of the bullying spat with Brad. And he did indulge in that thoughtless diatribe. But he was intriguing company; self-deprecating to a degree and rather witty. As she stared through the window at an ocean-going liner proceeding down the Derwent River to Storm Bay, she wondered if it was worth pursuing the matter. At what stage did something like this become a vendetta?

What irked her more at the moment was the fact that strings had been pulled. Someone, the academic or one of his contacts, had gotten to the press. Amanda could live with Cartwright sailing on through life without come-uppance for the lecture hall but she was beginning to feel a strange sense of being hamstrung by the faceless men: the people who really exerted power in this state. They were not the politicians. They were not the reporters. They were certainly not the voters. They were the wealthy and well-connected.

There were no gated estates in this town but there did not need to be. People knew their place, their station. Certain suburbs were kept cleaner. Certain suburbs were better protected. The richer residents south of the GPO may sneer at the police, particularly if they had been picked up for traffic offences, but what a song and dance if immediate action was not forthcoming to a call for assistance.

In that very day's paper, a disgruntled resident of Gagebrook had rather pithily nailed the situation. Another hooning incident in his suburban street had resulted in a verbal altercation and a man was shot by one of the passengers. Neighbors lamented that the reckless speeding was regularly reported to police but the complaints went unheeded. One railed, "You can bet if this sort of stuff went on in Churchill Avenue the law would be there in five minutes pronto." He was dead right, mulled Amanda. A drunken student party in that salubrious stretch of real estate had the week before made the front page of the papers. The subtext was that the unwashed rabble with their rowdy habits had no place in the nice suburbs.

And it was here that the powerbrokers resided … and ruled. They did it not by virtue of a legislature but by influence. It was not feudal but it was symptomatic of a traditional exercise of power by a group of privileged citizens.

Amanda was sure it must be some of these people who were manipulating affairs: incidents such as this with the pulled press article. But what could she do?

CHAPTER 10

Tuesday 9th March 4pm

Dr. James Cartwright could not help but check his profile in the lounge room mirror. Presentation was always crucial whatever the circumstances. Of recent months the question of hair color had begun to perturb the sleekly groomed academic. It was not that his dark thick head of hair was overly grey; tinting and comb-overs were for sad fools in denial of the inevitable path to decay. No, a silver lining of time suited his view of himself as a mature thinker, deserving of the same professional status as his university contemporaries who had gone on to become partners in accounting firms or take silk in courts of law. It was more that the grey hairs, somehow being lighter, showed above the mostly darker thatch and were a bit too obvious just at this stage of his life.

The mirror was a welcome addition to his sister's house. Perched above the sandstone fireplace before had been a ghastly painting of a white horse galloping through what looked like a blue forest. Unsure whether it was the product of some Adult Education class or some bizarre throwback to Mary's teenage obsession with Hobbytex. Cartwright always tried to studiously ignore it when visiting but his eyes were routinely drawn to it in the same way that one cannot help but stare at a phosphorescent pimple on another's forehead.

At least now the rampaging steed had been replaced by a reasonably proportioned mirror encased in a pine frame in sympathy with the recently sanded and polished floorboards. Perhaps the prosperity being generated by Larry's booming construction business might generate some more tasteful changes in the décor of the house. It would be a long road, thought the post-modernist, as his eyes caught sight of the mauve beanbags.

"Here you are then. It's pretty hot but I didn't want to over milk it." Larry had shuffled back in with two steaming mugs of tea.

"Thank you, Larry. Now I needed to meet with you because I believe you can assist me with the rather delicate situation I find myself in."

"Yeah, you are in a bit of hot water, Jimmy boy, a real dilemma." Owen had always barely tolerated his brother-in-law and was secretly enjoying the present discomfort of the arrogant academic. The big mouth deserved his come-uppance.

"Actually, Larry, there is no need to be alarmist. I know exactly what has to happen if my good name is to be restored. I am not on the horns of any dilemma. There is a very simple solution to this whole messy business and you are going to help provide it." Cartwright was standing before the fireplace and looking pretty damned confident.

Larry began to wonder why he looked so cocksure. "And how am I going to help you exactly? Assuming I want to which I don't really. You're the one who opened his bloody big mouth. Just cop the flack." The harsh edge to his voice was becoming more obvious.

Cartwright barely missed a beat. "I was stitched up. Anything I said to that cunning little bitch was off the record and she knew it. And as for sneakily recording a private conversation…well, you would appreciate the illegality of that." Even when calling in a favor, he was unable to refrain from patronizing someone. "My reputation, whatever you think of it, deserves to be maintained. I'm damned if she's going to bugger up my sideline as a pundit. The money is always welcome and I'm good at it. With the election on, I need to be seen as an expert without stain. I can muddy the waters with the local media and the disciplinary review will be more bark than bite. But this little slut needs to be taught a lesson. That's where you come in."

Owen could barely believe what he was hearing. He had half expected the shifting of blame and protest of innocence but the complete lack of regret was pretty stunning, even going by previous performances. And this stuff was way beyond the pale. "Bullshit. You're a dead duck and there's no way I'm getting involved in one of your devious schemes. Keep me and your sister out of it. I don't want to know."

Cartwright stepped forward. "Larry, hear me out. I don't need much from you. Just a short loan of one of your building sites. And just a little part at that. One of her friends is going to be part of the lesson. All you need to do is play dumb. Simple really. Your hands remain clean and this whole fuss will quickly fade away."

Owen was stunned. He had cut corners before and had to deal with some tough nuts but surely this was some sort of sick joke. "Absolutely not. No way. You dig yourself out of this hole. Keep me right out of it."

But Cartwright was completely unperturbed. "Oh, I think you will. I've two words for you, Larry. Jane Watson. I'll keep that tawdry secret to myself if you see your way to helping me out with this." Checkmate.

Owen's shoulders slumped. His carefully constructed house of cards had suddenly started to waver. If that affair got out then he could kiss goodbye to his marriage and, more crucially, to a bloody great slab of his business. He had worked too hard and taken too many risks to see it wash away through the Family Court now. The scheming bastard had him and, by the smug look on Cartwright's face, he knew it.

"Alright, I'll do it. One favor. And that's it? Forever?"

"Definitely." Cartwright was practically purring. Bouncing on the balls of his feet. "Just this one small thing and the problem disappears."

CHAPTER 11

Wednesday 10th March 10am

Mahoney's holiday was not as straightforwardly idyllic as he would have wished. On the Wednesday morning he was due to appear in court. The previous month the police had apprehended a young woman who had belted a neighbor about the head with a tomahawk. Hobart, not being Manhattan or even Midsomer, did not really have that many suspicious deaths so homicide detectives dealt with all manner of crimes involving violence. The attack, over an alleged case of infidelity, was sufficiently brutal to put the female victim into a coma.

As investigating officer for CIB, Mahoney had made the arrest and was therefore bound to appear at the preliminary hearing at the Magistrates Court prior to the full case being heard at a later date at the Supreme Court. No matter what the crime, even murder, all cases first went before one of the eight Hobart magistrates. Indictable offences, as this was, were then set for hearing at the higher court. Mahoney would not be needed as a witness but it was good form to be there to support the police prosecutor at all significant points and to respond to any questions the magistrate may have at this early stage.

He had driven up from Dover that morning. An easy drive on a clear day until he hit the bottleneck at the city end of the Southern Outlet. Even then it had not been exactly horrendous. Friends from the mainland were always amazed that locals would even complain about traffic: compared to Melbourne there simply weren't any problems.

Having parked undercover at Police HQ, he walked the twenty meters along Liverpool Street to the court building.

Opposite the Royal Hobart Hospital, the facade and interior had been radically updated since his initial stint as a uniformed officer in the '80s. The old brick Victorian frontage was now a double-storied construction of glass panels. So justice could be seen to be done, perhaps. It actually looked rather good and had a huge benefit of allowing in natural light to make the public areas feel airier and a bit more hospitable. It was a massive advance on the previously cramped and Dickensian atmosphere the old building generated.

He went in, proceeded through the body scanner and walked upstairs to Court Number Four. Inside, the room was modern and far less intimidating to average citizens. In the media box was Susan Hart, the designated court reporter for *The Mercury*. She walked over to chat. Dressed in a grey skirt with matching jacket, she smiled, tucking luxurious auburn hair behind her ear. "Detective, good morning. This one could be quite interesting."

"Susan, good to see you. You look well." Aside from being a damned good reporter, she was an attractive woman with bright green eyes. Keeping competent members of the media onside had many benefits, not least that it could mean an objective rendering of police conduct may eventuate.

"As do you, John. Bit of a tan there. Don't tell me you're taking a break."

"Sort of. Turning into a bit of a busman's holiday now but I'll get back down the Huon this afternoon. You're always welcome, you know. Seafood, sunshine, serenity." He was unsure if he really meant to extend the invitation: it had just popped out of his mouth.

"Thank you. Yes, that would be nice. This weekend perhaps." She gestured to the paper under Mahoney's arm. "Rachel's upset about what one of the subs did to her page 3 story."

"With good reason, I'd say. Thank God they didn't print 'boongs'. May as well have." A short article that morning announced that the former Premier had agreed to assist Aboriginal communities with the red tape of mining claims. The bold headline proclaimed he had a "job helping blacks". Mahoney had a vision of the subeditor chewing and spitting tobacco as he typed.

Susan smiled in acknowledgement. "Here's hoping he doesn't get this one. Probably come up with 'Axe murderer on loose in Gagebrook'. Anybody in those places must think society has got it in for them." She was referring to a cluster of suburbs on Hobart's northern fringe that produced a disproportionately high number of criminal offenders. Readers in more comfortable locales lapped up the seemingly endless parade of news stories involving seemingly random violence: theft, vandalism, alcohol-related driving offences etc. That these very same suburbs experienced disproportionately high levels of unemployment, teenage pregnancies, drug abuse, broken families and poverty rarely got a mention. Cause and effect.

Mahoney felt you generally ended up with the sort of society you allowed to be created. A recently retired magistrate had remarked that a very sobering aspect of his thirty odd years on the bench had been that he had been obliged to hand out varying sentences to quite a number of members of four generations from the same family. He noted that none of them had ever held a job. Inter-generational poverty was surely a contributing factor to inter-generational crime. This was the harsh reality of the Timsons and the Molloys.

Their amenable chat was curtailed by the entry of the police prosecutor and legal aid barrister. Mahoney acknowledged his colleague then took his seat. The Clerk of the Court announced the entry of the magistrate and another act in the theatre of jurisprudence was set to begin. Members of the accused's extended family had also filtered in and were seated to Mahoney's left in the front row of the public gallery. Apart from the slightly elevated bench, all the other participants in this small drama were on the same level, spatially at least.

In his grey suit and accompanying pieces of apparel, he felt at odds with the fashion choices of those seated nearest him. Despite the warm weather, the males were almost uniformly in boots, stovepipe denims and flannies. Echoing the latest craze among some professional footballers, shaved heads were on display apart from one blonde youth with a back to front baseball cap on his head. Females sported lurid tank tops with skirts at a fairly daring length.

The court having been called to order, the accused, one Montana Stripley, was brought up from the remand cells where she had been held over the long weekend and was ushered into the dock. Given that she had been delivered a change of clothes, Mahoney, and most probably the magistrate and most certainly the court appointed defense lawyer, were disconcerted to see her parading in a tight T-shirt emblazoned with the logo FCUK U 2. It reminded Mahoney of the old joke about the dyslexic agnostic insomniac. He doubted the bench would see the humor.

Her immediate apparent manner of ill-concealed aggression to all and sundry did not suggest remorse at her deed. In her home she had asserted that the "bitch deserved it for gobbing my Jamie". Mahoney's sardonic thought at the time was why wasn't it Jamie she had brained instead of the victim? Although that claim was inadmissible as evidence, she had, under caution in a taped interview, made further inflammatory comments that would lead any reasonable person to assume her guilt. As the prosecution had two seemingly reliable eye-witnesses to the assault, and that one of the uniforms had found the tomahawk in her carport with the victim's blood and her fingerprints only on it, her plea of "Not guilty, ya poncey nuff-nuff" was ill-advised as well as just plain stroppy.

Expectedly, the committal hearing was adjourned so that her case could be transferred to the Supreme Court. Mahoney doubted that a further week in remand would mollify her. The current imbroglio did not suggest that sentencing her would be an easy matter either. As he departed, Mahoney mimed a 'call me' hand signal to Susan Hart and began the journey back to his holiday idyll. And for most of the journey wondered how he would feel if she actually did take up his invitation.

CHAPTER 12

Wednesday 10th March 1pm

"You don't want much, do you?" Larry Owen sneered at the man opposite.

"Not really, considering the totality of things." James Cartwright was impervious to the sarcasm. In the exchange he held the trump card: knowledge. He had the whip hand and he felt no compunction in utilizing his advantage. Given the severity of his problem, there was no hesitation in turning the screws on his brother-in-law. Wasn't even greater pressure being applied to him?

In much the same way as a bookie laid off a dicey bet or an insurance company re-insured a risky proposition elsewhere, he was very prepared to re-direct the strife threatened him, onto others. His reputation and academic career were in peril. He'd been played and he felt sure he didn't deserve the potential repercussions. Even if the immediate danger had been defrayed by Fotheringham's influence, there was no guarantee the whole incident wouldn't come back to bite him. He couldn't allow that.

"You sure it's not just that your ego was hurt? Someone had a lend of you and you don't like it." Owen was on the money but there was no way Cartwright would admit to it.

"Ha. Good-looking Lebanese man."

"What?"

"Asif!"

Owen's puzzlement cleared. "Oh, that's a belter. You'd reckon you'd steer away from ethnocentric jibes given your problem."

"Ooh, my word, Larry. Well done." Sometimes it was just too hard not to be patronizing.

"Thanks, smartarse. We don't all have to go to a university to be able to use a dictionary. Anyway, being a smug prick doesn't exactly help you get what you want."

Cartwright paused to reconsider his next remark. The owner of the Citrus Moon café was on his way to their window table to take their orders. When he'd rung Owen that morning to arrange the meeting, this quirky café in Kingston had been agreed as the venue. Cartwright wasn't totally happy: too near the building site where Owen was working. He couldn't communicate this without tipping him off as to the exact nature of his proposal and he couldn't do that…yet. And Fotheringham had been very clear on the need to avoid giving too much away on a phone line. Dodgy things, phones. Tell him the deal face-to-face. No record. Gauge his reaction. Get him tethered to the scheme.

Both men shifted slightly in their rickety bentwood chairs to order coffees and salads. Tried reasonably successfully to keep a light tone for the tall Scotsman with a ponytail and ringed ears. After he moved back to the counter, Cartwright leaned forward. "OK, let's start over. My smart tongue ran away from me back there."

Owen nodded. Didn't believe a word of it. But he had to listen. There was a favor to be done. Might as well get on with it.

"So, as I was saying before things got a bit tetchy, we want you to make your building site available."

"We?"

Cartwright mentally rebuked himself. The change from domineering to friendly had caused him to be sloppy. He must bear in mind Larry was proving to be no fool. "Let's just say it's not me alone behind this bit of pay-back."

"Who's we?" The mule had hit the sand.

"Can't say, sorry."

"Can't say, or won't say."

"The first." He held his hands up in a gesture of pacification. "Believe me, the less you know the better."

"Need to know basis only, Philby."

His brother-in-law was proving to be a surprise package. "Nothing cloak and dagger. Just protecting you."

"How noble of you. Very altruistic."

"No need to be too sarcastic. I know I'm being selfish but I'm in a corner too, you know. If I could I'd leave you out of it, but I've been given no choice."

"What, someone else is blackmailing you?"

Cartwright felt they were disappearing into a maze. He had to keep this on track. "No. Not really. Look, it is complicated but this bit is simple. You do what I asked at the start and your part in the affair ends there. I swear."

Owen sat back and looked out the window. The food and beverage arrived. To anyone else in the café it looked like a quick business meeting, albeit a slightly tense one. A client and a tradie haggling over a contract. After of sip of his latte Owen spoke. "Right, just so we're clear. You, singular and/or plural, want me to make sure the unit construction site over yonder is free and clear this Thursday night?"

"Yes."

"No security checks that evening?"

"Yes."

A long, long pause. "And for this you swear to keep your nugget of information to yourself."

"Yes."

"Forever?"

"Yes."

"And nothing comes back to haunt me?"

"Nothing." Was the fish on the line? "See, it's quite a small thing to ask, really."

"Yeah, it is and that's what's worrying me. There's a hell of a lot you're not telling me. Not that I'd want to know anyway. Whoever's behind whatever's planned must have you by the balls."

"To put it mildly, yes. But it's the same deal for me. Get this done and my problem disappears too. Win for you, win for me." Cartwright hazarded a smile.

"Don't grin just yet. This scheme. How criminal is it?"

"Hardly at all. It's a bit iffy but I can assure you neither of us will be breaking any laws."

"But others will?"

"I honestly don't think so. No." To the extent that Cartwright had no real idea what the scheme actually was, he was being truthful. The Fixer had delegated this task to him and that was it. Less you know the better, Jimmy boy. The lack of information rankled as much as the dismissive nametag. He wanted to know. Wanted to be included. Yet he acknowledged that being uninformed could be a blessing here.

"Righto. Even if you did know I doubt you'd tell me. I'll sort it out. Turns out the concrete delivery for the foundation trenches won't be this Friday now. Company has asked if they can do it Monday instead. So, I'll knock the team off this tomorrow afternoon and the site will be clear for a few days. Suit you?"

Cartwright was instantly relieved. He hadn't felt like touching his food. "Yes, that will work. Thanks, Larry."

Owen stood to depart. At a low volume he imitated the Scottish café proprietor's voice. "Fuck you, Jimmy. Don't bother calling."

With that he walked out without a backward glance or a contribution to the bill.

Cartwright blushed. With embarrassment, not shame. He felt small and used. Not half as smart as he wished he felt.

CHAPTER 13

Thursday 11th March 9pm

The Metz was humming and the alfresco drinking area perched above Sandy Bay Road was filling up very nicely with a plethora of bright young things. On the balcony the pizza oven was casting a zephyr of charcoaled vegetable aromas as a succession of thin-crust gourmet pizzas were cooked and then transferred to waiting tables. The perfect food to snack on with a drink in one hand and to soak up some of the alcohol. And that was flowing very freely. A combination of a weekly special of $5 jugs of beer and a balmy evening had drawn another large crowd of freshly groomed twenty-somethings and a quite a few of them were drinking with both hands.

Tomorrow was another day: a day to recover with a bit of study or a cruisey day at work as the weekend beckoned. Friday on their minds. Tonight was a warm up for the serious partying of the weekend. Guys were mostly wearing T-shirts louder than the dance music being spun and long surfie shorts or jeans. Flip-flops were de-rigueur. Girls all wore summer dresses that bore testimony to lots of healthy skin, trim midriffs and long firm legs. It was half a world away from Ibiza but only geographically.

Brad Finch was in his element. Even the ordinary girls looked good and the better packages were getting into the swing of the evening. Training was done for the night. Finchy was on the prowl. His gelled hair was tousled just right and his deeply tanned face highlighted his smile.

He worked out long ago that by keeping it in reserve it was that bit more effective when a gorgeous woman was looking his way.

As was one now. A brunette with an olive complexion, dark eyes and a terrific rack. Just be patient. Smile a greeting. Then ignore her and talk to a few blokes he knew. Ten minutes later she just happened to saunter over. Just happened to perch herself by Brad's shoulder. The other males suddenly needed a re-fill.

"Hi, I'm Zoe, as in David."

Finchy got it straight away, thankfully. "Brad, how are you? Good spot to neck a few and wind down."

"Yes, not exactly Melbourne but pretty good."

"Yeah. That your hometown?"

She nodded. "Yes, a dreaded mainlander. I just wanted to get out of that posh school, rich kid scene and grow up on my own for a while. Away from Daddy, Mummy and the Beemer in Kew. I like it down here." The last sentence was delivered with an unreserved smile and comely eye at Brad.

"Good idea. It's not anywhere near as bad as a lot of people make out. Plenty of surf beaches, pubs, bands. And this summer. Right out of the box."

"Mmm, I'm discovering that." Another gaze straight into Brad's eyes. He didn't mind: it kept his gaze level which was not easy. Was she standing just a bit closer now? He could practically brush her left breast with his arm. He tried to concentrate on what she was saying.

"I'm pretty sure I've seen you at uni. Last week at the café I think it was. Talking to your girlfriend."

This one was easy. He could just tell the truth. "No, that's Amanda. We're buddies."

"FBs? Nice." She winked at him.

"Ay? Oh no. Well, we help each other out if you like. She helps me with study notes and I kick her along with her fitness program. We're mates, really."

Zoe gave him the full 100 watt grin. "I think you could get me rather fit." She ran a fingernail down his stomach. "Nice pack."

Done deal. Brad was about to suggest a quick exit when his mobile chorused the 'William Tell Overture'. He was the Lone Ranger after all. He mimed to Zoe that he had to take the call on the street. Better take it. Could be good news hopefully.

"Hi, Brad here."

"Brad, glad I've caught you. Not interrupting your recovery session, am I?" Doc Randall gave a generous chuckle.

"No, Doc. Just catching up with some friends. About to head home actually." As he actually was but not to rest.

"Goodo. Just wanted to update you. I don't think we need to worry too much about the uni problem. Your lecturer has become a bit distracted from that issue. Still, it wouldn't hurt for us to have a little chat about your footy."

Jesus, what now? Brad did his best to keep his voice bland. "Yeah, OK. There's no problem is there? I did an extra session with the juniors this week. I am giving it a fair go, Doc."

Randall's tone was as smooth as bowling green turf. "Of course not. Far from it. You're doing a grand job on and off the track. I want to discuss a role you could fulfil for one of our gold level sponsors. Easy stuff and a bit more cash in your kicker, so to speak."

Relieved. "Yeah, yeah, no worries. Thanks Doc."

"Good. Now it's just that the chap in question is at my house as we speak. You've met Roger Sproule, haven't you?"

Certainly have, thought Brad. Club President. A slob of a man. An opinionated, brash, insensitive prick. The starch of his shirt front matched his overbearing efforts to buddy up to the star players at functions. Corker of a wife, though. And a fantastic house too, the little bit of it he'd seen last week. "Yeah, sure. Good bloke." Sincerity plus.

"Certainly a strong supporter of the Devils. Well, he's here drinking my best whisky and wants to have a yarn to you tonight. I'd like you to come around."

No if about it. A directive. He must go. The Doc was his puppeteer. "Whereabouts are you now? On the strip?"

"Yep, at the Metz."

"Perfect. You know where my place is on Queechy Lane. Quickest way for you is to cut through the Bowls Club and hop over the back fence. Save a lot of foot leather."

"OK, Doc. See you in about ten minutes." Bugger. Zoe would have to wait till later. He rarely went without but this girl was a bit of alright. He went back in to explain and get her number. Then he was off to a meeting that could not wait.

CHAPTER 14

Friday 12ᵗʰ March 11am

The threatened change to the Indian summer being enjoyed in Tasmania's South had not materialized. A low pressure system had simply blown through overnight so the morning was again witness to clear skies and a benign sun. Accordingly, Tom Cunningham was out and about with his faithful golden retriever. Busby was let off his leash on the 'doggie section' at the far end of Kingston Beach and followed his customary romp across the sand to the low waves lapping the shore . Having made a futile attempt to catch any sea bird near him, he then darted in and out of the line of tussocks that fringed the small car park. Letting the dog gambol merrily, his owner ruefully gazed out across the bay to the Iron Pot lighthouse at the far end of the South Arm peninsula. It would never be the same without his recently dear departed wife, Maggie.

And now Tom completed the daily constitutional with Busby. They left the doggie zone and trudged along the Osborne Esplanade footpath to the far end of the beachfront. After the children's playground and the pub, they passed by the southern reaches of the street and, near the end of the flat section, crossed over so he could read a real estate billboard. Advertising yet another residential villa development, the spiel promised prospective purchasers that "there will be space to keep everything that makes you who you are…your boat, the motorbike and the golf clubs". As his own father had been fond of saying, it was the sort of language that stank up the place.

A light breeze was picking up as Cunningham turned for home but Busby was having none of it. He skeltered off to the foundation trenches and, ignoring his master's calls, began to scuff around the edge of some reinforced wiring. Tom sauntered over to see just what had piqued the dog's curiosity. After a cursory glance at the nearest work, he came upon an unusual sight. Wedged into a right angle corner was a large hessian bag that looked as if it contained something bulky inside. It was secured at the top with a length of thin rope.

Although he had never seen a body bag in real life, this was similar enough not to ignore. He got down on his knees and prodded the bag. There was a slight give just as flesh and muscle might give. Busby had calmed down a touch but the dog's reaction reinforced his growing conviction that something human was in there. Standing erect he pulled his mobile from his trouser pocket and punched in a number he had never before used.

CHAPTER 15

Friday 12ᵗʰ March 1pm

Mahoney received the call almost right on lunchtime. Call received number displaying 'Big Ted'.

"DI Mahoney speaking."

"Please hold for Commissioner Phillips."

"Certainly."

"John, it's Ted. How are you? Nice break?" Clipped and precise…a formality being observed.

"Just fine, Sir. But I sense my seclusion just coming to a grinding halt."

"Sorry, John. I need you on this one. It's not just a nasty homicide but the victim has a substantial public profile. Not only do we need a result but I want people to know we've got the best on it. Whether your modesty permits that view or not."

"As you wish. Who and where?"

"Call DS Robertson in the incident room for all the details but I can tell you it's Brad Finch. The gun recruit for the Devils. Hence the potential flak."

"I understand. Presumably I can bring in the people I need for this."

"Whoever and whatever you need. The media will be all over this so you can assume the top levels of government will show a keen interest. I need a safe pair of hands, John."

"Yes, Sir. Understood. You'll receive our best effort." Wanted to say 'as always' but knew not to push it. "I'll get started immediately."

"Thank you, John. A quick result without cutting corners would be ideal. Keep me posted." With that loaded request, the call ended.

Mahoney immediately called Robertson and was given an efficient briefing of the salient facts. Packing up took a matter of minutes and he departed his shelter very soon after. Once through the rigmarole of the gate he drove the kilometer to Taldana. As he came into the parking area, he saw a tanned figure in the garden. He parked and got out. Called to the green thumb, "Jerome, I've got some more for you."

The slim debonair man promptly dropped the weeds in his hand and walked over. "John, good to see you. Can you stay for a drink this time?"

"I wish but no. I've been called away on urgent business. I've packed up 'Bail' and I didn't want these mussels to go to waste so here you are." He handed over another largish package of fresh seafood.

"Thank you. Much appreciated. As you can see, we've got a full house so they will go down nicely as a pre-dinner treat."

Mahoney half-turned to observe the four cars in the guest section of the car parking area. Three guest rooms. One car with Victorian plates. Another a rental. Leaving two local automobiles: both very recent models. Jerome sensed the cogs turning. "Are you ever not detecting? Yes, in the Treetops room we have a lusty pair from Hobart who arrived in separate cars. Not a honeymoon couple is my guess but they are certainly giving a good impression of one. Arrived yesterday and apart from a spot of breakfast have barely been out of their room."

Half their luck, mused Mahoney. But he had a more pressing assignment. "Sorry, Jerome. Can't help it. Natural stickybeak. Anyway, I'd better go. I'm needed in town. Don't know when I'll be back down so please keep half an eye on my place. Ta."

"Of course. Good detecting to you. See you whenever."

Following that salutation he got back in the car, reverse-turned and took off for the highway.

Mahoney made good time from Huonville, thanks largely to the four lane highway. At Kingston the Huon Highway became Beach Road as it passed the links golf course and ran alongside the aptly named Brown's River. At the T-junction he turned right into Osborne Esplanade. Many of these weatherboard beachside homes had been 'spruced up' in recent times. One, in particular, had taken advantage of the magnificent view across the river to Opossum Bay by installing a large circular window in an upper story wall. Given the surging popularity in this stretch of real estate, it was little wonder a developer had sought to capitalize on the only vacant land available for housing. He parked near the laneway through to the recreation ground.

Unsurprisingly, the forensic team vehicles were already here. Mahoney strode forward to the huddle of officers standing a few meters from a foundation trench. As he neared them, he noticed that although the wire supports were tied in place, no concrete had been poured.

"Hello, John. We've got the real thing I'd say." The speaker was a tall rangy man with gold-rimmed glasses and a neatly trimmed salt and pepper moustache. He reminded Mahoney of an older version of the TV cop character from the '70s who patrolled the New York streets on his horse.

"Afternoon, Sergeant McLeod." Mahoney loved the fact that was the scene of crime photographer's real name. Resisting the urge to ask if Jim had ridden from town, he turned to the two female officers standing next to them. McLeod did the introductions.

"DI John Mahoney, this is Constable Lyn Manning and Constable Libby Postma who are organizing collection of physical evidence." The latter he already knew. Manning was new to him.

"Good afternoon, Sir," they choroused.

Postma took up the running. "It seems we have a fairly uncontaminated scene. There were no builders here when we arrived about half an hour ago."

"You can thank Rumneys Concrete Haulage for that." Nobody had noticed the uniformed officer approach. "Sergeant Wilkes, Kingborough District Section. I responded to the initial call. Arrived at 12.40pm and barricaded the area as best I could. I know there have been no workers on site today because the cement delivery trucks were postponed until next week. I got hold of the boss and he was resigned to the inactivity. They'd told him a few days ago. Guess that's good for us though."

"Yes, definitely," replied Mahoney. "With luck there'll be very few fresh footprints around the trench. So what have we got here, Sergeant?"

"A local retired chap out walking his dog happened on the body a bit after two o'clock. The dog sniffed it out and the chap swears he only prodded the bag. Thought it suspicious and rang us. One of my constables has escorted him home so you can talk to him later if you need. All I did was to open the top and check for any response. Otherwise it's as I found it."

"OK. Anything else?" The others stood silently by in deference to Mahoney's rank.

"Well, it seems you have a relatively tall male in a large hessian sack jammed at right angles into a foundation trench. Whoever did it must have loosened the ties on the framework to lift a section out, shoved the body in, threw in some dirt and then secured the whole thing again."

"Right, thanks Sergeant. If you could co-ordinate your available officers to keep unnecessary visitors off the site in the short term and then we'll look at the logistics of door-to-door later." Mahoney knew 'local knowledge' was always helpful and the more manpower the better.

As Wilkes moved off, he turned to the others. "Let's get on with it then. Jim, have you all the shots you need?"

"Yeah, pretty much. Just the ones of the body to go. Now Dr. Johnson has dragged himself off the golf course it's pretty straightforward. Fortunately he was just up the road so we didn't have to wait too long." It was common knowledge among the relevant officers that the contracted police pathologist resented having to leave the fairways for jobs such as these. Mahoney suspected it wasn't the cessation of the round that riled Johnson so much as the fact that the other members of the foursome were consulting private surgeons who always set their schedules to suit themselves.

His professional pique was understandable but Mahoney wished Johnson could see that his police work was more valuable to the working of a fair society than someone who did elective rhino surgery. At the heart of this situation was good old-fashioned snobbery. Some in the medical profession found the prospect of working with the police demeaning while others resented the fact that their lack of pertinent knowledge had been shown up in courts by defense experts. Johnson, despite the misgivings he sometimes aired, was efficient and very capable.

"Thank God for small mercies," Postma sarcastically chipped in. Mahoney was not surprised. A brief romantic liaison between the young redhead and the pathologist's law student son had been scuppered by the father. Some sons did take heed of paternal advice or veiled threats. Obviously, young Jack valued his free board and lodgings more than the tenderness of Postma's embrace.

"Well, he's here now Libby so it's probably best if you widen the search area, assuming you've got what you want from near the body."

"Yes, Sir. I'll sort that out. There were just the five sets of prints due to the circumstances. We've ruled out the dog, the old man and Sergeant Wilkes so there's one set of clear marks left by a size ten set of work boots and one set from what I'm guessing are Dunlop Volleys. Fairly deep impressions on the boots as you'd expect from someone carrying a pretty solid corpse. I've made plaster impressions of them. A few interesting nicks in the pattern that may help us. I'll get the wider search going."

"Good. Thanks, Libby. Lyn, anything?"

"Not yet, Sir. I'll check the bag and ditch thoroughly once the body's been looked at."

"Fair enough. Can you help Jim with the body photos? An extra officer on hand helps with the good doctor as well. I'll just be with the Sergeant for a bit."

Although he wanted to see the body in situ, Mahoney first wanted to square things away with the local officer. He made his way back to the entrance of the building site where Wilkes was directing a subordinate. The constable jogged off.

"Sergeant, have you got a second?"

"Yes, Sir. You want to know about the ID?"

He was no fool, thought Mahoney. "Exactly. Who else apart from you initially knew who the poor bugger was?"

"No one. I recognized the lad from when he did a footy clinic for our junior teams last year. Not a bad fella; turned up late but then ran really useful sessions for the kids. Took it seriously, unlike some of the boofheads who come down. Anyway, I know he's the franchise player and there'd be a fair bit of interest so I went straight upstairs. I figured the fewer who knew early on, the better."

"Quite right." So that's how Mount Olympus came to be delivering instructions. "Sounds like you made the right call. We certainly don't want any external interest right now. Hold off any reporters, actually anybody for that matter, for as long as possible. The Media Liaison Unit can deal with the press tomorrow. Keeping it out of tonight's news will greatly assist us."

"No problems. Door knocking?"

"How much light left?"

"Three or four hours? Should be a good time to catch people coming home from work. I'll put my best man on the gate and co-ordinate door-to-door."

"Yes, good. Usual drill. Noises, anything suspicious." Mahoney turned on his heel and strode back towards the trench.

Their southerly latitude, coupled with daylight saving, would mean a proper line search of the site by the cadets could be carried out. Using floodlights was an option but never the best one. As he neared, he could see the pathologist was intent on his task of examining the body. "Samuel, how goes it?"

"Ah, John. Early days but I'd say it's fairly straightforward." The stocky man stood up from his kneeling position. "There is a substantial fracture at the side of the skull which caused the death. A blow to the other side is probably what caused him to fall and crack his head on something very solid. That's all I can reasonably say at present but we'll know more from tomorrow's autopsy."

Dr. Samuel Johnson was not given to verbal circumlocution: indeed he was almost taciturn. He left the hypothesizing to the detectives but could be relied upon to provide astute observations upon the carnage he often had to witness. "The level of lividity suggests he was contorted into that position quite soon after death occurred and initial temperature readings suggest he's been dead more than twelve but less than twenty-four hours. Bodies left outdoors are problematic but the bag insulated the body so that will assist the calculations. As I've said, we'll know a lot more after the autopsy."

"Alright, thank you Sam. Sounds like we'll have no problem with the coroner releasing the body from the site. Highlight anything unusual in your preliminary report and we'll talk later."

"Of course. I'll be off then. I'm not sure if I'll be there in the morning. May have to delegate that one. Goodbye all." And with that the man Mahoney so wished to be an amateur philologist departed.

Mahoney turned to McLeod who was packing up his tripod. "Has anyone told Ballistics not to worry about coming down?"

"Yes, already done. Fortuitous really. McMullen's on leave and Burrell is off to a shotgun accident at a farm in the Coal Valley. And Constable Manning, before she went head down and bum up in the trench, contacted Dr. Geddy so he'll be here shortly."

The dental expert would be necessary for formal identification. The young man had probably not been previously fingerprinted and there had been no documentation found on the body. The process of accessing dental records for a match would be faster than using DNA and certainly more circumspect. Having been assured by the photographer that a full set of images would be available in the morning, they said their goodbyes and McLeod departed.

Although all suspicious deaths theoretically received equal time and effort in their investigation, Mahoney was shrewd enough to discern that this victim, by virtue of his public profile, would be the subject of a greater than usual amount of police resources. And that investigation would attract a potentially unprecedented degree of attention from the media. The former factor would allow for greater thoroughness but the latter necessitated that they work quickly to find a solution.

The Detective Inspector decided to start assembling his team for the task in hand. This particular death brought with it a series of attendant problems. Aside from the obvious challenges of finding witnesses, sifting through the myriad sources of physical evidence and co-coordinating the pursuit of the perpetrator or perpetrators, there was an extra element to this case. The publicity. The blowtorch would be applied from the word go. The call from the Commissioner had heralded the ignition.

Mahoney held no fears that he was up to the task of detecting but he preferred to go about his business quietly. Get the job done. No fuss. Had never hankered for publicity. In truth, he abhorred it. But now he would be right smack in the full beam of the headlights. And so would his squad. He must ensure nobody got stuck like a rabbit. The selection of key personnel was critical. Detective Sergeant Tim Munro was the first name he mentally inked onto his team sheet. Impulsive and at times stroppy, he was instinctively a good detective. People often misjudged him as a brutish bouncer type but that was merely a superficial assessment. Mahoney knew that Munro played to that perception in some of his dealings precisely so that unwary suspects would let down their guard in thinking they were cleverer than he. Then the tables could be turned. A definite asset.

The promotion of Detective Constable Susan Haig to an Acting Sergeant's position in the Drugs Squad had left Mahoney with a gaping hole. His fervent hope was that her designated replacement would be just as competent. He decided to call a bit later to inform the officer that the pending transfer was effective immediately and to report for duty early next morning. As would the rest of the squad and the uniformed officers who would be conscripted for this investigation. Very few would argue. It was the job after all. And anyone who did not relish the prospect of the hunt over their regular weekend activities could always be salved at the prospect of a healthy dose of overtime pay.

The duty-roster Sergeant would take care of the task of drafting in the extras and contracting the regular crew. And gently but firmly reminding them that a night on the hops was probably not the brightest option on the eve of the morning briefing. He could practically hear the veiled warning they would receive: "Bright-eyed and bushy tailed. Ease off the sauce tonight. This is a biggie." Anybody who ignored that could ruefully expect the fabled hairdryer treatment. A fire and brimstone telling off from the crusty Sergeant Manson was not something to bring on oneself. Well, at least not willingly.

Having assured himself there was nothing more he could usefully do at the crime scene, Mahoney walked to his car. He needed to get to headquarters to set up the receipt of reports that would soon start coming in. There may be some useful feedback from the door-to-door canvassing and the combing of the site by the cadets and forensics teams. He must organize the correct procedures so that every detail was recorded. Sir Humphrey Appleby would have nodded approvingly. And he had one phone call to make.

CHAPTER 16

Friday 12th March 9pm

The place was humming; voices were getting more raucous as the beers kicked in and off-duty cops started to forget the petty dealings with colleagues, surliness from the "disaffected youth" in the mall and general lack of co-operation from just about everybody in the community. In here, at the Central Social Club, the police force could comfortably be at play without any threat of aggro from members of the public: no chance of being accosted by anyone aggrieved, disgruntled or just plain belligerent as so often happened in other nightspots.

The Bluetones Bar only admitted Tasmania Police personnel (no partners) to its monthly function (all being well aware that this euphemism signaled a Bacchanalian frenzy). Booze was ridiculously cheap and the members of the constabulary who over-imbibed (the majority) or at least lifted their blood alcohol levels to over .05 (practically everybody) had their cab fares home covered by the profits of the various raffles held during the year and by a generous subsidy from the Occupational Health & Safety budget. In a not so earlier decade they could get away with the social secretary sticking orange labels on drivers to avoid the breath tests.

The beat from the jukebox carried another song by either Farnsy or Barnesy – hard to tell apart sometimes but perennial favorites of this crowd. If asked, most would have guessed the Buzzcocks to be a new motorcycle gang, thought Kate Kendall. She persevered with attendance at these nights because not to attend would have seen her labelled from newcomer to snooty stuck up bitch in the blink of an eye and curl of the lip.

Transferring from Melbourne had been a breeze, administratively speaking, but had involved more of a cultural leap than she had envisioned. Practically all the uniforms had gone to the local Academy and had plenty of shared reminiscences about initial postings to small towns ('bogan hotels') where they'd felt about as welcome as a black shirt at a bar mitzvah. Kate knew how they felt.

When Gerard, her partner, had suggested a move back to his home state, she had been enthusiastic. He was sick of teaching history to unresponsive high schoolers who thought last century was ancient, let alone the Middle Ages. His argument was that they could sell their weatherboard cottage in Yarraville for a small fortune and purchase a stucco brick inner city Federation cottage in Hobart for a song. The problem was he was basing his calculation on real estate prices from the mid '90s when he had first come over Bass Strait to teach at a mid-range Catholic boys' school. Then, Hobart prices had been seriously undervalued but had experienced a serious correction since. As it turned out, they just about broke even on the deal and still had a decent old mortgage to deal with.

Still, they did have a very cute little place – were previous generations that much smaller? – in South Hobart near the Adult Education building with an arresting view of Mount Wellington. There was a Graduate Course in Journalism at the University of Tasmania that was not steep in terms of fees and would give him a real chance to properly change careers. He could write instead of endlessly marking the slovenly essays of others. It would be a sea change for them: they could even contemplate the prospect of a beachside shack in a few years.

Twelve months of sheer hard slog to be accepted as an equal by her colleagues in Traffic had been marked by Gerard announcing he was not really happy with the course and wanted to head off to teach English as a Foreign Language in Hong Kong...solo. No, there was nothing to discuss: he would be leaving in a week to take up a post at a school in Kowloon. She could keep the cottage as the title was in her name anyway (as was the mortgage, she had thought ruefully). He needed a clean break.

Standing there, that cold August night, she had instantly decided to agree and let him go. If he could conspire to apply for and gain his job without her knowing, while keeping his true feelings from her, then he was obviously not a person she would ever miss, regardless of the decade long relationship with its trove of shared memories. She slept in the spare room for the rest of the week Gerard used to pack and move his belongings, then bidding him a calm good riddance set about making the cottage her own. Without his series of landscapes to clutter the walls and ramshackle library of travel books, she had room to place her own favorite mementoes and to decorate with scarves, mugs and candles. She considered taking in a flatmate to subsidize costs and repayments but decided that she deserved some breathing space for a while. That was almost exactly six months ago and tonight, God knows why, she was thinking of Gerard.

Somebody had chosen Meatloaf on the jukebox so before the drunken chorus of "Know Right Now's" started, she shuffled out onto the smokers' balcony and perched herself next to the rail and gazed at the view of the Domain.

"Five dollars for them," from just behind her right shoulder.

She turned. "I'm sorry?"

"Well, they're obviously worth more than a penny. Your thoughts. You seem pretty engrossed."

"Oh yes, I was. Just brushing off the week. You know."

"I most certainly do. TGIF and all that. I'm Rex, by the way."

"Kate. Nice to meet you." She shook hands with her fresh acquaintance and tried to comprehend his attire. He was dressed in a mustard colored dress shirt, grey slacks through which ran a purple checked thread and black winkle picker boots. She was not sure whether he was dressed for a dance party or an audition for the Rupert Bear comic strip. "That is a rather eclectic wardrobe. You certainly stand out in this crowd."

A quick flick of the tongue over his lips, "Well, I am the Department's resident metrosexual. And before you ask my feet are very nearly the size of Thorpedo's as well."

Unsure as to whether this was a come on from the twilight zone, Kate stuck to the realm of the here and now. "So you work here?"

"Yes, Internal Investigation Unit. Given I've tested the patience of my superiors in just about every other division, they thought I'd be best suited to sticking my nose in other people's business."

An aside from a previous conversation twigged Kate's memory. "So you must be Rex Chambers. I've heard of you. Aren't you the guy who was a bit careless with his weapon in a nightclub?"

"That old chestnut," he smirked. "From the old days in the drug squad, that one. A couple of us were watching at the Granada Tavern hoping to spring a few underage drinkers. Thought the safest thing would be to unload my revolver, put the bullets in one jacket pocket and the gun in the other. Trouble was I got a bit worked up doing the shuffle, tripped and the bullets sprayed over the dance floor and as I lurched after them, the revolver fell out. Now this was a slightly rough part of town but that cleared the dance floor pretty damn quickly. If the suit hadn't already given us away, that little piece of theatre scotched the undercover operation that night."

Kate could not help laughing. This was certainly one idiosyncratic copper; not the slightest hint of beige about him. "Now having so ruthlessly interrogated me, might I ask what you are doing here?" So she told him; the whole story over a pretty decent number of Coronas on the balcony. She even smoked a few of his Stuyvesant cigarettes ("Your passport to international smoking pleasure").

For the first time in months she felt relaxed in the close company of a male. She had not laughed so spontaneously for a long time and there was not a hint of a come-on. Perhaps he was gay. It was a bit hard to tell but he was certainly the perfect company for this particular evening. A short while later, after some dancing, they were back on the balcony and her mobile started ringing. The call, short and to the point, was from DI Mahoney outlining her immediate secondment to Serious Crimes. She quickly shared her great news with Rex.

He responded with something like a gospel singer's riff. "Maaa Honey."

"Sorry. What's that? It's certainly not Al Johnson."

"You're with the Beekeeper now. Well, under him, so to speak." A wicked roll of the eyes. "You'd better be on your game."

"I'm guessing that already. He seems very matter-of-fact. That call was almost terse. But he's got the track record, hasn't he?"

"No doubt about that. He even turns over the pebbles to find the truth, that one. Not the most flexible man I've ever met, however, he's got the clean-up figures they all want but won't ever admit to it. Let's toast your success with what is probably going to be your final drink."

Kate gave a generous smile. "Yes, let's. We should do this again sometime without all the others around."

"Certainly. I'll keep my eye out for an opening."

CHAPTER 17

Saturday 13th March 9am

As Kate crossed the corridor from the lift to the incident room, she felt a small surge of panic. Was she ready for this? Could she cut it? It was all very well wanting something badly but she was no use to anybody if she could not contribute. She had fretted over what to wear and finally opted for pump shoes and an olive two-piece trouser suit over a short-sleeved black cotton top. Smart but practical. Did the male detectives ever worry about this stuff? If she dressed like that awesome woman from *Mad Men* on TV, she would certainly command attention but hardly respect in this workplace.

Unfortunately it was still something of a minefield for females who could choose their own attire in a mixed sex work environment. Probably even more so in a workplace that could barely be described as progressive. The force may herald itself as an institutional benchmark of equality but the reality, as Kate well knew, was always more problematic.

Wardrobe aside, she was more immediately concerned with the dilemma of how to enter. Not even knowing how the room looked nor its configuration did not assist her. She was deliberately early so at least the embarrassing scenario of tardiness would not be an issue. As she walked through the open doorway, she edged her shoulders back, lifted her chin level and looked straight ahead.

Twenty feet across the room, next to a row of windows, was an officer writing on a large whiteboard. She decided to head straight for him. She greeted the man with the rather neat handwriting as confidently as she could. He turned. A not unpleasant face. Neither striking nor handsome, he had sharp green-grey eyes. They looked straight into her. He extended his hand.

"Welcome to the team, DC Kendall."

Of course he would know who she was. He would hardly request an officer without carefully considering the personnel file with the mandatory photo ID. Kate made a reasonable assumption. "Good morning, Sir." No negation so she was right, thankfully. "Thank you for bringing me on-board. I appreciate the opportunity." Not too much? She was actually ecstatic but this was not the time, person, place or emotion.

"That's perfectly OK. You wouldn't be here now if I didn't think you could make the most of it." He glanced over her right shoulder. "And here is the person with whom you'll most closely be collaborating. DS Tim Munro, this is DC Kate Kendall."

"Hi, good to meet you. Welcome to the team. This one could be very interesting. Need good people. If the boss can spare you, I'll show you round before the briefing."

Mahoney agreed so Munro proceeded to show Kate her allocated desk where she could place her laptop. He patiently went through the rigmarole of explaining where everything was on this level of the building: toilets, photocopier, tea room et al. She noticed he was not only thorough but he managed to conduct her familiarization with a deft touch.

They came back into a large room with windows facing over to the Royal Hobart Hospital. Behind the whiteboard was a glass partition that marked off what she assumed to be Mahoney's office. The desks were standard government department issue and the carpet was, well, serviceable was the most anybody could reasonably say. It was like this through so many areas of the Public Service. Foyers that were frequented by members of the wider community and executive officers were usually smartly fitted out but the facilities for the average workers were pretty basic. While the two colleagues were going over procedural matters, a number of other officers, some uniformed and some in plain clothes, filtered into the incident room.

Almost exactly on the stroke of 9am, Mahoney turned to address a group of a dozen officers. Everyone had made it well ahead of time and looked fresh and expectant. "Good morning, everyone." Mahoney sounded like a senior coach addressing a crack team. "Just quickly, I'd like to introduce DC Kendall who is joining this Homicide Squad. From my viewpoint she could not be more welcome, especially today." Kate acknowledged this with a nod to the group. This guy was pretty good alright. Inclusive language that conveyed a strong ethos of teamwork. The initial hint of praise mixed with an overriding sense of the importance of the fresh investigation. "Now to the case in hand."

All eyes were fixed on the Chief Inspector. "The corpse of a Caucasian male was found yesterday at a building site in Kingston. Initial identification is that it's Bradley Finch, a footballer with the Tassie Devils." A murmur of recognition went around the room. "Yes, I know, the great white hope for this season. So there'll be much more publicity and hence greater scrutiny of this investigation. From the word go, we must be meticulous and resilient. Every victim deserves our full attention but we're going to have to be seen to be doing it perfectly this time. I know that's a bit odd but there it is." He paused and slowly swept the room with a gaze that reinforced the warning.

"To the details. The body was discovered early afternoon by a retiree walking his dog through a new residential development on Osborne Esplanade. The scene was secured and forensics had enough light to get the job done. Absence of any identifiers at the site, apart from fresh footprints, suggests the attack occurred elsewhere. Supporting that is the lividity of the corpse. The patterns on the skin strongly suggest the body was moved after the heart stopped. We can assume the assault took place in another location and Finch's body was transferred. That he was contained in a large bag supports this."

Mahoney half turned to point to the photos on the board. "Two blows to the cranium. An autopsy being conducted now will determine the precise cause but you can assume it was being battered with a solid object that caused the trauma. When you look at these other photos, you'll see the body was wedged into a foundation trench. So far no eyewitnesses to this crude burial. Preliminary tests for rigor mortis and body temperature suggest all this happened sometime on Thursday night. Given the changeable external conditions, it is very hard to be precise, but we'll consider the hours of darkness between 10pm and 4am as our window, for now."

Munro gestured to speak. "We know it could not have been earlier. He trained with the squad early evening. Usual routine was to recover at the Metz." A few smiles. Well known spot.

From the back of the room. "Any sightings there?"

Mahoney answered. "Not yet. That's where you're straight off to, Constable Herrick. Take two other officers with you. Start there and then ask around the shopping strip. Someone must have seen him. He's hard to miss. Farrell, go with Sergeant Munro up to Finch's flat. See what you can find out about him. Senior Constable Marron, I'd like you to meet the parents when they arrive from Ulverstone. The local branch informed them this morning and they're driving down now. Should arrive early this afternoon. I'll be back from attending the autopsy with DC Kendall by then to assist you. Sergeant Munro has already sorted the other tasks. Scene of crime material regarding footprints and tire tracks etc. should be available by tomorrow at the latest. McLeod's team is working overtime to assist us. This is not your average weekend. So let's get cracking."

Mahoney allocated some further roles to particular officers and informed the rest to see the duty sergeant for any ancillary tasks. He was about to conclude the briefing when the Press Liaison Officer raised her hand. She had quietly slipped into the rear of the assembly. "Yes, Sergeant Gill?"

"Inspector Mahoney, two things if I may. There have been reports on the local radio this morning of the crime and I've been fielding calls from the major TV networks. All are in the process of sending down crews later today or tomorrow. There's the same high level of interest from the print media so we are about to be inundated. The spotlight will be shining on a few of our number."

And that will suit your career prospects oh so well, mused Munro. True, she would not be likely to have wished ill upon the poor guy, but if anybody was going to come out of this with a boost to her profile then it would be Sergeant Gill. She could not be blamed for any setbacks or mistakes and, as soon as any progress was made, you could guess who would be front and center proclaiming the good news.

"I implore you to avoid any doorstop interviews, refuse all external requests for information and to channel information through your commanding officers. The media en masse will be too overpowering to be our servant but it will be a PR disaster if it becomes our master. I do hope that's clear."

There were murmurs of assent that at least indicated a grudging acceptance. Mahoney spoke. "I cannot emphasize strongly enough how much we need to heed Sergeant Gill's warning. Top level football dominates the local media and even more so in Melbourne. Whether we wish for it or not, there will be greater downward pressure on us precisely because of the heightened external interest. Like it or not, that's a fact of life we have to accept. Now. Understood?" The volume of comprehension was more marked. "Good. I'm glad we all appreciate that. Sergeant Gill, the second matter was?"

"Yes, thank you Inspector Mahoney. Have you earmarked a name for this operation?"

How about 'catch the prick who did it', thought Munro biting his tongue. Senior Constable Evans could not help himself. A round shouldered man with sandy hair and twenty-six years in, he volunteered his take. "Dunstan."

"Who?" several voices chimed in.

"Dunstan, after Keith Dunstan. The old journalist from *The Sun-Herald* who founded the Anti-Football League." That generated a few laughs but the majority seemed to find it a bit macabre.

Mahoney resumed control. "Thanks but no thanks, Evans. For the present we'll go with nothing. I'll discuss this later with you, Sergeant Gill. For the present we all have work to do so get to it. That's it. Go."

*   *   *

As they walked out onto Liverpool Street, Mahoney asked Kate if she had breakfasted. "Yes, thanks. Well, just a coffee actually. I tend not to be particularly hungry early in the day. I know I should get something where I can but I didn't feel like it this morning." Too nervous to eat if truth be told but there was no need to divulge that. He probably knew that anyway.

"Might be for the best. A full stomach isn't necessarily a good thing for where we are going. I've never adjusted to what we're about to witness. Is this your first?"

They had crossed the lights with a smattering of weekend shoppers keen to cash in on yet another clearance sale at the CBD department stores. Out to shop whether they needed the appliances or not.

"Officially, yes. There was an induction session as part of training. That was certainly an eye-opener. Most of the internal organs don't look as you imagine them to be."

"Certainly. The human body is a conundrum in many ways. Full of quirky things. Today should be reasonably straightforward. At least the cadaver, as the TV pathologist says, is fresh. The ones where the remains are already decomposing or bloated from being in the water are never pretty. Here we are."

Mahoney gestured to the glass sliding doors that led into the Emergency Department of the hospital. Once inside, Kate followed him along the corridor for a few meters before they descended a set of stairs to the basement. At the bottom of the steps they faced a solid white door. Her superior pressed the intercom button, waited a few moments for a response, then identified themselves and the door was buzzed open. Kate was immediately struck by how brightly lit the area inside was. It made sense. A high level of wattage would be necessary to perform the clinical tasks that were performed here.

"Welcome to my domain." The voice was theatrically deep and belonged to a dapper man sporting a striking red bow tie. The rest of his attire attested to bespoke tailoring. The worsted grey wool, double-breasted suit and black oxford brogues could not have been purchased in this town. The tanned face was chiseled and piercing brown eyes fixed on Kate as he approached.

"Now, DI Mahoney I know but who are you, young lady?"

"DC Kate Kendall. And you must be Mr. Bede Harcourt."

"Pleased to meet you, I'm sure." A brief shake of his smooth but rather large hand. "John, welcome. Your new colleague is a commendable addition. Smart, attractive and savvy enough not to address me as the venerable surgeon."

Mahoney smiled. "You well know I could only bring my best officer to witness your skills." This was delivered so deadpan as to be a pointed remark. Nonetheless there seemed to be a genuine bonhomie.

"Well, we shall see if I need to draw on them overly this morning. Of course, I'm making no assumptions but I doubt I'll be late for today's regatta."

Harcourt led them through to the examination room. The white walls and tiled floor exaggerated the luminescence.

"I took the liberty of proceeding without you. Time and essence etc."

"Of course. We appreciate you getting it done."

The corpse of Brad Finch lay on the gunmetal stainless steel bench. In death he looked so composed. The lean musculature testified to a body previously capable of power and energy. But now he seemed serene. And pale. Kate was surprised by how waxy his face appeared to them now. Of course she knew it was Finch. That was the person they were to see.

But even though she had studied the available photographic images in the incident room, she was not totally convinced that he would be immediately recognizable to anybody save those few people who knew him very well. The fabled 21 grams, his soul, had departed the earthly body. However, the changes in the deceased's appearance were quite telling. With the eyes closed and all vitality drained from the visage, he looked nothing like the publicity shot on the AFL website. No bright smile. No lively eyes.

Kate remembered the Forensics module of her cadet training. The lecturer had put up a PowerPoint slide of a deceased person's head and opened it up to the class to guess the person's identity. The complexion was freckled and the face was not spectacular at all. After a short while he began throwing out clues.

"Billy Joel." No, it certainly was not Christie Brinkley. "Elton John." No, not Princess Diana either. "Arthur Miller." Who? "Joe Di Maggio." Who's he? "JFK." Finally, someone called out Marilyn Monroe but immediately said but that's not her, surely. "Yes, it is. There she is. An icon of the 20th century. The poster girl par excellence. Never assume an assumption about identity. One reason we cross the t's is to avoid horrendous mistakes. One sure-fire way to send people apocalyptic is to wrongly identify a corpse. Grief and rage are a potent mix."

And that had been a memorable insight into how the departure of one's vital spirit could dramatically transform a human body. Kate turned her attention to Harcourt who was now explaining the summation of his findings.

"There are two head wounds discernible. One, to the right side of the head, lacerated his ear and was caused by a blow with a flattish metal object. As there are soil particles attached to the hair, my guess is some sort of shovel. The second, probably fatal, blow was to the left temple, and was dealt by a hard edge. From the angles of the wounds, my calculation is that the victim was hit from behind. This momentarily stunned him, causing him to fall sideways and land with his head hitting some concrete curbing."

Mahoney nodded. He and Kate mimed the incident as outlined by the surgeon. "That seems feasible, doesn't it Kate?"

"Yes, given a pretty forceful blow."

Harcourt drew their attention to the right side of the head. "Certainly forceful. Had he lived, the ear would have been barely recognizable. A complete mash. There is plenty of damage but not terminal. The cranium is intact although there is some injury to the jaw. It was the fall and subsequent blow to the temple that caused the fatal brain hemorrhage."

Mahoney nodded his understanding. "Anything else of note?"

"Yes. There is ambiguous bruising and the loss of some skin on the principal knuckles of his left hand. Completely consistent with a fist hitting another's face."

Kate ventured an opinion. "Two assailants, perhaps. Finch hits the one facing him but there's another one behind him who strikes him down."

Mahoney nodded. "Most likely. Let's hope we can locate the spot where this took place. With luck, some decent forensic evidence could be there." He turned to Harcourt. "Thank you, Bede. Senior Constable Marron is coordinating the meeting with the parents. He'll be accompanying them to a viewing of the body and consolidating all information with regard to identification. The dental records will be with you very shortly but I'd say there's little doubt this is Brad Finch."

*   *   *

As Mahoney and Kendall were walking back to HQ, an ambulance pulled up at the Emergency parking bay. There was nothing particularly unusual about that, apart from the presence of a uniformed officer in the front passenger seat. The constable had the sort of deeply colored red hair that was way beyond strawberry blonde and coupled with azure eyes indicated a complexion not entirely suited to spending endless hours in the sand and surf. A fully fledged Bluey if ever there was one. Having escorted the two ambulance personnel and a patient prostrate upon a collapsible bed into the foyer, the young policeman returned to the street just as the detectives approached the sliding doors. Mahoney's curiosity had been caught.

He walked up and introduced Kate. "So, Constable Gibson, what's going on here?"

A smile broke through. "Hard to describe, really. A mix of theft, absconding, espionage and plain stupidity." He ticked them off on his long fingers. "We've just brought a fella back from K&D Hardware. Got a call about forty minutes ago about a suspicious looking bloke wandering the tool aisle. Trying out spanners."

"What was suspicious?"

"Just that his neck was encased in a titanium cradle. You know, one of those metallic doughnuts that neck victims have bolted to their heads." His slender hands made the shape around his own collar. "Meant to stop undue movement so the head doesn't fall off."

"What on earth is he doing up in Murray Street instead of in bed?"

"A get rich quick scheme." Gibson's voice betrayed his mirth. "Our patient is no rocket scientist. He comes round from the operation and straight away a nurse is there to reassure him and explain why this thing is attached to him. Goes through the spiel about saving his spinal cord and the need to be calm and still. Best equipment going, she tells him. All he hears is the bit where it's worth five grand because it's made of titanium. So, soon as the staff leave him alone, he's up out of bed and up to the nearest DIY shop looking for a spanner that fits."

"And then what?"

"Like I said, no brain surgeon. I dunno. Cash converters? Who knows?"

"Hard to believe he'd risk his head almost literally falling off for some quick cash."

Kate was bug-eyed at the stupidity of the man and was inclined to disbelieve the story but Gibson sounded convincing and Mahoney had no problem accepting the veracity of it all. As he wiped a tear from his eye and composed himself, he clapped a hand on the uniformed man's shoulder. "Thank you, David. You usually tell a good story but that one is right up there. Who'd have thought, eh? Hope our lot are as easy to find. By the way, I've asked for you to be with us for a bit, if that suits."

"Yes, Sir. For sure. See you soon then. Goodbye, Constable Kendall."

As they turned the corner of Argyle Street, a man in a red baseball cap called from a park bench. "Hey, Mahoney. Gallows humor already?"

The Inspector stopped abruptly and told Kate to wait on the pavement. He then strode over to the lanky figure lounged on the wooden seat. "I beg your pardon, Lester. I didn't quite catch that witticism. What with it being randomly barked out and everything."

The man in the cap smirked. Tapped what was presumably a mobile phone in the breast pocket of a lumberjack shirt. "Got a couple of good shots. You and the Missus laughing your head off with the Ranga. Bet the press boys would love to blow one of 'em up. Show how seriously you're taking it." The smirk had morphed into a sickly sneer. Lester McCann was not over-brimming with the milk of kindness.

Mahoney experienced one of those moments as in the latest Sherlock Holmes films where the sleuth almost instantaneously assessed the risk and potential outcomes before deciding on a strategy. He bent forward and in almost a murmur said, "Feel free, Toad my boy. I'll just tell them that we were laughing about how much a certain low-life would be looking forward to seeing Dwayne Lambert. Now he's out of Risdon prison, you see."

Toad saw alright. Saw his past flash right past his dial. Even a slimy creature like himself had sussed that paying a recreational visit after hours to Trish Lambert was not the wisest career move. For the vast majority of the three years her husband had been away for aggravated burglary and GBH, Toad had resisted temptation. But only last weekend the sweet allure of Sugarloaf Road had proved irresistible. McCann did not even bother asking how the copper knew. Small town. End of story.

And it would be the end of him if he hung around too much longer. Sliding his skinny rear back into the bench he sat upright. Taking out his mobile he pressed a few buttons and in Mahoney's view deleted the recently taken images. Looking very contrite.

"And you're sure that's all?"

"Yes, Inspector. Definitely. In fact I don't think I even need the damned thing anymore."

With that he took out the SIM card and dropped it in the adjacent bin. "Best to be out of contact for a while I reckon. Might take a hike."

"I know you're not a great lover of hard yakka but I doubt Dwayne's reach extends as far as the mines in West Australia. Could be an option. They're rather desperate for workers."

"And I'm pretty desperate too."

"Exactly. You're probably on the endangered species list now so a change of scene looks best I'd say."

Lester stood up. "Reckon I'll be off then. Don't s'pose you know anyone who wants a load of skunk going spare? Doubt I'll have time to offload it."

Mahoney could well believe the cheek of the slimeball. "Don't push it, Lester. You wouldn't want me involving your mates in the Drug Squad. They'd be straight onto Lambert. Whisper from a little birdie etc. Get out while the going's good." With that he turned and walked off to re-join DC Kendall without a backward glance. Truly good riddance to bad rubbish.

After they crossed Liverpool Street, Kate dared to ask what that had been about. Mahoney said, absently, "Oh that idiot. Well known supplier of strong dope on the Eastern Shore. Our lot never seem to be able to pin him down. He's cunning as a shithouse rat but he's gone and shot himself in the foot. Dalliance with the wrong man's wife so he's out of town by sunset. Nice bit of impromptu community policing, really. Some other scumbag will stick his head up and take the network over but at least he's out of the way."

By this time they had climbed the stairs and were back in the incident room. Kate went to her desk to write up their observations from the autopsy while Mahoney entered his office and closed the door behind him. He needed a moment. The altercation had been defused nicely. But it was a warning of something potentially much darker. When talking to Gibson he had temporarily forgotten that the Force was always on show. In uniform or not a police officer was constantly subject to public scrutiny. Innocent as the exchange with this colleague had been, it could easily be misconstrued as undue levity.

Toad was right in that respect. The media would have been interested and they would gladly have grabbed the wrong end of the stick. And pulled hard. As a young royal with hair the color of Gibson's was learning, some figures were expected to always wear their public face. They were fair game to a world that just relished any opportunity to pour scorn on the slightest error of judgment. He and Kendall had been fortunate. Cursing his oversight, he resolved to constantly bear in mind the very warning issued just a few hours earlier. They were in the full beam of the headlights. It would be relentless.

CHAPTER 18

Saturday 13ᵗʰ March 11am

There was one theory out the window. When Amanda had moved into her flat a little over two years ago, the landlord had assured her that, in his experience, it would be the odd-numbered years in this millennium that would yield clear summers. Thus far he had been pretty accurate.

That first summer, '08, had been mediocre while the next had been a big improvement but this year was just brilliant. Sunshine with little humidity – long clear days. And this Saturday was not going to break the pattern. Amanda packed her sports bag with beach towel, sun block, iPod and all the associated paraphernalia for a session at Cremorne Beach. She loved it there. Not really a surf beach, it was good for swimming and walking. As an afterthought, she popped two deck chairs in the boot of her Suzuki hatchback. Perhaps Brad would fancy a trip down too. She was not able to reach him on his mobile so she decided to simply zip over to his place and check out his plans.

When she arrived there was an unfamiliar car in the drive. As soon as Amanda started towards the front door, a woman sprung out of the blue Mitsubishi Pajero. Sunglasses perched atop her chestnut hair, she was wearing a breezy summer dress that left no doubt as to just how tanned her full breasts were. Obviously an acquaintance of Brad's. Amanda wished she had her own sunnies with her. The huge smile was nearly as dazzling as the most impressive rock on her ring finger.

"Hi, are you a friend of Brad's?"

Amanda nodded. "And you?"

"Yes, Felicity." She extended her hand.

Amanda shook it, introduced herself and politely wondered if she could help in some way.

"I was so hoping to see Brad this morning but he doesn't seem to be in. All the curtains are open and I can't spy anyone inside."

She was right. All the rooms of the basement flat he rented below a family house in South Hobart faced the front. Amanda stuck her nose up against the slightly grimy glass and peered into the far corners of the interior. The door to the bathroom was open but there was no light on or movement discernible there. In the foreground was a particularly tidy bedroom. Although very masculine in most respects, Brad was a bit of a stickler when it came to keeping his own place looking respectable. Obviously did not want any of his visitors thinking him to be a secret slob. Even the kitchen and bathroom were kept clean. They had certainly broken the mold with this one.

Amanda turned to the buxom visitor. "Well, it looks like the *Mary Celeste*."

"Yes, yes, it does. I called and texted him yesterday but no response."

Increasingly, it seemed obvious this woman was rather attached to Brad. She may be a bit more mature than his usual choice of playmate but the superficial attraction was clear, apart from the teeth that is.

Amanda could not resist taking a little more wind out of her sails. "I shouldn't worry too much. Knowing Brad, he's probably just giving the white shorts an airing."

The woman looked befuddled.

"You know, playing away from home. He's always good for a dirty stop-out."

That did the trick. The breeziness gave way to rueful anxiety. But she put on a brave face. "I imagine so. He is rather handsome, isn't he?"

Amanda merely nodded. Her earlier guess was spot on.

"I don't suppose there's a spare key somewhere?"

There certainly was but Amanda feigned ignorance as to its whereabouts. "Did you leave something here?"

"No, not really. Brad said he'd found some good fitness material for me and I could collect it here."

Yeah, right. As if, calculated Amanda.

"Well, I guess we're a bit stymied then. You'll have to catch him another time. As will I. See you."

She purposefully walked away down the drive. At her car, she looked up to see the curious visitor tapping away on her mobile. Good luck to her. She looked like she would need it.

Amanda could not be bothered hanging around to see if Brad would turn up so she drove off down Washington Street. Just past the soccer ground she pulled over. A takeaway coffee from Magnolia would not go astray. As she approached the counter, two strapping men in dark suits turned away from the barista machine with their coffees.

An incongruous sight of a Saturday in this area, she assumed they must be detectives. Mormons did not wear jackets door-to-door and the pair looked a bit hunky to be that zealous. Unlikely to be a real estate duo. They usually stalked solo unless there was an auction nearby. Probably detectives though. Had that look. As she made her order, she wondered what brought them to this neck of the woods. Maybe a break-in at the Lost Sock Launderette.

As the two detectives got into the car, Farrell could not resist a comment. "Did you clock that sort who walked in after us?"

"Yep, nice way to spend the weekend, I reckon. Marks out of one?"

"Shapely. Sparky eyes. Good tan. Yeah, I'd give her one."

Munro smiled to himself. Going anywhere with Farrell, even a funeral home, generated this level of banter. He figured it was easier to play along with the gags than have a go at his colleague. He wondered if the irredeemable one ever approached any of his targets of fancy. In his experience, the constable was a 'gunna'. Gunna do this; gunna do that.

He knew Mahoney found the whole routine puerile and had torn strips off the subordinate quite recently. He had asked the Beekeeper for an HB pencil so he could take notes. When asked why he needed that pencil specifically, the gormless fool had said it seemed right for their interview with the manager of a modelling agency who was being subjected to stalking by a disgruntled client. Farrell had described her as a horn bag. The Beekeeper had given him the full angry hornets' nest treatment. It obviously did not seem to have improved the most un-PC PC going around. Still, he possessed some good qualities. Not many, but some. And one of those was he followed instructions clearly.

So when they arrived at Finch's address there was no need to emphasize the requirement for proper procedure. The drive was deserted, as was the flat, seemingly. They found a spare key underneath a garishly colored gnome so entry was uneventful. The front door opened straight into a compact lounge room decorated without any acknowledgement to interior design trends of the past decade. Opposite a wood frame sofa with beige upholstery was a large flat-screen TV perched atop a low hardwood table. Beneath it were a digital receiver and small DVD player. And that was it. No posters, lamps or shelving save a free-standing electric panel heater underneath the window next to the front door.

Separating this space from a functional kitchenette was a waist high bench with a lurid orange Formica top. A solitary stool stood on the lounge side of the bench. The appliances in the kitchen space looked like they were still there from the original installation, sometime in the 1980s. Everything, the policemen noticed, was spotless. Farrell was incredulous. "Well, either he's batting for the other team or someone's been through here to clean up any traces."

Unsure whether to first address the homophobia or the predilection for the CSI entertainment franchise, Munro reserved judgment. "Perhaps he didn't want to live in a pigpen. Some people have a bit of pride in their dwellings." Despite a well-founded reputation for sloppiness in the police section house, his offsider did not flinch. The man's an armadillo, thought Munro. "You go through everything in here and I'll sort out the bed and bathroom." His partner looked a touch aggrieved. Probably hoped he would find a wardrobe full of lubricant and sex toys. Best leave him with the pots and pans.

Munro walked through the open door into the double bedroom. Again it was a fairly Spartan environment. Next to the made-up bed was a table on which were a black metal lamp and an iPod dock. Opposite the bed on his immediate right hand side, Munro found the built-in wardrobe. He opened the mirrored sliding doors to reveal the clothes of somebody who had a place for everything and liked everything in its place. He made a mental note to make sure he kept a blank face when he told this to Mahoney.

A window similar in size to the living room area let in light to the room. As in there, a timber pelmet was sitting above the curtain rail: a practical nod to the need to retain warmth in the flat. A sliding wooden slat door opened into a bathroom-come-laundry. No towels on the floor. No soiled clothing dumped in the corner. Finch might be a gun sportsman but he was also Mister Neat. Nothing wrong with that. Munro just secretly hoped the guy did not wax his eyebrows. That really would tip the sympathy barrow over the edge.

As the banging about continued in the other room, Munro carefully looked through the cabinet underneath the washbasin (toothpaste and brush, anti-perspirant deodorant, condoms, massage oil and band aids) and the wardrobe (jocks, socks and tops) before sitting on the bed. What had he expected to find? A diary. Incriminating letters. A Gladstone bag full of cash. Unlikely, really. This generation used a mobile phone device for everything. Why bother even with a laptop when an iPhone could do practically everything you wanted?

Mahoney had told him a while ago that death stripped away a person's privacy. And as a person's private life could often open the way as to why they were killed then they should have no qualms about intruding on that privacy. Munro could see the logic of that but it was not going to be much help here. They had squat. Even the bed revealed little. Finch had obviously been intending to come home for a 'clean-sheet' night. The bed linen looked and still smelt freshly laundered. A batch of washing was out on the line fluttering in the light breeze. Even the fact that there was nothing, despite the evocation of sinister deeds, signified nothing. The guy was clean and tidy. Not much more to it. He hoped Herrick and the guys down at the Bay were having more luck.

*   *   *

In his office, Mahoney took a call from Constable Herrick. It lifted the gloom a little. The manager remembered seeing Finch there on Thursday evening. Couldn't be sure how long for but he was sure of the night. Nobody else working at the Metz on Thursday night was there today. Herrick had the duty roster with accompanying contact numbers to be followed up. Aside from that, the canvassing of local businesses had produced nothing. With a terse instruction to call everyone on the employee list, Mahoney finished the call.

Almost immediately Munro called through. Same scenario. No one in the dwelling above Finch's flat or any of the neighbors had noticed anything untoward. The flat itself and the occupant's car parked in the street had yielded nothing of consequence. The first twenty-four hours were generally held to be the most crucial in a homicide case. An initial velocity could be transformed into a momentum that would carry on to a positive result. They were certainly garnering a reasonable amount of information about the corpse but far too little material was forthcoming from the relevant scenes including, most worryingly, the building site in Kingston. They were fast becoming mired in a bog.

The victim's parents had been most understanding, despite their obvious distress. There were no hysterical demands for something to be done immediately or for any sort of miracle for that matter. Marron had informed him that they had not minded the routine questions he was obliged to ask. After all, living three hundred kilometers away, they were hardly suspects. Marron sensed that it was the father who was the most shaken by the events. A sense on the officer's part that the father was immensely proud of the son but had never taken the opportunity to tell him. Now it was gone and would never come again.

They sounded like good people and the least they deserved was for justice to be done. To find who had snuffed out the light. As Mahoney started to read the initial report from the building site, his phone distracted him again. Caller ID on the handset indicated Assistant Commissioner Newman was about to throw in his two cents worth. If only it was worth that much, thought Mahoney, as he contemplated ignoring the ringing tone. May as well take it. It could even be an offer of more resources. It was not.

"Yes, Sir."

"John?" Who on earth did he expect to be on the other end of the phone? A cadet from the Academy?

"Yes, it is." Mahoney waggled his jaw in an attempt to relax his voice. Moving house would be easier than conversing with this particular man.

"Good. John, I'm just making a quick call to let you know I'm right behind you on this one." Mahoney mentally debated whether this was because the AC was holding a knife or so his chief investigating officer could shield him if the offal came flying in their direction. Hard to say. "The Commissioner and I know the importance of this case and would not wish it in the hands of any other officer. Needless to say, there is already an unprecedented amount of interest and speculation so I exhort you to obtain a speedy result. Sergeant Gill has personally briefed me on the current situation and she and I will be conducting a doorstop shortly for the media. Is there anything else we can tell them?"

Bugger off and let the real police get on with their job. "No, Sir. We are pursuing every angle as tightly as possible. All procedures are being followed to the letter. The squad is on to everything, I assure you."

"Well, that's good, John. Keep Sergeant Gill in the loop. Must go. The Fourth Estate awaits."

The unwitting subtext was obvious. The oily Newman was relieved it was someone else, preferably Mahoney, who would carry the can if things went wrong. The media may be pushing hard but that suited the prima donna upstairs beautifully. He could soon do his impression of the earnest and authoritative statesman. Sergeant Gill could not be trusted out of sight in a dust storm. Par for the course.

But what really irked Mahoney was the gratingly false bonhomie of being addressed by his Christian name. Surely Newman must know how much 'John' loathed him. Perhaps not. Mahoney was always scrupulously careful to maintain a professional demeanor around the top brass. Especially around the very superior he truly had a strong reason to despise. Resolving to not give the smug bastard the satisfaction of seeing him fail, Mahoney bent to his task. Digging in the assembled reports for a speck of useful material. The grind continued.

CHAPTER 19

Sunday 14ᵗʰ March 9am

Mahoney had woken early as always nowadays. Long gone were his days of youth when he would slumber till the late morning of a weekend. His body clock was locked-in to an early awakening, whether he was dog-tired or not. Today that was hardly a problem. A case such as this energized him and as he eased out of bed he knew why. Homicide was the ultimate crime for the victim, the perpetrator and those who sought to solve any mystery arising from it. As a detective, it meant putting all distractions, pleasures and most of life's necessities aside until the case was closed. This required determination and skill if it was to be done correctly and expeditiously.

Regardless of whether his squad attained a quick result or the investigation became an arduous marathon, it was necessary to grind relentlessly away at all aspects that should be covered. Luck could play a part but one could not, and should not, hope too much for it. As one of Mahoney's sporting heroes had asserted, "Luck on the field of sporting endeavor is mighty helpful but I find that the harder I train and the more committed I am to the fray, the luckier I get." Exactly.

A DI had a multifarious role in any investigation. He need not be the marquee player, though that helped, but he had to be the captain in the field who led by example in the work of detection as well as being the able coach, who could organize, delegate, cajole and inspire. He may not be as well paid or well known as Sir Alex Ferguson but the consequences of getting it wrong were far weightier. The victim's family would certainly think so and the wider community definitely expected the thin blue line to do its job.

Mahoney showered quickly and then dressed himself in his 'uniform' of black shoes, navy single-breasted suit, sky blue shirt and red tie. Although not the most practical attire at a crime scene, the principal investigating officer chiefly needed to look…Chiefly. Even on the occasions he didn't necessarily feel it, he must look authoritative: his officers and public alike expected it. He may prefer to doff the jacket and roll up his sleeves but people desired a particular image and it always paid to look the part; to appear unflappable.

As he was closing the front door behind him, his mobile rang. "Mahoney."

"Sir, it's DC Kendall. Sorry to disturb you…"

"Kate, stop. You've used up your one 'sorry' for the course of the investigation. I want you because I hear you do things properly so don't apologize. What is it you have to tell me?"

"Understood. We could have an original crime scene. Down at the Sandy Bay Bowls Club. The curator was there to do a final prep of the greens and spotted blood and hair on a concrete curb at the end of one rink. I've called McLeod, Libby and Lyn and they're all on their way. I'm here and have informally sectioned the site to minimize fuss. It could be it. It's very near the last sighting of him."

"Yes, good work. Call for some uniforms to close that street and move the cars that are within ten meters. I'll be there shortly. Good stuff, Kate."

This was quick. Maybe a spot of luck wouldn't go astray. From his flat in Dynnyrne, it was no more than five minutes at normal speed so Mahoney was there as soon as predicted. Another sparkling morning in a seemingly endless summer.

Upon seeing his ID, the young uniformed constable let him drive through the roadblock. He parked in one of the spaces reserved for committee members. There would be precious little bowling today. Perhaps the club could re-schedule the pennant match if one was on. A minor matter but keeping people onside never hurt in the long run. As he got out, he was approached by McLeod.

"Morning, John. I've just arrived myself. Any particular stuff you need?"

"Jim, thanks for being prompt. Though you always are, aren't you?"

McLeod smiled. "Yes John, I always snap to it. Boom boom. Now we've done the Basil Brush routine, shall we start?"

Mahoney nodded. "Yeah. OK. Usual stuff but could you also take some broader location shots of all entrances and exits and fence lines. We will need to know how anybody got in or out of here. I'm assuming the gates are locked out of hours."

"Yes, they are. Don't want hoodlums traipsing all over my greens." This from a short nuggetty man dressed in old style white tennis shorts and little else. George Hamilton would have swooned to see his tan. His skin was the shade of dark brown boot leather and quite possibly the same texture. His acquisitive eyes were even darker beneath a pair of eyebrows to which Lord Kitchener would have given the seal of approval. His wispy grey hair could not cover a couple of impressive sunspots.

"Bloody kids get in and stuff up all my good work. Need the buckle, some of 'em, if you ask me." Mahoney guessed he was being addressed by the curator and introduced himself while McLeod strolled off to follow instructions. "I'm Fred Cooper, as in barrel." He held out a large knuckly hand which Mahoney shook. "Looks like a bit of a punch up. How come so many of you fellas swooped down?"

Mahoney always figured on a need to know basis. "There was a report of some trouble we have to follow up. Could be related to an ongoing inquiry. Sorry to mince words but I can't say too much."

The senior man nodded wisely and tapped his nose a touch theatrically. "No worries, Inspector. I'm no gossip. Go for your life. No matches on today so it's pretty free. Just a bunch of blokes having a stags do about 4 o'clock. All the go these days. Barefoot bowls and cheap beers. Can put 'em off, if you like."

Mahoney got the feeling Mr. Cooper would like nothing better than to jettison the booze-up. "I'll let you know in a while if that's OK." He made to walk off but hesitated. "Apart from the blood you saw, were there any other signs of something odd?"

"Yeah, too right. After I called the cops I sort of stood guard near the spot. That's how I spied it."

"What?"

"My work shovel was tossed down near the end of the rink. Wouldn't leave it there. Bloody untidy, I reckon. Didn't touch it. Told the pretty lass when she arrived."

"Thank you, Fred. If any of this lot stuff up, I'll get you in. Could do with sharp eyes." Mahoney winked and continued into the club.

At the far end of the nearest rink a small open-sided tent was being set up. There might be little chance of rain to contaminate the scene but this was part of the established process and needed to be done. It helped demarcate the immediate area of interest and alerted all personnel not to go wandering near what could be vital trace evidence. Lyn Manning was in front of the clubhouse delegating various tasks to the three uniforms at her disposal. He would need to speak to her later for an update on any information than might have been gleaned from the site at Kingston.

But first Kendall commanded his attention. He walked down the smoothly grassed rink to where she stood with a man in white overalls who was pointing downwards to some dark splotches on the ground. Mahoney stopped at the edge of the enclosure.

"Good morning, Sir. Sergeant Wall was just about to start looking more closely." Kendall was astute. No doubt. She knew to be formal in front of the officers and was canny enough to hold off initial examination so he could be present but she was still unfamiliar with the correct identities of many of the personnel with whom she would be working.

"Thank you, Constable Kendall. Before that may I re-introduce you to one of the Forensics officers?" He gestured to a grinning face that was gaunt to say the least. "This is Sergeant Don Baxter. Bit of a gun triathlete, hence, the lean and hungry look. I thought by now he might have foregone the offensive nickname but there you go. We can't all be sensitive to new norms of sexuality in our community." Mahoney was terse. It had the requisite effect. The grin was gone.

"Sorry, Sir. Sorry, Constable Kendall. I just thought I'd have a bit of a lend of you. You being obviously new and everything."

Mahoney was not finished. "Don, we know you're valuable and I'm grateful you're back from leave a day early." Baxter's eyes were wide with surprise. "Don't gape. It was a calculated guess. Our superiors want a result here. Lots, as in tons, of pressure. So you've been dragged in. A good forensics person is needed. And that's you."

Baxter puffed up a little.

"But for God's sake don't piss about with change room humor. Kendall is new to my squad but she's not green. Understood." No question about it. "Right. So what can you tell me? Apart from there's blood."

"Not much, yet. I just got here and togged up. I'll get to it now."

"Good. Meanwhile Detective Constable Kendall and I will be talking to DC Manning."

Mahoney took Kate by the crook of the elbow and they stepped up onto the central pathway that separated the normally pristine patches of lawn and started walking to the clubhouse.

"Thank you. What was all that with the names about?"

"Frat house jokes. Baxter is competent. No doubt about that. Skilled and careful. But a bit insecure maybe. Was quite plump for a few years. Working in the lab, not much active work. Very ordinary diet. Then he decided to get fit. Twelve months later he's competing in triathlons and his skin folds are unbelievably good. He feels better and life is on the up. But he's still not totally sure of himself. Body's great but his self-esteem hasn't quite caught up. So when some buffoons from the Clarence Station start asking him if he's got AIDS, to explain the weight loss, instead of telling them to grow up he plays along. Goes along with the daft nickname. Baxter the Wall. The height of wit."

"Blokes." Kate's voice conveyed all anyone needed to know about her attitude to bullying of any kind.

They were now standing under the clubhouse veranda. Manning joined them. Introductions done, Mahoney asked for an update from her. "I've managed to snare three probationers who weren't out on the booze hunt last night."

To help curb the late night outbreaks of damaging violence that was cursing the waterfront nightspots, an increased number of uniforms had been patrolling the city streets on Saturday nights. The net result was a dramatic increase in arrests for disorderly conduct but not, as yet, a commensurate decrease in trouble. Perhaps the proposed restriction on licensing hours would help alleviate that if the powerful hotel lobby could be acquiesced. Apparently, serving intoxicating beverages to young people was not the reason frustrated teenagers started belting people at all hours of the night. Seemed cut and dried to the police but what would they know.

"They're checking the perimeters and the surrounding laneways for anything that might be left. I'm assuming, Sir, that this could be the scene of the initial assault from last Thursday."

"Correct. We'll work on the basis that if this is the scene it happened then. Baxter will provide that link, I hope. And something could turn up in the surrounds."

"We've been lucky in one respect then. The old fella that looks after everything told me that there have been very few people here lately. The club was closed to players for the past three days while he did some essential upkeep on the surface. So nobody clumping about much at all."

Kate did not want to state the obvious but decided being shy was not the reason she was included in the enquiry. "Why would Finch be here? It fits with the last confirmed sighting of him just up the road at the Metz. But his flat is back up the hill off Huon Road. Was he here for some alfresco fun or en route to something similar nearby?"

Mahoney breathed deeply and slowly exhaled. "That's the nub of the problem. My guess is he was going somewhere else. This was a short cut." He gestured behind him. "The way the streets run around here this club provides a quick way down to the houses on Marieville Esplanade and the Yacht Club."

Manning was watching the uniforms scouring the grounds. She turned back to the detectives. "One of the football people perhaps." She pointed towards the river. "Just over there is a house belonging to the Vice-President of the Devils." She had their full attention. A small shrug of the shoulders and a half smile. "I just know because my boyfriend, he's a horticulture teacher, and I visited an open garden day there a fortnight ago. Beautiful property. Belongs to this university guy. Um, yeah, Dr. Bruce Randall. He could have been going there. I mean, it could be a start."

Mahoney knew it was tenuous, but did not say so. A cloak of confidence was necessary in order to encourage people to think and to proffer ideas. There was precious little use in playing safe. The man lived nearby and a quick visit would not be untenable given his link to the player. "Jane, that's a good suggestion. As soon as we have confirmation Finch was here, I'll contact him. There's always a chain. We just need more of the links."

Mahoney's mobile rang. He answered. "DI Mahoney speaking."

"Inspector, hello. I know it's Sunday but I needed to speak to you. About Brad."

The voice was not one he knew. "Don't worry about the day. They're all work now. But could you tell me who you are?"

"Oh, sorry. My name's Amanda Pattison. I've just heard about Brad's death. I was a close friend. It's horrible. It's suspicious, isn't it? That's what they said on the radio." The phrases tumbled out. Emotional.

"That is certainly what we presume. But why have you been given my number? How can you help?"

"Sorry. I badgered the officer on the phone to give me your number. I'm away down the Tasman Peninsula today but I know I can help. A few weird things have been happening lately that might be part of this, this horrible mess."

Her tone was urgent. And Mahoney's antennae were alert. "I certainly want to speak to you as soon as you can arrange it. As you can guess we need to gather as much information as we can about Brad's movements prior to whatever it is that's happened. So anything you have is appreciated."

Her voice was now more level and, if anything, more steely. "I can definitely do that, Inspector. I will be back in town tomorrow morning."

"OK. Does 8am at Kafe Kara suit you? You know it?"

"Yes, yes. That's fine. I'll be there."

Could be nothing. But if it was something it could only help.

CHAPTER 20

Sunday 14th March Noon

So this is what a crisis meeting is like, thought Bruce Randall. In times of emergency – invasion, natural disaster, economic collapse – the powerbrokers assembled and decided what was to be done. This was hardly one of the aforementioned catastrophes but from the demeanor of Roger Sproule you could be excused for thinking so. From the moment he'd arrived at the Football Club offices he had been edgy. The customary arrogance was nowhere to be seen. Rory Fotheringham was behaving true to form. Unflappable, brisk and in command of the situation. Cold-blooded didn't quite cover it.

Just the three of them. When Sproule had called him one hour earlier, he had stressed that it was best if just the executive be there. They were seated in the boardroom; all three oblivious to the southerly view of the Derwent River as it ran out into Storm Bay.

The club's base was here. On the site of the former Tasmanian Cricket Association Oval the new stadium was a testimony to how a vision could be transformed into a stunning actuality. Two decades before, the Cricket Council had transferred operations over the river to Clarence. It was believed that revamping the existing Bellerive oval would give the capital a much better chance of hosting Test matches. And so it had proved. Blundstone Arena was now the home of cricket in Tasmania: a regular schedule of Test and one-day matches were now a staple part of Hobart's summer. This nettled the sensibilities of sports followers in the north of the state but that was part and parcel of the senseless parochialism that infected the place.

The TCA ground had moldered for a number of years. Local cricket matches in summer and some football games in winter. Deciding to use it as a major part of the bid to bring an AFL club into existence had been a masterstroke. Randall knew the kernel of the idea had stemmed from Fotheringham. He was a callous manipulator but he definitely had an eye for the main chance. And knew how to bring a scheme to fruition.

In retrospect, it seemed that the current structure seemed perfectly placed but no one else had seen it at the time. Fotheringham had. The ground was perched on the plateau atop the Queen's Domain, a large area of land on the edge of central Hobart. Apart from the small suburb of Glebe in a corner of the precinct the area was mainly bushland. Government House and the Botanical Gardens occupied prime position on the eastern side of the hills facing the river. Within one kilometer of the oval were the Domain Tennis Centre, Hobart Aquatic Centre and the Athletics Track. The whole area was bordered by the principal arterial highways that fed traffic into and out of Hobart. From the airport to the ground took fifteen minutes by car: a fact not lost on the marketing firm that drafted the submission to government and the AFL Commission.

A private consortium took a bold proposal to the State Government. Let us take over the site of the TCA oval and we will deliver an AFL team to Tasmania. The case for a team was compelling: tourism numbers would surge and an underused venue would be revitalized for the benefit of the local community. The public consultation process was duly carried out but in this football-mad area, little real opposition emerged. In truth, it was simply a bloody good idea. The transport infrastructure was largely already in place. Plenty of room next to the ground for car parking. Shuttle buses from the CBD and the two suburban transport hubs had easy access to the site. And what was music to the ears of government was that a spanking new facility would come into being with a minimal outlay of public funds. A piece of public infrastructure that wouldn't become a white elephant. Hobart City Council and the State Government clambered to get on board. More crucially, so did investors.

The masterstroke there had been the provision for a state-of-the-art hotel and convention center. The southern end of the ground would be flanked by a sweeping grandstand that could seat twenty five thousand patrons. Behind the terraced seats would be an outer ring of buildings to house club facilities, offices and a two hundred room hotel. The topography of the site meant that guests would enjoy views of the Tasman Bridge, Derwent River, Hobart's waterfront or Mount Wellington depending on their choice of room. Given its proximity to the sights of the State's south occupancy levels would be high all year round. And so it was proving. Since the end of construction the previous August, the Royal Domain Hotel had been very nearly full for the whole summer. Within weeks of opening, the Conference Centre had been deluged with booking requests. The home football matches would guarantee a solid income stream during the traditionally slower winter months.

Geography greatly assisted the oval itself. The tall grandstands at the southern end would shelter the playing surface from the sharp prevailing winds during the season. The northern 180 degrees of the ground's boundary was flanked by smaller grandstands built at a height to ensure the sun could still hit all areas of the turf from April to September. Every seat in the house had a great view and the curators experienced none of the constant resurfacing issues that plagued the roofed Docklands Stadium in Melbourne.

The beauty of the deal for the Tassie Devils Club was that use of the oval, training facilities and corporate offices were available at a peppercorn rent on a long lease. This had been a tipping point in the consortium's pitch to both the government and the AFL Commission.

Start-up costs for infrastructure would be unusually low which meant revenue could be directed to ensuring the club would have a solid platform on which to build. Due to the restrictions imposed by the salary cap, the Devils couldn't just lure whatever players they wanted with hefty contracts. But the list they had assembled was still pretty formidable for a start-up team.

The recruitment manager, Colin Thompson, had a two-pronged approach. Firstly, he pointed out to targeted players that although the money on offer was not better than available in the mainland capitals, it was absolutely no worse and that sort of money goes a long way in Hobart. On your contract, son, you'll be a property magnate in no time. Try that in Sydney. The particular players targeted were not the marquee players of their competitors. Rather, Thompson adopted the money ball strategy that had been so successful for the Oakland Athletics Baseball franchise in the United States. While his craggy features dictated he would never be played by Brad Pitt if Hollywood showed any interest, Thompson knew how to assess underlying value.

At trade time the previous October, he had worked the phones arduously, looking for players with a couple of season's experience who could hold their own but were considered expendable by their existing employers. Guys whose salaries wouldn't be rocketing up when their turn came to sign. Players who knew, come contract re-negotiation time, it would be take it or leave it. So why not take a good offer and go to Hobart. Thompson's expertise was that he sourced the players who were solid mid-range performers with a team ethos. Mix a majority of such personnel with a few higher-level performers and you had the makings of a competitive team. And the Devils had used their selections in the national draft wisely so that the younger players coming on board exhibited strong potential and were injury-free. Season preview articles in the mainland media had heralded Thompson's recruitment period as the shrewdest smash and grab raid in the previous decade. Pundits had them as odds-on chances to make the finals: a bold prediction given the initial fortunes of the other two most recent expansion clubs in NSW and Queensland.

Secondly, Thompson lured players south with the prospect of a working environment equaled only by the mighty Collingwood club. Faced with the across-the-board limits that applied to the wages bill of all clubs, the Magpies of Melbourne had realized that the next best way to spend their unrivalled amount of income was to provide their team with superb facilities. There was no cap on the amount of money you could spend on having the best gymnasium and treatment rooms, the most expert medical staff and training camps in Arizona.

"It may just be Hobart but the only club with a set-up as good as this is Collingwood. So come down and be part of it," he'd enthused to each recruit. "And that's not the only point of comparison, as I'm sure you know."

They did know. Knew that in a remarkable coup the Devils would have the former Fitzroy champion player and Adelaide premiership coach, Mick Squires, in charge for the coming season. Squires had spent the previous season commenting on radio but the competitive zeal was far from sated so he had literally leapt out of retirement to take over the reins for the Devils. No matter whom you were, footballers wanted to play for him.

The club was built … and they came. Randall grudgingly admitted that although ice probably ran in his veins Fotheringtham was a genius. Surely an A type personality. Saw the big picture and puts the nuts and bolts in place.

Only now was the club facing its first major hurdle. Hurdle was not the word Randall would have thought most appropriate. But that is how Fotheringtham had put it and it was his take on proceedings that most people acceded to. They did that or he put them in their place. The week before, Randall had appeared on the local ABC station's statewide current affairs program. It was felt that his traditional image would give an impression of gravitas for the public broadcaster: it was Sproule who was trotted out for any spruiking on the commercial station. Towards the end of the studio interview, the presenter had asked about the effect of regulation on the financial affairs of the sporting clubs. Were the draft and salary cap a good thing, he was asked. Randall gave an emphatic yes. Even in America, where regulation was something of a dirty word, the NFL imposed a similar set of stipulations on its member clubs. This helped bring about a spread of success. Otherwise big clubs like the Dallas Cowboys would gather all the best talent and steamroll the opposition.

One only had to look to the United Kingdom where the inequities of wealth and the absence of a salary cap meant only a handful of clubs could realistically hope for premiership success or compete for the lucrative places in European competitions. The exclusive dominance of Chelsea and the two Manchester teams in recent years could not be genuinely healthy. Even a grand club such as Arsenal was hard pressed to keep up. So, Randall concluded, provisions such as the salary cap ensured a mostly level playing field which, in Australia's egalitarian society, was quite apt.

The next day Fotheringtham had called to say well done on his appearance. It sent a good message to viewers, he said. And the guff about a fair competition in an egalitarian society had been a winner. Guff? Randall expressed a modicum of confusion. How so? Fotheringtham explained. The AFL has got the cap and draft for two reasons. One is so they can exert control over the clubs. Keep people in line. Second, is to make money. That's why it's that way in the US. To maximize the pot of gold from TV rights. If all the success is enjoyed by Dallas and San Francisco then couch potatoes in Cleveland, St Louis and New York will tune out. Spread the talent and you spread the opportunity of success. More people tune in so more advertisers want to get on board. The Commission can demand more for the TV rights. So it's really the use of socialist practices to feed the goal of capitalism; make more money. And it's the same here. If Melbourne clubs dominate, then the tellies in Perth and Sydney won't be turned on. There's your bottom line.

And so another bedrock in Randall's slab of principles had been ground to dust. As he got older he began to feel that one's life was a process of developing articles of faith only to see them demolished by the reality of existence. Was it really just dog eat dog? He believed not. The Fotheringhams of this world held sway sure enough. There had to be another way. But his own light on the hill was dimming. The younger ones may provide some answers. He hoped so.

His feeling of melancholy was heightened by the tenor of the discussion around the table. A young man's life had been brutally ended and his colleagues were talking as if a discrepancy in the annual audit had been found. Well, Fotheringham was. Sproule seemed slightly distracted and had to be brought back a couple of times.

"Roger. Earth to Roger. Come in please."

Sproule shook his head as if coming out of a bad dream. "Sorry, Rory. Kid's death is having a bit of an effect. Sort of delayed shock."

Randall was quietly amazed at the change in the President's demeanor. He'd assumed the man must have some reflective moments but he had never seen him around other people as anything but irrepressible. Something had shaken him. Something more, he privately wished, than the problem of finding a talented tall forward a few weeks out from the season opener.

As if on cue, Fotheringham went on. "As I was saying, the club's priority, in terms of moving forward, is to find a half-decent replacement in the attacking half. I've spoken to Colin and Mick earlier today and there're a few options available. Blood some of the green youngsters early. Scour the locals for anybody we've missed. Admittedly, that's unlikely given the job Colin did last year. Tweak the game plan. Finch was a great talent but nobody's indispensable. Mick agreed with me that we treat the loss as any club would a long-term injury to any star. Except it frees up a nice whack of money to get some fresh talent down the track."

Randall had shut his eyes for the last bit in the hope that it would heighten his olfactory senses. He was pretty sure there were rasping hints of Darth Vader somewhere. He opened his eyes to see Rory tick off that item on his list. Job done.

"Now to funeral arrangements. I met Mr. and Mrs. Finch for dinner last night." He pointed to the end of the room. "We're putting them up next door for the week. Waiving the bill. Do the decent thing on behalf of the club."

And slip a mention of that into a press release, thought Randall. He said, "I'm glad we're doing something. It must be a very sad time for them. No one wants to ever have to bury their children."

"You're right, Doc. Not the natural order of things by any stretch. So the club is doing all it can to take the stress out of arrangements for them. I spoke to the Assistant Commissioner this morning and there's no indication as yet for the release of the body from the mortuary. Autopsy was done yesterday and it seems pretty straightforward. Bashing gone wrong. Tragic accident. AC Newman reckons there's no reason to delay the funeral so I've penciled in next Saturday."

Before either of the others could speak, Rory ploughed on. "The lad's parents agreed that having the funeral down here would be appropriate. He'd become a Hobart boy anyway. And it fits in with plans for everyone who will want to attend. Club people, local friends etc. And the politicians will want in on the act. So the likely venue is St David's Cathedral, nice and central. Easy for media to cover and afterwards the police will sort the traffic so a funeral procession can head out the Brooker Highway to the Cemetery. A reception will be held here in the Conference Centre."

An event orchestrated to maximize publicity for the venue and the club. Fotheringham did not miss a trick. As the President continued to sit mutely, Randall hazarded a question. "Did his parents ask for a hometown ceremony?"

"No."

And that was that. Once they'd seen Fotheringham for a few minutes, they would have realized it was a *fait accompli*. Resistance is futile. May as well go along with it and adopt their set role as chief mourners. They had precious little choice, apparently.

"Well, on behalf of Roger and myself, I have to commend you on your efficiency. A very brisk response. You're not by any chance conducting the police investigation as well, are you?" The delivery was deadpan.

"Are you taking the piss, Doc?"

"Far from it, Rory. I'm pragmatic enough to know that history demonstrates what you need in a crisis is strong dictatorial control. Committees phaff around. Best for you to take control. Especially as Roger isn't firing on all cylinders at present."

"I'll take that as a compliment then." He smiled but the eyes negated any warmth he tried to generate. Clapping Sproule on the shoulder he said. "Old Roj here has been knocked for six by it all. Had a lot of time for the boy, didn't you Roger?"

Sproule blinked as if trying to remember the script. "Ah, yeah. Lad had a bit of spark to him." He sounded hollow.

Randall knew this was not the time to ask how much of a spark Felicity Sproule had found in the young footballer. But it was time to ask about the elephant in the room. "I'm sorry to have to ask this." He looked straight at the President. "Roger, does Finch's death have anything to do with the *tête-à-tête* you wanted last Thursday night?"

Sproule roused from his torpor. "No. How could it? Why would I want our prize player to get done over? Give me some credit."

Randall could think of one reason. A bit tenuous but Sproule was renowned for taking a bulldozer approach. The Fixer chimed in. "Strange question, Doc. Roger tells me Finch didn't front up. Next thing anyone hears is that his corpse turns up in Kingston. Bit of a stretch if you ask me."

As he wasn't asking Fotheringham, Randall maintained a fixed gaze on the President. "The thing is Roger, as I was departing my house to come to this meeting, there was a lot of police activity at the Bowls Club. Not quite such a stretch if you ask me."

Sproule wouldn't meet his eyes. "Jesus, how am I meant to know? Could be pissed vandals for all I know about it." The customary vigor was back.

Randall was unconvinced but short of a direct accusation he felt it prudent to let it go. "Alright, it just seems curious. Probably unconnected."

"Almost certainly, I'd say," Rory put in. "Could be anything at the Bowls Club. Coincidence, Doc, pure and simple. As Roger said why would anyone in the club be involved. Robbery gone wrong is what the police are thinking. Best we leave the hypothesizing to the experts, eh."

The words of Sean Connery in an old film floated into Randall's head. I wish you'd met me twenty years and thirty pounds ago.

Fotheringham wouldn't patronize him then. But right now he felt old. Stick his head out and get it kicked in. Not likely. So he acquiesced. "Fair enough. Silly thought." He got up from his chair. "I'll be off. Let me know if there's anything to be done."

Sproule mumbled a farewell as he continued to stare out the window. Fotheringham stood. "Righto, thanks for coming up, Doc. I'll be in touch."

As soon as Randall was out the door, the Fixer sat down and set his focus on Sproule. "Get a fucking grip and get it right fucking now." The harshness broke the spell. "If you don't your arse is grass and the lawnmowers are queuing up. Understand?"

Some hurried nodding. "Yeah, yeah. OK. I'm right."

"Good. You'd better be. For your own sake."

"Yeah, righto. Tone it down a bit. You gottta admit the pigs being at the Bowls Club was a bit of a shock."

"Not to me."

"What do you mean?'

"Newman told me about it." Someone tripped over something and the upshot is that it looks like a bashing went wrong. There's trace evidence of an altercation, the techies think. Cops will probably join the dots. There's nothing to think we're part of the picture. I made sure of that. I trust you did."

"Yeah, followed your instructions. They can't connect any of us up, can they?"

"The thugs who botched it have no idea who hired them. They certainly don't know why. Randall is just a curious old fart. Won't say anything. You just need to make sure you don't go jumping at shadows. And keep your trap shut."

CHAPTER 21

Monday 15th March 8am

For a brief diversion from the hysteria of the sports pages, Mahoney turned back a few pages to the classifieds section. Oftentimes these pages provided a more telling snapshot of what was going on in society than the news section; certainly so in contrast to the clinical media releases of the politics of the day. It always paid to scan the flea market section in case any petty thieves were trying to offload any items. Unbelievably, some actually tried this.

If the advertising was any guide, the rental market looked rather healthy…for landlords. He could scarcely credit that, according to comparable figures, his own flat would cost nearly $300 per week to rent. Thankfully, he did not. He recognized nobody in the hatched, matched and dispatched columns before flicking to see how the job market was faring out of curiosity and to see the sorts of salaries on offer. The Cadburys factory at Claremont had a couple of positions advertised. One was for a 'Logistics & Materials Manager', presumably to run the warehouse. The successful applicant would 'ensure the flow of goods across the site is optimized and synergies are gained across inbound and outbound deliveries'. What the…? There could only be one person for that job. Hercules. If the advertisement was any indication of the quality of communication within the company then all his experience from the Aegean stables would be necessary. In spades.

He took a final sip from his flat white as a confident young woman came down the aisle between the teak tables and bentwood chairs. Mahoney was fairly sure this was Amanda Pattison. He could immediately see she was attractive. That was obvious. Moreover, she was stylish in a way not many local women managed to be. Without mimicking foreign fashions, she obviously took care with her apparel. She even managed to make the wearing of a beret look natural.

She paused just short of his table. "Inspector Mahoney?"

"Yes, and I'm safely assuming you are Amanda."

She nodded and sat opposite him. "Yep, that's me. Thanks for taking time to see me."

"No problem at all. In truth it is me who should be most grateful. Your insight into some of the permutations could prove very valuable. What was Brad like?"

"Brad and I were good friends. Buddies without benefits." Mahoney smiled. Encouraged, she moved on. "Believe me; he didn't go wanting in that department. Anyway, we got along really well. I wasn't part of his footy social life. We caught up for coffees and chats. There was a side to him that was deeper and gentler than many saw."

A brief pause. Happy memories acknowledged. One of the staff arrived at their table. A perky young woman with the svelte figure of a gymnast. Mahoney ordered the same again and Amanda opted for a skinny latte. Neither was hungry, thank you. The hiatus gave Amanda the opportunity to settle herself. The waitress pirouetted away.

Mahoney let her think. "I understand what you mean. He displayed a social face because that was expected but with you he didn't have to keep it up. He could be him."

She let out a small exhalation. "Exactly. He was young Mister Studly around town and the gun recruit at football but when we hung out he was just himself. A nice simple guy. Not Oxbridge material but a lot brighter than he let on. It kind of pissed him off that some people would automatically assume he was a type just because he was a bit of a jock. Sure, he could be blokey and everything but he was pretty smart, too. Not many people gave him any credit for that."

Their coffees were served. A smile, some wanky Italian and a ramrod straight-backed Gen Y male strode away. Mahoney rolled his eyes and Amanda stifled a laugh. "This is good to hear. You'd think from all the media noise that what was lost was a prize yearling from a horse stud. There is always quite of lot more to people than we necessarily see. Either we want to see or they let us see." Mahoney methodically stirred just a bit of sugar into his coffee. "What in particular is worrying you?"

"I think you should talk to Dr. Cartwright from the university. Not that I think he did anything violent to Brad. I don't think he could do that but he's mixed up in this somehow. I mean everything was going well until the other day when there was a clash in one of his lectures. Cartwright just went off at him in front of the whole class."

"Can you tell me your version of what happened and what that led to?"

She sipped her coffee and wiped some crema from her top lip with a napkin. "Alright. Long story short. I'd seen a bit of Dr. Cartwright at these Pilates classes we were both doing. Didn't know him from Adam but noticed him at the studio. Not many men do those types of classes. Probably not butch enough for many males. Have to pump iron. At the start of semester it was him lecturing us in Australian Political Systems. One morning before a class he starts flirting with me at the refectory. I played along out of curiosity and cattiness. I mean, a meal with him could turn out interesting and if not I've been wined and dined gratis."

Mahoney admired her frankness while being grateful they were just having coffee. "So you agreed to have dinner with him?"

"Not then. Later. Another reason emerged."

"Arising from Cartwright lambasting Brad in front of the whole class?"

"Pretty much, Inspector. Yes, but not just that. Cartwright complained to one of the board members of the Tassie Devils. Then whoever he had the ear of gave Brad a telling-off as well."

"How so?" Mahoney was doing well to keep his voice level.

"Well, they couldn't threaten him with any football sanctions. Imagine the uproar. If unicorns returned they wouldn't be as protected as some of these wastrels who parade around as professional sportsmen. So Brad was told his enrolment in the athlete tertiary scholarship program would be in jeopardy if he stepped out of line again. Well, that stung. Some players, a lot of them probably, wouldn't care less but Brad really did want to study. Wanted some quals for later on. And his dad would be spewing too, if he found out."

"Hard man? Old school?"

"I'll say. Well, at least according to his son. Brad really liked him but he did admit that his upbringing on the North West Coast was a bit 'my way or the highway'."

Mahoney nodded and breathed deeply. He knew exactly what she meant. But that was another story so kept quiet.

"So Cartwright has got Brad a beauty. Seemed a bit unfair to me so I engineered a bit of a reprisal. We went to dinner and I played him. Flirted full on. He got a bit pickled and made a few very un-PC comments about overseas students. He wasn't to know I was recording him on my mobile. The new ones are fantastic. I teed up with a student doing a journalism placement at *The Mercury* to write a scoop. Take him down a notch or two."

Mahoney was unsure how to react. It was unlikely a quick lecture on fair play or the intricacies of the Telecommunications Act would get them very far. He was just glad he wasn't taking her on. "And where did this material end up?"

"Nowhere. That's it. Grace, the budding journo, wrote the article, submitted it and thought it was good to go. It was even advertised on the Monday evening TV promo as a story in the next day's paper. But then it just disappears. Wasn't printed. Grace was fed some line about legal concerns and it's been buried deeper than nuclear waste since."

Mahoney frowned. This was redolent of week old fish. "And the copy of the article and the recording?"

Amanda gestured as a magician sending an object into a puff of smoke. "Grace took my phone in with her to the offices to write the article. Was too keen to get going on it to make a copy. Sent the article through to the news editor's desk and handed over the phone. Silly girl."

"Then what?"

"Well, the article doesn't appear. Grace asks what's going on. Gets given a load of rubbish about legalities. Blah, blah! Goes back to her desk and discovers that the article has been wiped from her hard drive. No back-up copy made. She was in a rush, you see. But what is really strange is that the recording is gone too. And now nobody knows anything about it."

"And that was your only corroborating evidence of Cartwright's conversation with you?"

"Yep. Foolish, I know. We were so hot on the scent and wanted to get it in Tuesday's paper that the whole thing was rushed." A rueful smile.

"We could have done with a few tips on securing the chain of evidence, couldn't we?"

Too right, thought Mahoney. "So the scheme has come to nothing. Have you heard any more?"

"No, Grace has tried but just gets stonewalled. I tried to rouse some interest but made even less ground. Then the events of the rest of the week sort of overtook us."

They both declined an offer of more drinks. Mahoney pressed on. "When did you last see Brad?"

"Thursday afternoon. We had lunch. He was off to training later in the day and then out. I didn't hear anything from him on the Friday. Not so unusual. I went round to his flat on the Saturday morning to see if he wanted to go to the beach. It was a stunning day. I didn't know then but obviously I was never going to get him swimming that day."

"No, no, you weren't. Did you call him or actually go to his flat?"

"No answer on his mobile so I went round. No sign of him. Just another visitor there."

Mahoney could not help reacting abruptly to this news. He leaned forward. "Visitor. Inside?"

"No. She was just there when I arrived. About midday. Bit of a cougar but nice enough, I guess. She seemed a bit concerned Brad wasn't there. Something about leaving something in his flat. Anyway, Brad wasn't there and we both left."

"Did you get her name?"

"Yes, Felicity. No surname, sorry."

"No problem. Probably nothing." He stood and put some gold coins on the table. "Well, thank you for this information. I think I have a visit or two to make. You understand that our conversation is completely confidential?"

"Yes, you can trust me on this one. I hope you get somewhere. I'm going to miss him very much."

"I understand. We'll certainly be doing our best. Goodbye for now."

CHAPTER 22

Monday 15th March 10am

The two detectives drove from headquarters up Liverpool Street, past the Pickled Frog Backpackers Hostel. After literally two minutes, they were out of the CBD and Munro steered the unmarked Commodore sedan into Liverpool Crescent. In that instant, the built environment altered from businesses, cafés and workshops to a much quieter street, lined with an eclectic collection of old houses. A further half kilometer on, it was hard to believe they were anywhere near the city center.

The road cut along a steep hillside that ran down to the South Hobart rivulet. Amongst the large gum trees were perched a series of pole houses and double storied bungalows that clung determinedly to the precarious slope. The occupants were thereby afforded a glimpse of the Derwent River and a perfect view of the congested Victorian workers' cottages on the strip of Macquarie Street.

As they neared Cartwright's address, Mahoney, in the passenger seat, could see the freshly labelled precinct of SoHo. It was nothing like the raffish den of iniquity that was its London namesake. There was, however, a tenuous link to the uber-groovy doppelganger in Manhattan by virtue of its variety of florists, delicatessens and cafés. One of his favorites, Magnolia, was at the Darcy Street end of the area. Excellent coffee and a breakfast item of spicy fruit porridge had constituted a very sound start to his day.

Munro pulled the car into the curb outside number 78. As they got out, the senior officer spied the green expanse of the South Hobart soccer ground. He had played many, many games there in his younger years and wished he could still play in the veterans' competition. Certainly, the odd match here and there was possible but the constraints of work meant that being consistently fit enough to survive the rigors of those matches was not really feasible. He simply did not want to be left hobbling around for forty-eight hours after the final whistle.

Almost as soon as they were on the curb, Munro typically verbalized his first thought "Christ, what a monstrosity."

"Yes, it is startling, isn't it? It certainly makes a bold statement."

They were standing in front of a three-story concrete block construction that looked as if someone had plonked a gigantic ablutions amenity direct from Santa Fe into the Tasmanian bush. Instead of being rendered a potentially harmonious adobe color, it was painted cream. The color scheme was further devalued by the streaky rusty run-off down the sides of the walls from the chocolate brown metal window frames.

To say it jarred with its surroundings was an understatement at the very least. The building allowed for a magnificent vista reaching from the river right up to the heavily forested foothills of Mount Wellington. The reverse view would hardly be as pleasing. Perched atop the house's tower was a castellated deck that gave the whole place the feel of a tacky fortress.

They strode towards the front door, an impressively solid chunk of oak with a grille over a small glass viewing panel at head height. Munro banged on the black iron knocker just below it and stood back. Quite quickly the door was opened by a dark haired man wearing a crimson robe, sandals and the sort of glasses that had become rather popular: narrow rectangular lenses with broad black temples. Munro thought "wanker". Mahoney said, "Dr. James Cartwright, I hope?"

"Yes, it is. And who has come calling at this hour?"

"Detective Inspector Mahoney and Detective Sergeant Munro." They both displayed their warrant cards. "We would like to briefly chat about a serious matter you may be able to assist us with."

Cartwright looked over his lenses at the two men. They younger man was brawny and his nose seemed a bit crooked. Pugilistic tendencies? The rest of his face was boyishly handsome and he had enough product in his hair to fuel a dozen fry-ups – the same upswept style favored by that bloody footballer. His colleague looked far more somber with his dark suit and more normal closely trimmed hair. Old school or just plain boring? But the eyes were sharp.

The academic adjusted and re-tied the robe's cord around his midriff. "Did it occur to you to call ahead instead of rolling up here unannounced?"

Of course it did, smarty-pants, thought Munro. But as the whole aim of our visit is to find you unprepared for us we're not going to telegraph our arrival, are we?

"Yes, it did and we apologize for dropping in so early," offered Mahoney. It was 9.30am and Munro knew Mahoney didn't care one iota for decorum during the hot phase of an investigation but his boss could soft-soap people as well as anyone. "It's just that when we contacted the university, the department secretary informed us you were working from home and, unfortunately for us, was resolute about not releasing your private number." Nice touch!

Mahoney could have insisted but he did not want her letting on to Cartwright about their immediate interests though she'd probably called anyway. "We found your number was unlisted so we thought it best to simply pop around." Munro managed to keep a straight face. Something the Beekeeper had effortlessly mastered.

Cartwright let out a theatrical sigh. "Oh well, may as well come in then." He led the detectives along a slate tiled hallway and through an open door to a large room with a far wall of floor to ceiling windows. The floor was polished pine and on it was perched a single plush leather lounge that faced the southerly view. That was it in the furniture department.

What also rendered it unusual, weird even, in Munro's mind was that there was no ceiling. The double-storied room (the top level must be the tower) was completely lined with oak bookcases and where the ceiling should have been was a gallery landing on three sides that meant all the hundreds of books were accessible to a six-footer. What a waste of space, thought Munro. He kept his mouth shut. Mahoney could not. "This is magnificent. Are you sure we haven't wandered into the abode of Professor Higgins?"

Straight over Munro's head: not Cartwright's. He swelled at the chest like a robin and managed a modest reply. "Thank you, Inspector. I had serious reservations about this house when I first viewed it five years ago but I could see the potential for this space and purchased it almost on the strength of that alone. Because we're on the southern slope there isn't a great deal of sun but the aspect from here is golden. I hope you didn't judge this place by the cover. It's the inside of a house that matters to me."

Mahoney thought that was alright for him. Unlike his neighbors he didn't have to look at it. But he could not help expressing his genuine admiration. "This is a striking library. It could have been a bit OTT but it's in proportion." Mahoney sauntered to the nearest wall. "Even arranged by genre, I see. I take my hat off to you. A genuine reading room."

"Yes, it is. And if you could excuse me briefly, I'll get changed into some more conventional attire."

"By all means. As I said, we'd just like a quick chat."

Cartwright exited. In his absence Munro sat himself in the luxurious sofa and gazed at the surrounding hillside. Mahoney ventured up onto the gallery landing and perused the titles. He noted with approval the bias towards certain fiction writers: Barnes, Hornby, Lowry, Faulks and Banks et al. Cartwright's tastes were certainly catholic.

"This place suits you, Sir" piped up Munro after several contemplative minutes. "I reckon my partner, Jackie, would like it too. She's big on books. Loves organizing her bookshelves at home. Once, to wind her up, I took a whole heap down and replaced them in groups according to the color of their spines. Geez, by her reaction, you'd have thought I burnt them. Took a pretty expensive restaurant meal to cover that one." Munro smirked at the memory. The make-up sex afterward had been fantastic.

Cartwright reappeared, dressed in a button down green shirt, canvas slacks and loafers. "So, gentlemen, what would you like to know? I assume this is not merely a social call."

Mahoney descended and took up the running "Just a formality. As you may know, one of your students, Bradley Finch, died late last week in suspicious circumstances. We're at a bit of a loss at this early stage so we hope to shed some light on the case by talking to those who had any dealings with him recently. Background, you could say."

"So I don't need to alert my lawyer then," joked Cartwright.

Yes, you do, thought Munro.

"I'd say not," soothed his superior. "I understand he was in your class last Tuesday week and there was some, how to put this, tetchiness."

Cartwright made a show of thinking back carefully with a slightly overdone frown. "Oh, you mean the lad who thought he could take notes by texting on his mobile. That's the victim?"

"Yes, it is unfortunately." It beggared belief that Cartwright did not admit to making the connection but Mahoney let it slide. The feigning of such blissful ignorance could come back to bite him. Stow it away for later. Munro knew his boss had a mind like a steel trap. Fresh ideas might penetrate it but it was rare if anything got out.

"Yes, yes, Inspector, very unfortunate. The incident was over in an instant and forgotten by me just as quickly. It's just that I abhor the prevalence of the damned things. Did you know that along Brick Lane in London the local council has put padding around telegraph poles so that people texting don't hurt themselves when they walk into them? Ludicrous, isn't it?"

Mahoney had heard but feigned mild astonishment. "Yes, remarkable. So that's it, a brief verbal altercation. Nothing more?"

Cartwright looked his questioner levelly in the eye. "As far as I can recall. A minor spat. Over and done with in the blink of an eye."

Munro would have liked to push him but averred to Mahoney who seemed perfectly content with the response. "Out of interest, Dr. Cartwright, how many pupils attend this class? What is it again, Australian Political Systems?"

"Yes, that's correct. It's a compulsory unit for first year political science students. About one hundred and sixty regularly attend. Quite popular really."

"It would seem so. I bet your colleagues in Classics would love those numbers."

Munro observed with admiration as his boss quietly engaged the academic. Get them talking and keep them talking. You never know what might slip out.

"I dare say, Inspector. It's a sign of the times. For this generation Alexander the Great will remain very much as Ancient History. Admittedly a fair number of students opt for my unit as it's relevant to the law course some will transfer to. There's a smattering of radicals and even some who are genuinely interested in the content for its own sake. I doubt anyone chooses it based on the reputation of the lecturer." He raised his eyebrows and shrugged in a play of mild disappointment.

Could such a man be seriously aggrieved by a dearth of attention? Mahoney thought so. "And the manner of your presentation. How did that go?"

"In the traditional manner, mostly. A straightforward lecture for fifty minutes. Some PowerPoint slides for diagrams and images of significant figures from the past. It does help if you know what former leaders such as Menzies and Whitlam looked like. Questions are dealt with in tutorials. I talk and the students write. Some a lot and some a little."

"And Bradley Finch was one of the latter?"

"No, he wrote nothing. Turned up without a pen or notebook. Bit arrogant, I sensed."

Pot, kettle, black, thought Munro.

Mahoney tried to tease out the irritation. "You mean he just sat there?"

"If only. He obviously felt it amusing to text his buddies and to try and distract the serious young lady next to him by showing her the responses." Cartwright managed unsuccessfully to disguise his agitation at the memory. He snorted. "Stats of his training probably."

Before the alarm bell could be noticed, Mahoney quickly changed tack. "This young lady you mentioned. Do they regularly sit together?"

"Yes. Amanda, I think her name is." Butter would not melt. "Very able student from what I hear in the faculty. Why she would sit near that oaf is a complete mystery to this mere mortal."

But not half as much as how this lecturer was so well apprised of these two particular students a couple of weeks into the academic year. Cartwright was fudging the truth but until he knew more Mahoney decided not to press the point. Assuming Amanda Pattison had been giving a true rendition of events, there were some telling holes in Cartwright's version of what transpired. There was little to be gained at this stage by confronting the man with his duplicity. When a few more strands had been woven into place would be the time.

Munro had gotten out of his chair and was casting an eye over a collection of framed photos on the side table. "Are these family snaps, Jim?"

The immediate reaction was electric. "Please do not touch those." Their host hastened over and took a picture out of the sergeant's hand and delicately replaced it. "And I would appreciate it if you would address

me by my professional title as your superior officer has the good grace
to do."

Munro did not bat an eyelid. Looked slightly amused if anything.
"And what would that be, if you don't mind my asking?"

"Dr. Cartwright."

"So you've done medicine too?"

Before Cartwright's eyes could fully pop out, Mahoney yanked on
the lead. As much as he was enjoying the way Munro's act wound up the
academic, he knew it could go too far. "My apologies for the confusion.
Sergeant Munro isn't very bookish. They are very nice shots by the way."

Cartwright breathed. "Yes, my parents. Both passed away now. And
this is my sister, Mary."

"With?"

"Who? Oh, her husband Larry. She's just retired after a distinguished
career as a teacher and principal." There did not seem to be anything
of note to distinguish Larry so Mahoney thanked Cartwright and they
began to exit the room.

He patted his suit pockets and made to go. "Well, thank you for
your time. Sergeant Munro and I had better push on. We have a lot of
ground to cover."

Just as they were about to walk out the front door, Munro uttered a
parting shot. "Not a bad place really. If you like that sort of thing. Not
my taste." Cartwright's shoulders stiffened ever so slightly. "My girlfriend
would love it though. She's into all that." There was a vague gesture with
his arm. "You got a missus here?"

Cartwright bristled. "No, I haven't. Not at this stage." And with that
the officers departed.

CHAPTER 23

Monday 15ᵗʰ March Noon

If any of the various members of the Murder Squad were unsure of the level of public interest in the current case then the media conference that morning was a telling guide. That there was a media conference at all was something of an anomaly. In some cases of suspicious death, journalists from the local newspaper and television stations would be briefed and a request made directly to the public for assistance. Mostly the relevant authorities got on with the task of sorting out the problem and life went on with little regard outside of the dead person's family.

Of course, there were celebrated or notorious incidents that drew all manner of media organizations to Tasmania. The chilling and horrific events of April 1996 at Port Arthur turned the Apple Isle into one of the most newsworthy locations on the planet for a week. A rock fall in a mine in Beaconsfield in the state's northern region also brought the spotlight. Two miners were trapped underground for many days as way above them the interstate television and radio crews jostled for information, any information. This potential catastrophe ended fortuitously for two elated men who walked out arms flying high in victory. One man was killed by the accident but the exposure was on the survivors.

Heroes made for better stories. You cannot interview a dead person and his grieving family would not boost the ratings anywhere near as much as valiant tales of endurance and survival. So the duo became temporarily famous and then went on with their lives.

Soon after, the normal state of affairs was resumed. Tassie just disappeared. It was not unlike a British author's remark about American newspapers. You could perform your very own conjuring trick simply by virtue of being a European in the continental United States. Buy a newspaper and see your country disappear. Tasmanians could do just the same. Fly over Bass Strait to Melbourne and maybe find a paper in a week that mentioned the state.

But this case would obviously redress the balance. The victim was a footballer. And not just any footballer. A rising star in the Tassie Devils Australian Football League team. After years of being ignored by the mainland executive, a license to run a team in the upper echelon national competition had been granted. In its debut season, interest in the expansion club was at fever pitch.

Locals felt vindicated after decades of shabby treatment by interstate authorities. The cream of the local talent had been plundered by wealthy Melbourne clubs. Some of these players became absolute legends in the Victorian Football League and, by also representing that state, helped make it the powerhouse of Aussie Rules football. Precious little was done to compensate the local leagues. They still drew excellent crowds and enjoyed strong indigenous support. All that was changed now. The move by the VFL to create a national league in the 1980s had, by the 1990s, created a behemoth that effectively destroyed the Tassie competition.

Now, if youngsters asked which football team you followed and you mentioned a team in Hobart, they would say, "No. AFL?" For a few years a powerful Victorian club had become the Tasmanian team simply by virtue of agreeing to relocate a few home matches to Launceston in the state's north. Their adoption of the role of quasi-ambassadors seemed heartfelt but most doubted they would be quite so genuine if the Tasmanian government withdrew the ludicrously generous backing that was provided.

Pressure mounted. Furious lobbying of the League's Commissioners went on. Powerbrokers assembled a sound business plan for the proposed Tasmanian team. Still no dice. And then a strange thing happened. A young singer-songwriter who was plying his trade in Melbourne sang a song. Not on the radio and not a song about football. He was singing the national anthem as part of the pre-match ritual at a headline rugby league match. He did it well but that was not the noteworthy thing. On his guitar was a "Tassie for the AFL" sticker that was picked up by TV cameras and the press photographers.

Next day it was all over the media. Pundits, former players and the fans all practically simultaneously threw their support behind the bid and it became an unstoppable force. Functions were put on at the Commercial Club Hotel in Fitzroy, a bohemian suburb in Melbourne. The venue was apt. The Fitzroy club had been the first casualty of the transition from a traditional suburban competition to a national competition that was more akin to a marketing company than a sport. The fresh momentum bore fruit and come the 2010 season there really was going to be a Tasmanian team in the AFL.

And Brad Finch was one of the local marquee players. Big things were predicted for him. Now, with the season a few weeks away, his death had sparked a media storm. Mahoney, Kendall and the Tasmanian Police Press Liaison Officer were startled by the flashing bulbs and the bright television lights as they walked into the Conference Room. They seated themselves behind a rectangular table facing the assembled throng. A few journalists darted forward to prop recording devices on the front edge of the table. The microphones were tested for clarity and lights were up for the circus.

Sergeant Joanne Gill, the press officer, opened proceedings with a very carefully worded statement. The circumspect address was concise, clear and completely lacking any real insight into the case.

So far, so blah. The hacks patiently sat through it, waiting for the opportunity to launch questions at the operational officers. DC Kendall, as planned, responded to the general enquiries regarding the basic facts of the case. Yes, the location of the body's discovery had provided some crucial leads. No, she was not able to disclose that information. And so the tennis rally pattern was established. A reporter would serve a terse question; Kate would return with a carefully considered answer but would not continue much further with the immediate follow up. Mahoney had forewarned her that very few of the experienced journalists really expected to elicit from her any critical information but the show needed to be played out.

After ten minutes or so, the pack shifted their attention squarely on DI Mahoney. To him they directed the queries regarding the potential impact of the loss of Finch from the football world. They must have felt his female colleague unqualified to deal with the important stuff.

Mahoney was barely qualified to assess this either, but did have the requisite experience to treat the exchanges with sufficient gravity and seemingly satisfy the sizeable contingent of sportswriters that had boosted the size of the gallery. All in all, the conference went relatively smoothly. A call for community support in establishing the movements of the deceased had been made and would duly be forwarded in the forthcoming news bulletins.

Just as Sergeant Gill was drawing the conference to a close, one more query slipped its way through. A local stringer who wrote copy for the national press. "DI Mahoney, can you verify the comments made earlier by Sergeant Munro?" Of course he could not. What would he be verifying? So he asked. Wished he did not have to.

"Earlier, he asserted that this case was one suspicious death. No more, no less, so if the people making the fuss would bugger off quicker, it would be solved."

Shit, shit, shit, shit.

*   *   *

Half an hour later in the incident room, the aforementioned excrement collided with the fan. Munro was sitting at his desk methodically reading the autopsy report. The whole team had been apprised of the preliminary findings, and potential conclusions to be drawn, by Mahoney but he knew he needed to be fully aware of the details if he was to do his job properly.

Kendall walked into the room and went straight to her laptop. Seconds passed. Munro looked up "So how did it go with the pack of hounds? Were they happy with the scraps?"

Kendall breathed deeply as she waited for her log on to finish. "Mostly OK. There are plenty of them scouring for material, for sure. This is turning out to be a pretty big deal." Kate was about to pass on the sting in the tail of the conference but Munro was winding up.

"Pity they aren't baying when some poor old bugger gets done over in a smash and grab. Bloody weird priorities if you ask me."

"Well, next time somebody asks you perhaps you could zip your stupid mouth." Sergeant Gill was in the room. "You've gone and done it this time, you clown." Her procession to Munro's desk was paced to time with the invective streaming from her own mouth. "What were you thinking? No, don't answer that. Because you don't think, do you? You're an instinctive cop. A man who gets the job done." No steam, just pure fire.

Gill's hands were by her side but her voice clearly enunciated the inverted commas of sarcasm and contempt. While the other officers in earshot, about the whole area, suddenly found pressing tasks to focus on, Munro swiveled in his chair to face the PR officer. She was literally standing over him. "And don't even think of giving me that moronic grin. You've obliterated a great deal of goodwill in one fell swoop. You couldn't do the team thing, could you? Had to spout off with your own opinion. Couldn't stop your own bloody-minded prejudices seeping into the operation." She ran her hand through a thick mane of dark shining hair.

Kendall was unsure how to react. Munro was her closest team member. Should she stick up for him? How would he feel about her support in dealing with this Valkyrie? Yet she was forced to admit to herself that the tempestuous visitor was onto something. And she was really rather formidable. Not some ditsy girl who whipped up press releases and looked pretty for the cameras. Striking but not pretty. But it was hardly some sense of ovarian sisterhood that led Kate to bite her lip. It was simply that the female sergeant was on the mark.

Munro liked to tread his own path sometimes. That was the word from other officers who worked with him on other cases. Very competent, strong instincts but liked to be lone gunslinger in town. Gill's invective was interrupted by her mobile beeping. With a finger pointed at Munro in a 'stay right there, I'm not finished yet' gesture, she flipped her phone open to take the call.

Just as Gill was concluding what was fairly obviously a conciliatory call, Mahoney entered. He went straight to Kendall and stood with his back to the combatants. Sotto voce he said, "I take it this is not a classic URST situation?"

"Sorry, Sir?"

"Unresolved sexual tension."

"Err, no." Kate rolled her eyes theatrically as she smiled with her superior. Mahoney turned. Gill snapped her phone shut. Before her jaw could open, the senior officer spoke.

"Sergeant Gill. Thank you for arranging the press conference. Very thorough. I don't think anybody should walk away feeling short-changed from that." Kendall was dumbfounded. He was obviously attempting to placate her and she must know it. But he was doing it in his clinical voice so no one could accuse him of that. And also what he said was accurate. Even Gill's detractors ("she's too assertive, you know, pushy") admitted she was good, very good, in her role.

"This case is going to be a huge challenge for all of us. Particularly for you, so I'll be adopting every measure I can to assist you in dealing with the mob. We all must come together for this or we'll be picked off. And no one wants that." A knowing glance to Munro, more to indicate to Gill he was aware of the incendiary that needed to be defused.

Sergeant Gill was left with nowhere to go. Face-saving was accomplished and the point was made. She thanked Mahoney and left, having promised to call him later for any updates. Mahoney faced Munro.

"We need a chat."

"I don't." Munro spoke to his desk.

"My office." Practically a whisper.

Mahoney was sitting on the front edge of his desk with his arms crossed as Munro entered. "Close the door behind you." Even Mahoney could not hide the irritation in his voice. Munro did so and then stood six feet from his boss. Mahoney opened his arms, palms facing his junior officer. "Tell me. The whole and nothing but."

"Hicksey caught me at a bad moment."

"No justifications. Just the who, when, what." Mahoney's tone was now terse and the words clipped. This was no time for excuses.

"Paul Hicks. A freelance journalist. Cornered me at hockey training last night. I made a forthright comment about all the hoopla." He shrugged. "There it is."

Mahoney believed 'forthright' to be self-justifying obfuscation. He simply said, "SNAFU."

"I guess so, Sir. Sorry."

"No guessing about it. It is so. Even if the woman who beat you to three stripes says so." That one stung. It was meant to. Part of the problem was Munro's ego. He could not see that some people really did attain promotion because they deserved it. Munro, in his own eyes, was the honorable exception. His view was jaundiced, Mahoney knew, but he had his strengths. "What prompted this outburst?"

"Frustration. I told our coach that training would be hard to make this week. He said it's the season opener. Big week. First real chance for our club to grab a Senior Hockey Premiership for a decade. Didn't I realize what's at stake? What are my priorities? I tried to explain but he just said my place might be up for grabs. Really pissed me off."

"And right after this, Hicks, a fellow clubman, asks about the case, correct?"

"Yeah, pretty much. Didn't think he'd bring it up. You know, off the record and all that. Prick's probably after my spot." Munro's indignation was again building up some steam.

"Well, in this instance your professional responsibility will have to come first. We have a murder to solve and that takes precedence over your recreational activities."

Munro could not help rising to the rebuke. "So my life and its commitments have to go totally on hold because the bloody Tassie Devils are down one player. Jesus wept." As soon as the words were out he grimaced, realizing a crucial boundary had been breached.

Mahoney stood, went to the window and breathed deeply. His own first superintendent, if spoken to in such a manner, would have flayed the subordinate alive and ditched the remains in the incident room as a warning to others. He needed to keep the younger man onside yet ensure he appreciated just what was at stake. His voice was measured. "Tim, you are a good detective and should become an exemplary one. Your instincts are strong and your basic values are sound. But you cannot forget that it's not just success on the sports field that demands high levels of perspiration. Much of what we do is sheer hard slog and we must be flexible enough to commit full-time to the job at hand."

Mahoney turned to face his associate. "We are experiencing an undue amount of pressure, I agree, and not necessarily for the right reasons. Nonetheless, we do not help ourselves if we fracture our efforts. Regardless of our opinion of the victim, the suspects and community expectations, our focus should always be solely on finding a solution. It's much more than some sort of sacred trust: it is a fundamental responsibility that we do what we can to bring about some sort of justice."

Munro's shoulders relaxed. Partly from relief that he was still in one piece but mainly because he had been praised by the Beekeeper. Some officers spent yearlong secondments in Serious Crime without even receiving a "Well done" so to be unequivocally told he could cut the mustard was news indeed. "Yes, Sir. Sorry the fuse was a bit short then. It's just that Jackie has been on at me about balance in my life and instead of telling her to give it a rest, I snapped at you. It won't happen again, Sir." He continued to stand rigidly.

"I may not have some of the external commitments of my men, Tim, but I am very mindful of them. Nothing is ever asked of you that is not absolutely necessary. The reason I need you on the job is that your presence seems to somehow rattle Cartwright. It's barely perceptible at the moment but there is definitely a tiny fissure there that will crack right open with sufficient well-directed pressure. He seems to feel quite comfortable jousting with me but you, without even seeming to mean to, unsettle him. It's only little things but he reacts in a much less charming manner to any of your questions. If we talk to him again, the rough sandpaper of your interrogation may start to ruffle his smooth surface. Let's hope so."

CHAPTER 24

Monday 15ᵗʰ March 2pm

Kendall and Mahoney were sitting in the latter's office when DC Manning entered.

"Lyn, take a seat. We're keenly awaiting whatever you've got. By the looks of it, there's some good news in there."

Manning was certainly looking quite chipper. "Hello, Kate. Yes, Sir. Plenty of traces. At both locations as it turns out."

"Good. Start with Kingston."

"OK. Not quite as telling as the Bowls Club but still good material. The line search by the cadets on Friday and again on Saturday produced nothing of any use. Same with the door-to-door. What we do have are two sets of freshly made footprints left in the immediate vicinity of where the body was discovered that cannot be accounted for. One set made by a pair of Dunlop Volleys with that easily identifiable sole pattern. And the other tread from what seem like work boots. Both sets follow a path to and from the trench. For both the depression on the way over was more marked, presumably because they were lugging a substantial weight."

"About ninety-five kilos worth."

"Yes, Sir. On the return, lighter indentation but still observable to the naked eye. All photographed and very serviceable impressions made. Same with the tire tracks. As you suggested, I've released the site back to the building company. The manager was there this morning. Flash ute. There's money in construction. Seemed relieved his crew could get on with the build."

Mahoney cut the observation short. "That's as maybe. Any ideas on the make of boots?"

"Well, they're not Blunnies. One of the guys at the lab reckoned they might be Mack steel toes. He's checking this afternoon." Mahoney nodded. She was back on message.

"And the car? Any luck?" As she took notes, Kate was very careful to sound as an equal to a fellow female officer.

"Excellent tire tracks. Again the lab is running various makes for a match and will have details this afternoon." A slight pause. "If I can say so, this pair were in a pretty big rush or they're just not very good at this type of thing."

Mahoney had been doodling on a jotter pad. "It seems so. I'm more inclined to the former but they made precious little effort to cover their tracks. What interests me is the choice of locale for the disposal of the body. Was it organized beforehand? And why there?"

Kate scanned her notes. "Well, it's a readymade trench so no need to allow for digging time and that decreases the chances of being caught in the act. Given the distance they drove, it would seem that they already had this spot picked out. Which suggests a specific plan as opposed to randomly attacking Finch and dumping the body anywhere. Or even just leaving it at the Bowls Club. So it really gets back to what was the intention of this scheme? Why bundle the body into a bag and then take it twenty kilometers away to a building site?"

Manning chipped in. "Were they hoping for the body to be concreted over? When we were building, all the foundations were minutely inspected just before any concrete went in. Surely the body would be seen in that case."

Mahoney brought them back. "Whether or not it was a pre-arranged dumping spot or they wanted the body to disappear is not the crucial point. We need to determine why there but we may not know that until we have found one of these people. Until then we're just hypothesizing on the mentality of the thugs who did this. It's all well and good acting as if we're in an Oxford pub supping pints and being lateral-minded sleuths but we've got a bit sidetracked." Realizing he'd lost both women with his last reference, Mahoney curtly moved on. "Lyn, what do we have from the Bowls Club?"

"Oh, yeah." She shuffled the second folder to the top. "See what you mean. Good traces of bodily fluids. Also samples of his blood on the concrete curbing at the end of the rink. So he was there for sure but we knew that already." Her eyes had skimmed ahead to the next paragraph and she immediately kicked herself for not reading the reports more thoroughly before racing back to HQ. "There's a second blood sample from a different individual."

The atmosphere became rather more charged. Both of the other officers were too tactful to say anything. It was not her call in which order the material was being dissected but this did look a bit like a smug conjurer pulling the rabbit out of the hat. Maybe it did not matter. She hoped so.

Thankfully, the DI was unconcerned with how the cards were falling. Made a joke of it. "Lovely, Lyn, bit of a grand finale." Genuinely pleased. No irony at all. "I don't suppose you can top that with an ID for the sample."

"Not just yet. Sometime this afternoon," a relieved Manning replied as she scanned the report. "Says here it's definitely a different blood type from Finch. Deposited at the same time as the victim's trace." Her voice was slightly halting as she paraphrased the text in front of her. "Cannot be absolutely certain due to environmental considerations but very close to almost definitely the same time."

"No matter, that's close enough. As I'm sure Kate would agree, there's enough probability to credibly place at least one perpetrator at the scene. Enough to closely question whoever that may be."

Just then there was a knock on the door. Munro entered. "Good news, guys. I've just been speaking with a girl who was talking to Finch for a while on Thursday night at the Metz. Staff and a couple of his cobbers confirm he was there but she was the last sighting. Says they were getting along beautifully, or words to that effect, when Finch took a call on his mobile and then all of a sudden he had to scoot off. She reckoned at the time he was blowing her off. Last she saw of him he was off down Russell Crescent. From there you can duck down through the Coles car park and into the Bowls Club. Could be the call that took him to the altercation." Despite gabbling at the rate of knots, all had heard him clearly. He was right to be excited.

Kate spoke first. "That last number received would be very handy. I'll try and hurry up the phone company. Get them to stop dragging the chain and see the urgency. It's far more vital now. May be able to circumvent the warrant." Left for her desk.

Manning stood as well. "I'll chase Graves at the lab for our match. Excuse me."

"Right, good. Report back as soon as either of you have any news." The two detectives were alone in the space. "Sergeant Munro. Good man. You've just reversed your own goal. Need I ask how you tracked her down so quickly?"

"Bit of rat cunning, Sir." Almost a grin. "And a fair dose of luck to be fair. She's a bit of a stand-out. Did some promo work for the bar last year so the number was dead easy to get. A lot of people want whoever did it found. And, needless to say, strung up. Anyway, sorry about earlier. Won't happen again. I've got the scent now."

"And if it goes cold?"

"No problem. I'm selected whether I can train Thursday or not. All good." The full 100 watts. "What needs doing now?"

"Speak to the Council and the construction company." Mahoney waved to the incident room. "Kate can bring you up to speed." A theatrical projection. "And if Constable Manning could get that DNA match."

A raised voice called back. "Got it but I don't think you're going to believe it."

*   *   *

An hour later Mahoney and Kendall entered the interview room. Seated on the far side at the wooden table was a wiry male with a classic mullet hairstyle. Behind him was a uniformed constable whom Mahoney excused from the room prior to acknowledging the subject. As the door closed, Mahoney addressed the man.

"Thank you for making yourself available, Mr. Knapp."

"Didn't have much choice. Smartarse in the suit reckoned it was this way or an arrest. Don't need that."

"No, that would be inconvenient." Mahoney said. "Anyway, at this stage you are helping us with our investigation, so informal is best."

"What bloody investigation? I've been out of trouble for yonks so why drag me in."

"Well, fairer to say you've been operating under our radar, Matty. Unlike your brother, eh?"

"Yeah, stupid bugger. Those Godfrey pricks dropped him right in it."

Mahoney leaned forward on his elbows. "No more drive away work for a fair while for Troy. Have to re-sit his license after a few years at Risdon. Still, his mates might show a bit of gratitude for copping it all by himself and not giving them up. Thieves' code of honor and all that."

Knapp shifted in his chair. "More shit scared, like. Hey, got a burner for me?"

"Sorry Matty, you know the new rules. Can't have smoking in a government building. Enough crime as there is. Get you a drink of the house dishwater if you like."

"Nah, let's just get this over. I ain't done any newsagents or nothing so why am I here?" He leaned back in his chair and clasped his hands behind his head. As he was wearing a blue work singlet, this afforded Kate not only a whiff of his rancid armpits but a glimpse of tattoos on either underarm that invited her to move away or words to that effect. Charming in all respects. It was her turn to speak.

"Have you heard about the Devils' forward who got bumped off?"

"So Miss Prim can talk." Cockiness was often the opening stance of suspects who wanted to avoid something. "Yeah, I heard about it. That'll stuff 'em up for the season I reckon." Knapp smirked, not an appealing sight. It made him look even more like a weasel.

"Well, we're more concerned with the fact he was murdered than the finals prospects of his club. There have been some interesting forensic developments and you may be able to help us with some of the discoveries."

"Whatever." Knapp had now crossed his arms and was staring at the ceiling. It was a master class in acting the unconcerned innocent citizen. Kate wondered how long he could maintain it.

"You see, Mr. Knapp, the person who bludgeoned the victim seems to have left some forensic evidence at the scene. Have you by any chance been down to the Sandy Bay Bowls Club lately?" The first strand of the web.

"Do I look like I'm retired? Never been there. Don't go in for all that malarkey. Waste of bloody time, if you ask me."

Kendall pressed on. "You're entitled to your opinion. Regardless, at the crime scene there was some puzzling material. Someone had left a beautiful deposit of bodily fluids right near where we calculate the actual homicide to have occurred. Whoever it was must have had a bit of a summer cold because he must have gobbed up a very hearty scallop of mucus. An absolute ripper, you might say." Knapp was no longer fixated on the ceiling. "Oh, and some blood. The forensic boys were very pleased until they tried to find a match. They couldn't find a suitable one."

Knapp let his shoulders relax. Decided to hazard a remark. "Bit of a bummer for youse then?"

"Close, Matty, but no cigar. As Detective Kendall said, they were flummoxed. Having DNA at a crime scene is only any good to you in the short term if it correlated with a person we have on the database already." Knapp may have been unsure of one of the verbs but he still felt secure. He'd never even been fingerprinted, so what were these galahs up to?

"But we did find an almost identical match as it turns out. Trouble is the person identified has been behind bars for six months." The interviewee smiled: the teeth needed a lot of work.

"The spooky thing, Matty, is that the match was with your brother, Troy." Knapp was silent. Perhaps he was now aware of the web. Kate concentrated on maintaining a bland stare even though she knew the coming sting in the tail.

"And the marvelous thing about DNA is that siblings have such similar strands. As Troy is highly unlikely to have been at the bowls club we have to assume it was you, Matty." The grin was well and truly gone. "Would you care to reconsider your earlier assertion about your whereabouts last Thursday?"

"I've got nothing to say."

CHAPTER 25

Tuesday 16ᵗʰ March 8am

Mahoney had already been at his desk for over an hour when the summons came. The local press had the story of the investigation plastered across the front page and the editorial asserted that 'not nearly enough was being done to discover who has committed this loathsome crime'. As he pored over witness statements, he experienced a nagging feeling that the powers-that-be would want to exert their authority. This would most likely manifest itself in the form of Assistant Commissioner Newman demanding a briefing – "just so as I can be across all the issues, you understand" – on the current investigation. And so, at 8.40am, the desk phone trilled. "Mahoney here."

"Detective Inspector, it's Bridget Scanlon. The Assistant Commissioner wishes to see you in his office at your earliest convenience." Her voice was almost a parody of formality as if this businesslike tone was her way of staying sane while the bullshit poured past her.

"Which means I'm immediately required on the Footy Show set." A cheap shot but who cared.

"Yes, that's correct, Detective Inspector." A stifled giggle. Newman was not exactly well liked by his immediate staff.

Mahoney pressed on. "Will the Mirror be there?"

"No, the Commissioner is in meetings with the Attorney-General this morning."

"Thank you, BS. I'll be right there."

He slipped on his jacket and took the lift six floors up to the Executive Level. Rare air. Adjusting his tie, he strode past the PA into his superior's office. "Shut the door, John." The clipped tone of a man who just loved giving orders.

"Yes, Sir." Maintain a level pitch and do not let the charlatan rattle you. Get this over and done with, with minimum hassle and get on with the real work. He could feel himself on edge.

"Sit down, John." Newman indicated the chairs at his round table. Camelot. Only it had been Newman who had cast himself as Sir Galahad years before and it had been Mahoney who felt the loss. He was grateful he rarely saw the loathsome Lothario. Sitting down, he declined the offer of coffee. Why prolong the encounter? His superior joined him at the table. Adopted his stern we-are-in-something-of-a-crisis face and proclaimed, "John, we are in something of a crisis. The media are eating us alive on this one."

Mahoney momentarily thought he had tuned into a television soap opera before registering that it was merely Newman displaying a customary predilection for dramatic cliché. It was bandied around downstairs that he prepared for the rigors of the working day in a hyperbolic chamber.

Mahoney could not let that pass unchallenged. "Sir, with respect, we are making strong progress on the Finch case. The press can feast as much as they like. My detectives are flogging their guts out on this one."

But Newman had a message to deliver whatever his DI wanted to say. "I do not care if they are sweating blood. This department can ill afford any negative media treatment in the run-up to the Budget discussions. Commissioner Phillips is at the Executive Building as we speak, desperately trying to gain us the resources we need to properly police this state. His efforts, and mine dare I say, do not need to be handicapped by the ineptitude of a task force that can only turn up one suspect, and a pretty spurious one at that. So, with respect John, do not go on to me about excruciating effort when we are not getting any results." The Saint had meted out his judgment.

The indecorous idea that extra resources probably amounted to government drivers for top brass was shunted aside by another thought that steamrolled over the edit button on Mahoney's tongue. "You're right, Sir. My use of language was inaccurate." Pause. "I don't respect you in the slightest so I won't pretend I do when speaking to you."

A distinct rise in volume. "You're a lizard – not a snake because they can pose a threat – but a gormless lizard. A pompous fool who bathes in the sunlight of success afforded by your subordinates and doesn't have the gumption or courage to stick up for his officers when the breeze of public opinion wafts the other way. You slid behind my back into Lisa's bed years ago and you've slimed your way to the top. I have gotten over your white-anting long ago and I've learned to operate under your ineffectual leadership but I cannot, and will not, listen to you spout unjustifiable rubbish about this homicide case when sound officers are giving their all. You couldn't solve a child's riddle, let alone a halfway decent crime, so how about you stick to monitoring traffic flow and let us do the real work."

Newman's ears were practically smoking: the jaw had slid open but nothing came out. He knew from his network of stooges in the department that Mahoney barely showed emotion let alone raised his voice so to witness a tirade was as much of a shock as the venom of the attack was fearsome. Mahoney upped and departed leaving the AC slumped in his chair, bewildered and hangdog. He had been told.

*   *   *

DC David Gibson wasn't sure if he was doing the right thing or not. In one sense he was: taking the weekend offer to move into CIB for this case was a gilt-edged opportunity. He'd had no hesitation when the Duty Sergeant confirmed on Monday that he was temporarily out of uniform and 'working with Columbo'. "No need to get too many ideas, son. They're short staffed, that's all. My granny's on the short list too. Don't stuff it up." That counted as encouragement. In another sense he felt clueless. At 9am he had reported for duty and no one seemed to know who he was. The boss wasn't in his office when he made it up to the incident room. When he re-appeared about 9.30, he didn't look in the mood for an induction. Fortunately, he had recognized DC Kendall and he gravitated to her desk. She looked up just as he approached. Clocked him instantly. "Good morning, Detective."

Gibson smiled. "Well, actually I stay as a constable for the duration. I'm not even acting, I've been told."

"But you get to ditch the blue cap so it's not all bad." She looked him up and down. "Sound choice. Not too flashy. Plain tie. Very wise."

"Thank you. There's nothing in the manual about that sort of stuff."

"KISS. Best policy."

Gibson was blank-faced. "Not the band?"

A fitful memory of Rex's taste in music flashed through Kate's mind. If they were going anywhere as a couple, she'd need to address that. When he told her he got dressed up in all the kit (boots, leather, make-up) to go to a concert in Melbourne, she'd laughed loudly. A bit too loudly. He was serious.

"No, certainly not. Keep It Simple Stupid. Low key. Same for your first few days here. Head down. Do whatever you're allocated. As well as you can." She paused. "Oh don't worry. You'll get it."

"Have I been allocated anything?"

"Don't think so. Boss looks a bit pre-occupied just now so you can help me. Grab a chair."

He pulled a spare one over to her workstation. "Right, read this."

She passed over a neatly stacked sheaf of paper. "It's my equivalent of a murder book. A summary of incidents and developments in this case. I update it on the computer and add to this hard copy each day. That should bring you up to speed."

"Thanks, DC Kendall. For this, and noticing me and that."

"You think I'd miss that hair."

* * *

Mahoney was back at his desk. So one domino had fallen. But it was not going to spark a chain reaction. Knapp was recalcitrant. Not due to any unwritten code of conduct. More likely because he held fears for his brother's ongoing safety in prison. If he ratted on anybody then not only he, but also his sibling, would endure the consequences. Troy may be incarcerated but if somebody wanted to, they could easily organize for him to come to harm. Serious harm. The sort that put you in critical care.

As a cadet, Mahoney was told about a rock spider that had been taught a gruesome lesson whilst in Risdon Prison. The man had been put away for anally raping two young boys. It would have been very hard for the perpetrator to commit a crime that ticked more boxes of contempt for fellow prisoners than that. Short of doing the same thing to his own children perhaps.

Rock spiders were considered lower than India's untouchables and the greater punishment was not the withdrawal from society but the anticipated reception they faced behind bars. Ben Clarke was to find life in Risdon truly horrendous. After five months of catcalling and blatant threats, one day he was in the shower block at the designated time for ablutions. Thus far, this had been a relatively safe procedure during the early part of his twelve year sentence. But not this particular day. The attention of many prisoners and staff was fixed on the cricket match being held on Risdon's postage stamp ground within the forbidding walls.

Every so often, outside sports teams agreed to come into the confines of the prison for a game of cricket or football to do their bit for the community. And so it was on the afternoon that Back Door Benny was brutally shown an alternative use for one's anus. Somehow or other, collusion maybe, there was no staff member anywhere near the shower rooms at the time 'Door' shuffled in.

He stripped and tiptoed across the cold white tiles to the taps. Before he could even turn them on, he was grabbed by the arms from behind. Thrown down face first. His nose bashed on the hard floor and a few teeth broke loose. Two smashing rabbit blows to the ribs knocked all the stuffing out of him. A harsh voice in his ear. "Just keep your trap shut or a knife goes in. Right?" Benny grunted. Had little choice. Gaffer tape was smacked over his mouth and his hands manacled behind his back. He could barely breathe.

Suddenly that was the least of his worries. A lubricated tube was shoved up his backside. "Feel good, brother?" Different voice. Two of them. He had no hope. Spread-eagled face first. A cold chuckle. "This ain't a dildo, brother. It's a hollow tube of plastic. We'll take it out again but there might be a bit of discomfort as the good doctor says." The same sick chuckle.

How could it be worse, thought Benny. Cut my nuts off. He very soon found out. The tube was whipped out and instantaneously his rectum contracted on what felt like jagged glass. The immediate agony was unbearable. "Just so's ya wondering, there's a half a foot of barbed wire up your jacksy. We're off. Enjoy your next shit, faggot." Benny was left sprawled on the floor writhing in agony and contemplating a fate worse than 'a fate worse than death'.

Little wonder Matty Knapp felt genuine concern for his brother's safety. Mahoney decided a few eggs would have to be broken. External pressures aside, he wanted to crack this case. Sure it was his job to do so but, moreover, he was determined his squad would pursue this further because it was the right-minded thing to do. Let something like this linger and another breech in the wall of civility eased open just that bit further.

He made a call from his office. A brief conversation ensued. All set. He collared Munro and went downstairs to the divisional car park. Instructed his driver to take them to Queens Domain. The morning traffic on the Brooker Highway was building as they headed north.

Just past the Federal Street turn-off, they saw two uniformed traffic officers sharing a joke. The younger of the pair was shaking his head and smiling ruefully at the sergeant who watched his subordinate operate the laser gun on the oncoming traffic. It was a perfect spot to nab unwary drivers who thought the double lane arterial road allowed them to ignore the 80km speed limit.

"Those two are happy in their work. Wonder what the joke is?" enquired Munro.

"Just Digger boosting his coffers."

"Eh! Bit of grafting?"

"No, far from it. The big fella is Sergeant Duigan. Been on traffic for ages. He's so attuned to that job he can guess the motorists' speeds almost exactly. The young constables rotate through the assignment. They operate the laser and every so often Digger throws off a guess as to the car's speed. Young bloke assumes it's a fluke so gets lulled into a bet that his boss won't get ten in a row accurate to a couple of k's or so either side. Digger reels 'em off without breaking sweat and pockets a lazy $20. Swears the constable to secrecy or he'll tell the station how gullible he is. Watertight."

"Cunning bugger. Know him well?"

"Oh, yeah. He's solid. In all ways. Puts his takings into the charity jar. Old school but one of the most reliable cops I've ever met. Take the Domain Highway turn-off."

They were on the Tasman Bridge scenic route. Munro turned right again as instructed and the car wound its way up the hill through Crown land. Just after the start of the Soldiers Memorial Walk, he was told to

turn again and, after a series of hairpin turns, approached an open air
car park that overlooked the northern suburbs.

"Drop me here and come back in half an hour."

"Sure?"

"Yes, this is strictly one-on-one. Don't hang about here. Grab a coffee
or something at the Botanical Gardens café. You don't know where I
am, right?"

"Yes, Sir. Crystal."

Mahoney got out and Munro drove off. He walked over to the rock
wall edge of the gravel car park. The aspect of the estuary splitting the
valley in two was quite amazing. On one side there were a few houses in
the lee of Mount Direction but mostly it was bush, while to the nearside
of the water sprawled the working suburbs of Hobart. The industrial belt
covered a substantial area. The smaller cottages and bungalows sat in
and around the metal roofs of the factories. A light wind from the north
meandered through the native trees on the hill where he stood. Behind
him, a motorbike idled to a stop. Seconds later a gruff voice turned him
around.

"John, how are you?" A huge bear of a man walked towards him.
Silver-studded black boots, black jeans and a red-checked flanny, over
a Southern Cross Union blue singlet. At the top of the six and half foot
frame between axe-handle shoulders was the head of a wild Scottish
Highland chief. Unruly red hair and a beard that would have provided
enough stuffing for at least a pillow or two.

"Alright, Heinz. You?"

"Fair to middling, no complaints but. Better than being down there."
The man gestured towards the Cornelian Bay Cemetery.

"Yeah. Right enough."

The biker took out the makings of a rollie. As he licked the papers
and massaged the Drum tobacco into a dart, they contemplated the view.
Mahoney had played club soccer with Heinz what seemed like many,
many years ago. The Catholic schoolboy alongside the rough as guts
teenager at the heart of defense. Heinz sorted out the main striker and
Mahoney swept up. An unlikely but effective pairing that became an odd
but enduring mateship. There was nothing Teutonic about Heinz. It was
simply easier to call that out on the field than his preferred nickname
Big Red. Now no one called him by the former name apart from the
old teammates.

"What can I do for you, Detective? That I can do, that is." As Sergeant-at-Arms for the Bezerkers' Bike Club, it was pushing things just to be seen together. Mahoney had to tread carefully.

"You've heard about the football bashing?"

"Yep. Not us, in case you're worried. Sounds like it was a bit of a stuff-up."

"From what we can gather, yes. As far as I can tell, it wasn't any of the gangs involved. But it certainly wasn't the guy we've got acting solo. Matty Knapp, Troy's brother. Trouble is he's clammed up. Tight as."

The giant blew smoke out the corner of his mouth as he scratched his shaggy head. "And you're wondering if there are any new pricks about causing mischief?"

Mahoney nodded. Heinz squinted into the late morning sun laying shadows over Geilston Bay and turned back to the Detective. "None of this came from me. Nothing comes back to us." A wave at his bike.

"No, definitely. We weren't here."

"OK. Couple of weeks ago a new fella finds his way into the clubhouse. None of the regulars had clocked him before, round here or on the big island. Just fell out of the sky. Weaselly looking fucker. Greasy hair, Zappa moey and the ears practically metallic. Drank shorts for hours and tried to hustle some eight-ball. Good player as it turns out.

"Anyway, caused no hassles but wanted to offload some gear in exchange for some tools. Barney tells him we ain't got none. What about in the strong room, he says. Barney tells him again. No guns here, mate. Silly bugger persists. Barney drops him. Gives his ribs a tickle with his boots. Throws him out and re-locks the door. Heard from the Wildmen he tried the same stunt there a week later." He stubbed out his smoke.

"And?"

"Wouldn't have thought anymore of it. Not a whisper of any B&E's, like. But I saw him at the Russell Hotel when I was putting a few bets on last week. Had your Napster eating out of his hand."

"Could be something. Could be nothing."

"Yeah, I agree, mate. But I don't think you got much, so anything's better than nothing."

Mahoney smiled. "Too true. Name?"

"Ronny Coutts. Reckon he might be staying over that way." Heinz pointed to the old EZ company site on the bank of the river.

Mahoney followed his gaze. "Much maligned suburb, Lutana. Might pay it a visit."

CHAPTER 26

Tuesday 16th March Noon

In the ten minutes or so until Munro returned to collect him, Mahoney got his fingers walking. Directory assistance brought up an address for a Mrs. Gaylene Coutts in Ashbolt Crescent, Lutana. Must be it. Staying with Mum. Use that as a base for some local fundraising. Not the smartest choice for a hideaway probably. But then it had to be said that criminals were no different from any other category of society; there were always going to be a reasonable number of boneheads. Stood to reason. Then a quick call to headquarters. He instructed Kate Kendall to bring Knapp up from the cells for further questioning at short notice. She was kept guessing of any developments.

Munro duly arrived spot on time. Another tick in the box. The young detective really did have potential. Not quite Kate's level of emotional discipline but getting there.

"All good, Boss?"

Mahoney was in the car and belted up. "Yes. Just needed to clear the air to see where we're going."

Yeah right, thought Munro. He remained circumspect. "And where is that right now?"

"Back down the hill end over to near the Zinc Company. We're making a house call."

En route via Cornelian Bay, past the cemetery and onto Risdon Road, Mahoney told his colleague the current situation. Could be something good. As the sedan pulled over, the DI gave his final instructions, got out and ambled across to the pedestrian walkway that split the residential block in two. Munro continued around the loop of the crescent, parked and, as he'd been told, alighted from the car with the maximum of fuss. Even got his ID out of his jacket pocket as he crossed the bitumen to the pale weatherboard house at number 33.

He rapped loudly on the glass pane of the front door. Called out who he was. Finally, the door was opened by a woman in her middle years. The color of her hair was streaky and it was unlikely any food would get stuck between her front teeth but she was not unattractive, thought Munro. She was dressed in a black nightie and golden colored necklace. Shift worker or afternoon delight. Hard to tell. But she was smoking.

"Yeah, can I help you?"

"I hope so, Madam." Before he could continue his phone started ringing and he bolted to the top of the laneway that ran alongside the paling fence of the property. He got there just in time to see a figure turning away from his boss and setting off towards him. Saw the burly partner and halted in his tracks, bent over, hands on his thighs, swearing to himself.

As Munro approached, the man jerked upright and swung at the policeman. Having expected this for the past five steps, Munro leaned back, watched the fist sail past, swiveled his weight and slammed his would-be assailant into the fence. He then smoothly pinned both arms behind the guy's back and cuffed him. All according to script. "What are youse doing to him?" The woman they presumed to be Mrs. Coutts screeched over the fence. "He ain't done nuthin'."

"Actually, he's attempted to assault an officer of the law so he is required to come with us to the station. We'll take him to Hobart."

They paraded Coutts, now sullenly silent, to the car. "Effing pricks, the lot of you," from the front garden. It would have to pass for a farewell in the circumstances.

On the drive back in, Mahoney texted Kate with very precise instructions. She quickly replied her understanding. Coutts had said nothing on the drive into the CBD aside from confirmation of his identity.

Having parked out front, the two policemen walked him through the foyer to the charge desk. As the trio stood in front of the sergeant on duty, Mahoney tapped his mobile. In a matter of seconds, Kate Kendall just happened to guide Matty Knapp around the corner of the corridor.

It was exactly like the proverbial rocket up the arse. Coutts went nuts. He jerked at his handcuffs and lunged forward. "You fucking weak arsehole. You've done it now. I'll fucking do you. You fucking prick."

Knapp reared back. He thought he was being brought down to meet a duty solicitor. Kate Kendall shielded him while admiring the new chap's consistency. It reminded her of *Hamburger Hill* with the addition of extra spittle. The man was apocalyptic with rage. Obviously, Mahoney had generated something of a reaction with the 'chance' encounter. Munro held Coutts in place. The volcano subsided. "You two seem to know each other," Mahoney dryly observed.

Immediately following the fracas in the foyer, Matt Knapp was taken back to the interview room. Mahoney allowed him to stew for a short while before going in with Munro. He opted for his briefed offsider to take up the running. Munro sat.

"So Matt, it looks like you've met Coutts before. Care to let us know how you're so pally?" He was particularly careful not to smile. Knapp sat staring at the patch of cement floor between his feet. "Help us out here. Things may not be as bad as you think."

"Yeah? Just how bad do they have to get?" He sat upright. "That prick's trouble with a big T. And not just for me."

Mahoney moved from the corner of the room to the side of the table and spoke softly to Knapp. "I agree he's trouble. But for himself mainly. He's nowhere near the threat to you, and yours, that he probably told you."

A lift of the head. "How so?"

"Well, for a start, he's not the big wheel he's made himself out to be. Nowhere near as influential as he told you at the Russell Hotel." That brought on a spate of eye-blinking. Mahoney knew they were onto something. The measured tone remained. "All that stuff about getting to your brother or your family was wishful thinking on his part. He's about as well connected as a burnt out fuse box. He's a blow-in. None of the players round here want anything to do with him. We checked. He's got no influence on the inside or out here. He's flying solo. A chancer. There's never going to be a Carl Williams scenario for your brother. He's safe. You're safe."

He let that sink in for a few moments. "You're in a decent spot of bother but nothing like Coutts has got you imagining. Now this is a good time to revisit the goings-on at the Bowls Club, don't you think?"

Knapp took a full minute to think it over. The lifebuoy had been thrown. Seemed no good reason not to grab it. "It was a cock-up. Pure and simple. Yeah, he set me up. Got hold of my number through a mutual mate, he said. Arranged a meeting and laid out a deal. Be his right hand man or Troy would be in all sorts of strife. Had me by the short and curlies, didn't he?" He leaned back in the chair and crossed his arms. "So I went along with it. Just meant to be a job of putting the frighteners on some bloke. Some bloke. Sweet Jesus. Didn't tell me the target was a tank." He blew air through his fringe.

"Anyways, we're meant to surprise this fella down at the Bowls Club behind the Mayfair Pub. Somebody tips Coutts off the guy would be there. Good place to give a bloke a warning, he reckons. Well, next thing this well put together snoozer comes sauntering through in front of the clubhouse and over the lawn. I step out and tell him to hold it right there. Next thing the bugger dabs me one. Great jab. Right on the hooter. I'm a bit dazed and the claret starts. He's about to sling another one when out steps Coutts and smacks him round the head with a spade. Big clout. Boxer boy falls sideways and cracks his skull open on the concrete curb. Does not move. Must have died instantly. No pulse. Nothing. Just this eerie quiet. We both just stood there.

"I knew then we were in deep shit. I was too stunned to move. Not Coutts. He swings straight into action. Plan B, he reckons. Plan A had been to overpower him, truss him up and leave him in a ditch for the night. Scare him good and proper. Now we had a body to get rid of. Can't leave him, reckons the criminal genius, so we lug him into the van and drive to Kingston. Plonk him in the ditch. In the rush I'd forgotten me blood was probably on the concrete. Had no choice but to play along and keep me trap shut. Well, until now that is."

Munro almost smiled.

*   *   *

Ronny Coutts was a suspect who, in a previous era, would have been a prime candidate for a hefty dose of old style rough justice. As a junior constable, Mahoney encountered a handful of detectives who believed wholeheartedly in the concept of noble corruption. These men were not on the take as such. That brand of unethical behavior involving bribe taking belonged more to the bigger cities on the mainland. In fact, they were some of the straightest coppers in the local force. They did not excuse mates who were caught over the alcohol limit as some traffic police did. They did not enjoy the various sexual services offered to members of the Vice Squad who turned a blind eye to the existence of illegal brothels dotted around the inner suburbs of Hobart. They were straight. Unsullied by graft.

But they were not impeccable. They prided themselves on belonging to the old school. Criminals in their eyes were invariably guilty and simply needed to be nudged towards divulging the truth. One raging bull of a detective, Reg Varney, built a legendary status for himself through the '60s and '70s by not so much nudging suspects as "belting the living suitcase out of them", as one of Mahoney's mentors enthusiastically described it. Rarely did the subject of interrogation refuse to sign the statement that had been scrupulously prepared by the investigative team.

By the '80s, practices had mellowed somewhat. Brutality was now deemed illegal but sheer physical intimidation was still considered a useful strategy in some cases. But it became clear to many detectives that there were surer ways of extracting the truth. The example of the Monsignor reinforced this. An unprepossessing DI standing five and a half feet and weighting sixty kilograms wringing wet, "Monsignor" Darcy Rogers possessed an enviable strike rate in the interrogation room.

When he lectured the police cadets in Mahoney's graduation year, the class was meticulously taken through his methodology. It was no miracle that suspects were struck with an overwhelming desire to confess. It was simply that Rogers appreciated one salient fact: many people involved in wrongdoing wished to unburden themselves at some point. It was getting them to that point that required the skill. Wearing a suspect down was still par for the course but the process of attrition should be mental and emotional rather than physical.

Having filed into the academy classroom prepared to be underwhelmed, the cohort of forty-three cadets began to hang on every word of the Detective Inspector's lecture. The presentation was impeccably prepared, which was exactly what every interrogator who strode into an interview room should be, asserted the mild looking detective. Although he dressed in the sort of mid-range off the rack suit that suggested mediocrity, Rogers soon convinced even the most skeptical cadet that being totally in command of all the available evidence was the most basic preliminary for any discussion with a suspect.

Behind the metal-framed bifocal glasses was clearly a mind that functioned like a computer. Become versed in the tell-tale quirks of body language and verbal patterns, he encouraged the class. Ask your questions matter-of-factly, do not be afraid of silences and listen as attentively as humanly possible to each and every response. The greatest skill of all was to get the criminal to come to terms with his guilt. And then to sell the idea that the truth of the matter, if divulged, will suit the suspect. The class was a resounding success. It formed part of a new policy adopted by the Executive of the State Police Force to formally tutor embryonic officers rather than leave it to senior officers to pass on the secrets through a process of (mis)trial and error.

The times were changing. As courts, and the public at large, began to demand a more accountable means of delivering all forms of evidence to court, so the police had to amend their approach to interrogations in particular. Still, the evolution was neither consistent nor popularly embraced by all detectives. Mahoney regularly heard tales, some wildly exaggerated, of how some officers went about the business of seeking the confession they wanted. In one Melbourne police station there was even a sign that read, "You enter here with good looks and the truth. You can't leave with both."

As recently as a few years before, there had been a short-lived scandal over comments made by the Premier when visiting a refurbished station. Having commented favorably on the fresh conditions in the holding cells, he wryly commented that something was missing from the new interview suites. "What was that?" queried the accompanying Superintendent. Just within earshot of a journalist, the Premier smilingly said, "Phonebooks, of course." Nobody laughed aloud. And there were precious few guffaws in the Commissioner's office upon reading it in the next day's paper. The old days were gone but the force was not going to be allowed to forget their often sullied heritage.

As Mahoney rehearsed his opening preamble for his meeting with Coutts, he mouthed again his formulaic ABC "Always Be Calm". In the same manner that salesmen should "Always Be Closing", he decided to follow the classic structure of the archetypal insurance agent's meeting with clients: Relax, Disturb, Relieve. He would assuage Coutts' obvious anger, point out carefully the trouble the suspect was in and then offer him a solution. Although he could not script the interview, Mahoney felt confident he and Munro would prise the truth from him.

So both officers walked into the interview feeling that the investigation was at a tipping point. Over an hour later they walked out with the shared conclusion the encounter had been an anticlimax. Initially, Coutts had been full of bluster and smarmy denial. At about the twenty minute mark, DC Herrick interrupted proceedings with a very helpful piece of information; one of the shoes Coutts had been wearing was an exact match for one of the distinctive prints at the Kingston site. Faced with the sort of fact even this very shifty character had to accept was incontrovertible, the bull dust blew away.

Previous denials of Mahoney's assertions were grudgingly reversed. Yes, he knew Knapp. Had recently recruited him for a bit of business that had come his way. And it had gone pretty much as Mahoney outlined it. Some rough stuff gone wrong, badly wrong. It seemed the garrulous thug was now relishing the opportunity to spill the beans. And then it became clear why the switch from dissembler to plain dealer: Coutts believed the death was not his fault. Admittedly he did smack Finch round the head but it was the stupid bugger's own fault for thumping Knapp. That fallacy was immediately stripped from his reckoning. The disposal of the body could hardly be forwarded as the action of blameless men.

Sensing that a plea of self-defense wasn't going to fly, Coutts shifted tack. It wasn't really his responsibility because he was put up to it by another bloke. At this point Mahoney sensed a distinct shift in the wind. The link between this pair and the victim was the tenuous link in the chain. But when pressed for further details Coutts could offer little verifiable material.

Last week he took a short call to his mobile: a gravelly voice told him to check his mother's letter box for an envelope that would show the level of the caller's intent. Two hundred dollars got his attention. Five minutes later another call from the same man. Was he interested in keeping that down payment plus tenfold that amount for a bit of physical work? Coutts certainly was.

He was instructed to recruit another male and be prepared to 'teach some bloke a lesson'. More instructions followed via a series of short calls in the next few days. The chosen places for the altercation and subsequent dumping of the body, the timing of the encounter and the ID of the victim were laid out. The man had identified himself simply as "the Colonel" and caller ID showed number withheld. Coutts deleted all call records as instructed.

So Coutts and Knapp had carried out their end of the bargain with disastrous results. It had all gone very pear-shaped. And to rub salt in the wound neither had seen any of the money. The phone calls ceased and the promised second envelope hadn't turned up in the letter box and probably wouldn't now. Stitched up good and proper. So he would love to cough up who this guy was but he had no idea. Knew it sounded flimsy but there you go. Why else would he get involved in all this?

And that is exactly what puzzled Mahoney. Why else? They had two assailants under arrest and their motivation was clear: money and fear respectively. But it was still a mystery as to who had a motive for harming this particular victim that could also feasibly arrange this sort of crime. Having prized Knapp and Coutts open, Mahoney was still left with a can of worms.

CHAPTER 27

Tuesday 16ᵗʰ March 5pm

Kate felt good in the passenger seat as Munro drove up Liverpool Street. The traffic gradually thinned as motorists branched off to the major arterial roads that drained the city of the evening rush hour traffic. Back at the station, Mahoney had quickly briefed them. Kate was tasked with the few simple questions. Munro was to ride shotgun and annoy their quarry simply by being there, the quarry being Dr. James Cartwright.

Munro pulled the sedan into the curb outside the academic's residence. They got out and walked up to the impressive wooden door. Munro knocked loudly and then stepped slightly back and aside so Kendall would be the first person to be seen. They waited patiently. A Skoda was in the driveway so presumably the occupant was home.

Eventually, the front door opened. "You again." Not the warmest of welcomes.

"Good evening, sir. I'm DC Kendall, and DS Munro I think you know."

"Yes, I do."

Good. His voice was on edge already. "We thought for a moment there you were sporting your oak." She indicated the door with a small wave of her hand.

He softened slightly. "You've studied then, Detective. Which university?"

"Not me, sir. The sergeant was telling me about the old university custom while we were waiting."

Cartwright looked as if he'd bitten into silver foil. He didn't acknowledge Munro: there was no chance he'd let that buffoon get one over him. "I see. And what can I do for you, young lady?"

Invite us in. "We have a couple of queries arising from findings in the homicide of Bradley Finch. You're familiar with that, I'm sure."

She was so straight as to be almost sincere so Cartwright had little wriggle room. "As I'm sure you know from your colleague, I am aware a man by that name is dead. Neither I nor my solicitor are sure why you consider me a person of interest."

Seeing as you've contacted a lawyer is a pretty good reason, thought Munro. He said lightly, "I don't know I'd go that far, sir. Just background."

"Oh, really. And that's why you came and badgered me yesterday? And why you're here now on my doorstep embarrassing my neighbors?"

Take us inside then. You're the one getting antsy. The sergeant kept his voice very level. "Our apologies if you feel that, sir, but we have our jobs to do."

"Then do them and stop harassing me."

No wonder we're here, thought Kate. He doth protest too much. "Could we just start again here, Dr. Cartwright? DI Mahoney simply wants to tidy things away from yesterday so we can move on with the main thrust of the case."

"He couldn't just call me?"

Of course he could. But you are again proving to be a very interesting kettle of fish. So here we are. "He is tied up with a suspect at present. This is a routine matter so we decided to clear it up in person." Her tone mollified the man in the doorway a touch. "So, to confirm, we have a suspect in custody and we wish to eliminate you from our enquiries. Normal procedure."

"Nice try, constable. But nowhere near good enough. That phrase is a furphy."

"I beg your pardon, sir."

An exaggerated aerial twitching of his index fingers. "'Eliminate from our enquiries.' Sounds good but it's absolutely meaningless if you're talking to an innocent man."

If.

"You can eliminate me from your enquiries because I had nothing to do, whatsoever with any bashing. I am wholly innocent. Nothing, repeat nothing, to do with this case has anything remotely to do with me. Is that clear for your enquiries?"

Bashing?

"I understand your position, sir. You put it well. But I'm sure you'll agree we're in a bit of a spot. Under authority, if you will. Our boss is such a stickler. He was pleased to meet you, by the way. Admires your writing. Anyway, he's wondering if you've met Amanda Pattison recently? We understand she's one of your students."

"Yes, I have. You know that already."

"Yes, yes, you're right. Clumsy of me. You did say that the other day. What I meant to say was have you met up with her socially at all in the past fortnight?"

"Yes, I have." He felt like saying and you know that already as well. He knew it was prudent to stick to the absolute essentials now.

"Was that last Thursday night?"

Great question, thought Munro. A few birds with one stone.

Cartwright blinked rapidly. Where was that going? Breathe. Frown. Look like you're thinking calmly. "Ah, no. It was the other weekend. A Saturday. We had dinner. Just a chance to enjoy some different company."

Yeah, right.

"Didn't the death occur last Thursday?"

"Yes, that's right sir. Where were you that evening? Just to tick the box."

"Burnie." He made very sure he didn't betray any relief. "I was due to speak to a group of students at the Cradle Coast campus early on the Friday so I drove up Thursday evening and stayed overnight."

"Nice accommodation?" Munro had picked up on the idea of throwing in a random question. Prevent Cartwright from settling on what was obviously a rehearsed spiel of responses.

"Ah, yes, it was. Surprisingly so. A revamped hotel on the waterfront. The Harborview. I'm sure they'll have a record of my stay."

Of course they will. You've organized your alibi rather tidily, he thought. "We'll take your word on that." Not that they would. What was interesting was that he should break off from his work in Hobart to be so far away on that particular night. An odor of decaying crustaceans pervaded the arrangement. "Why surprising?"

"Well, Sergeant, Burnie hasn't always enjoyed the most salubrious of reputations. Didn't some rock band sing that it was a place without a postcard?"

Munro nodded. Midnight Oil. "Yeah, that's right. You had to be up there even though the election's in full swing? You weren't needed here for a sound bite for the news?"

Kendall began to fully realize what Mahoney had meant earlier. Munro had a way of riling Cartwright when asking even an innocuous question. The hackles rose immediately.

"They do vote up there as well, you know. And for your information I do provide something more than sound bites on the radio. As your superior acknowledges."

Kendall was straight in. "So you felt no ill will to Bradley Finch?"

"What?" The exaggerated frown returned. "How could I? He was a student, apparently, in my class. One of my classes. I lecture to a great many pupils. How can I be expected to be familiar with them all?"

Just the ones you publicly berate. Munro aimed one just under the rib cage. "It would be hard to be as close to them all as you are with young Miss Pattison."

It was not often you genuinely saw hatred in someone's eyes. As now. "How dare you. You come to my house to humiliate me. I don't have to justify my behavior to the likes of you."

Yes, you do, thought Kate. Seeing as you've been lying through your teeth to investigating officers. "Sorry, Dr. Cartwright. We've gotten a bit side-tracked here. Obviously, we don't wish to intrude into your private life." But we'll trample all over it if you prove to be as implicated as you seem. "Your professional reputation is important to you. Rightly so. As I said earlier, we were just dispatched to clarify a few matters. I think we've done that." You're a liar and you're very touchy whenever your possible connection to the homicide is mentioned. And a prickly prima donna. Yes, that had all been clarified.

"I don't see how. It seems to me you've trotted up here to fire off a series of petty insults. You and your brute of a sidekick. Be assured I'll be speaking to Detective Inspector Mahoney, among others, about this flagrant misuse of your powers."

Munro smiled. "I'm sure he'll welcome any information you can provide that helps move the case forward. We may need to see you again. Goodbye for now."

From the look on Cartwright's face, it didn't seem to be a circumstance he would welcome. The two detectives returned to the car.

As Munro started the ignition they looked back through the windscreen to the figure still standing at his front door. "Not a happy camper."

Kendall agreed. "I see what you guys meant before. He's shifty about the Pattison thing and even more so whenever Finch is mentioned. We may never have thought he did the deed but he's a good chance to have organized it."

Munro completed a three point turn in the narrow street. "I don't think he's got the balls for that. And a guy like Coutts is way removed from his circle. He's in this up to his neck, yeah. Definitely hiding stuff. But I can't see him as this Colonel guy. He's linked in but we need someone else."

The two detectives retraced their route back into town. As arranged, they met with Mahoney in the back bar of the Duke of Wellington Hotel. None of the trio had managed more than a quick coffee during the day so a debriefing over a meal was deemed a good move.

They walked in the Barrack Street entrance and saw their boss already seated at a table set for them. He was talking on his mobile but caught their eye and beckoned them over. As they sat he finished his call.

"I've ordered herb pizza bread for us and some water. I could do with a drink as could you, I presume. But alcohol consumption with Joe Public watching won't go down too well. Fair enough?"

Kendall nodded. Munro said, "Kate, are you having anything else?"

"No thanks. I'm feeling a bit tired to have a full meal. I'll just get a snack when I get home."

"How about you, Sir?"

"Same, Tim. I just don't feel all that hungry now we're here. You go ahead."

"No, I'll be right. We've got some stuff in the fridge to reheat."

"Stuff. Yum, sounds good. Does that come with something or other sauce?"

"Probably. And an oozywhatsit dessert to finish."

Mahoney smiled to himself. It was a relief to see how quickly Kendall was fitting in. Right now he needed to know how the pair had operated professionally.

"How did Dr. Kissinger behave?"

Munro left it to Kate. "Badly, in a word. His antipathy to Tim is obvious. A few manly insecurity issues there. That's also a by-product of something else. He's guilty of something. Lying to us, obviously. His reactions indicate that he's known who Finch was for some time."

"Probably from about ten minutes after the altercation in the lecture hall."

"Yes, Sir. Most likely. When he's asked about him, it's like a master class in feigned ignorance. Aside from the odd slip."

"Such as?"

Munro spoke through a mouthful of the crusty pizza. "Bashed."

"Sorry, Sergeant." Mahoney leaned forward as he theatrically cocked his ear. "Didn't quite catch that."

"He got very uppity when he was banging on about how he shouldn't be involved in any enquiry. Said he had quote, nothing to do whatsoever with any bashing, unquote."

"That's not public knowledge, is it Sir?" Kate asked.

"Not that's been officially released. But there are various channels that sort of detail could get out into the wide world, alas." Mahoney drank some water. "There's an assumption in your question that I agree with though. I don't think he was there. He's not up to that sort of thing."

"That's what Tim said. He doesn't seem the sort to get his own hands dirty. Bit esoteric."

"And he wasn't in Hobart on Thursday night. Was in Burnie for his work. Four hours away. Kate checked on the way down. He stayed there. A function at the hotel that evening and a presentation on campus next morning."

Mahoney nodded. "Bit too neat, I'm thinking." He exhaled slowly as he gathered his thoughts. A few other diners sauntered past their table. When they were out of earshot he continued. "He's involved. But removed from the deed itself. His motive is clear. Finch embarrassed him in public. It may not seem much to those of us who deal with that sort of flack on a daily basis. However, he's an academic who wants to shine. To be looked up to. Everybody wants to be noticed these days. The big dream is to be on television. Being invited to conferences isn't enough for him. He craves publicity of a brighter sort. There's an underlying insecurity, I'd agree. Anyway, Finch pricked his bubble. And that business with Amanda Pattison compounded it. We've no reason to doubt her story. She played him and he's somehow avoided an even more humiliating ordeal in the media. I don't know if he connected the two: the lecture hall and the recording at dinner. Quite possibly. Even if he's only seen it as coincidental he's fuming at those two. And he wants to lash out at them: one or the other, or both."

Munro asked, "But is that motive enough for murder?"

"Not to us, no. And I don't think even for him. I believe he's the sort of person who would answer in kind. Find a way to make life difficult for the two of them, sure. But not violence, no."

Kate thought you'd be a fool to underestimate Munro. He might seem a thicky to the likes of Cartwright but he was proving to be right on the money. His comments expressed in the car were being echoed here. She expressed the obvious point. "So he's not the Colonel character Coutts referred to? But he's involved somewhere or other."

"Yes, I think so. We know from Amanda Pattison that Cartwright had already engineered a reprisal through a colleague at the university. He's lorded it over Finch already." He stopped abruptly and placed the salt shaker in the middle of the table. "That's a reminder. Ask me at the end what I need to remember." They both nodded. "Following that, Pattison decides to teach him a lesson. Sets him up a treat. Unscrupulously so but eggs get broken. Anyway, she does enough to frighten the horses. The damning article never got to press but it was a close run thing. As you arrived I was talking to a friend at the paper. She's checked for me that a story along the lines Pattison suggests was set to run but got pulled before printing. It was even mentioned on one of those crosses to the newsroom they do on WIN TV to publicize the next day's main stories. At 8.30pm. But by 9.30pm it had vanished. Never to be seen again. All my journalist friend could find out was that the night editor pulled it under advice from their in-house legal counsel. And his ongoing advice has been not to touch it. She couldn't be sure but she thought the guy on that night was a bit forced when telling her it was no big deal. Amanda's work placement friend who wrote the story is away interstate somewhere. The story just disappeared."

Munro was staying silent on all matters dealing with the media so Kate was left to ask, "Who has that amount of pull? Cartwright? To muzzle the press like that."

Her boss shook his head. "I doubt it. He's not that precious to them. He's one of their own, in a sense, with him composing articles for them. But they were prepared to run with an exposé regardless. Muck sells. Someone else sat on it. I'd say the editor-in-chief. But who sat on him? *The Mercury* has been blessedly free of pandering to sectional interests for the past decade. So whoever wielded this axe has plenty of pull in this town. An amazing amount." He held up his hands in mock surrender. "It certainly isn't me. And I've no earthly idea who it could be."

"The Colonel," Munro quipped.

"What luck with that? That's George Castanza's dad's 'worlds colliding' for sure. Right, speaking of neatness, back to Cartwright. Amanda Pattison becomes his *bête noire*. How to stymie her? Not by getting Finch done over. It's a bit Godfather-horsehead-in-the-bed for Cartwright's situation: rather over the top for him."

Kendall was slightly confused. "Then why do we think he was involved?"

"Because his alibi is excellent."

Munro could see it. "Why does he cover himself so well for that night in particular?"

"Exactly. Sorry, I forgot to tell you about another call I made while you were up at the castle. I rang the departmental secretary who told me Cartwright was a late replacement for another pol sci lecturer who was originally scheduled for the trip but withdrew due to illness."

"How late?"

"The email asking for someone to fill the breech went around Wednesday afternoon and Cartwright volunteered almost immediately."

"Doesn't strike me as the selfless type."

"Absolutely. Never shown any interest prior to then in visiting either of the northern campuses. But jumped at this chance to ensure he was out of town. As my cousin says, 'you may need a peg for your nose'. Cunning but actually a bit stupid. We're never really going to pin a guy like that for GBH stuff so he's no need of an elaborate smokescreen. An alibi like that, so orchestrated, actually draws suspicion on him. Needlessly. So now I'm thinking he's definitely involved. His evasiveness, straight lies, attitude, getting legal advice, lack of co-operation, unnecessary alibi. It's a potent mix. He's guilty. But I'm buggered if I know of what."

"I don't really think he's the Colonel, I was just kidding," Munro offered.

"I know. I doubt he knows that people like Coutts and Knapp exist. But his conscience is working overtime. We'll find out soon enough."

Kendall sensed they were drawing to a close. "The salt shaker, Sir."

"Oh yeah, I need to talk to the uni chap who ticked Finch off over the lecture hall stuff."

CHAPTER 28

Tuesday 16ᵗʰ March 8pm

Assistant Commissioner Newman felt at home in his current surroundings. Seated in a well-upholstered, high-backed leather chair, he was cocooned from the other conversations in the reading room of the Colonial Club. Perched on the coffee table shared with two identical chairs was a bottle of Church Block Shiraz and three glasses. One for himself and one each for his two companions, Rory Fotheringham and the Minister for Sport and Recreation, Bill "Dusty" Rhode, so named because he represented a country electorate with few sealed roads. Or so he claimed. Detractors believed his promises slid about all over the place like a "car with bald tires on a gravel track". Friends charitably insisted it alluded to Bill's liking for a beer or three: it was usually 'hot and dusty' causing a thirst that needed to be parched whenever he was near a bar.

This evening the glass of wine was his first drink for the day. Mind you, parliament had been in session until 7pm so that the wait till 7.36pm was understandable. Rhode was no great fan of this tipple, the room or the company but current circumstances dictated he must sup with the devil, the devil in this case being Fotheringham. Fothers had him over a barrel, a very deep stout barrel. A few backhanders here, a few private donations there and over time Bill Rhode was snarled in a web of patronage. It wasn't as if Fotheringham demanded much. There was never any request for proper laws to be bent: it was more that he received a discreet heads-up about any policy developments the government may be considering. And every so often an indication of what ballpark figure might be acceptable in the tender process for certain government contracts; certain lucrative government contracts.

Most people, Fotheringham's competitors included, assumed his operation was simply more efficient and professional and so deserved to get over the finishing line. Having the one-one sit in racing parlance didn't hurt at all. It was corruption, certainly, but Rhode figured that if economic development occurred then the government of the day benefitted, as did the electors upon whom he relied. If Fotheringham getting filthy rich was the by-product then so be it. He was hardly going to blow the whistle: not if he didn't want a decade's worth of slightly dodgy dealings to see the light of public scrutiny. So he was no great fan of Rory F and he thought even less of the chameleon to his right. AC Newman reminded him of an oil slick: smooth, superficial and unnatural. Word was he was deeply unpopular with the police rank and file but he glided up through the ranks with a combination of guile, false bonhomie and a Teflon coating. Rhode wouldn't trust him out the door of a broom closet but he had his uses.

As he was most likely to prove now. Fotheringham had convened the meeting at the exclusive members' only club. The reading room was not for the discernment of printed material but rather a moderately quiet space where you could read more closely the reactions of others without the distraction of snooker, phones or too many people.

Fotheringham swaggered into the room. Was in no mood for chin-wagging. "Thanks for meeting up, guys." As if they had a choice. "Need to check with you how the Finch case is playing out." Newman, as the Police Commissioner's right hand man, and Rhode, as a member of Cabinet, were ideally placed to report on how the constabulary and executive arm of the government were responding to the crisis. Anybody who didn't regard the death of a local sportsman as a crisis or didn't see what concern any of this was for a business consultant was simply ignorant of how things were in Hobart. If Fothers wanted to know then he needed to be told. Simple. Power.

Newman eased forward in his chair. "We're throwing the kitchen sink at it. Phillips wants a result, of course. My guess is he's going to his retirement farm pretty soon so he dearly wants this sorted."

And you want him gone quickly so you can ease into the big chair with the executive toilet, Rhode thought. He said, "Bully for him. How's that going to fix this PR mess? Season's starting in three weeks. Boys don't need this hanging over their heads. Government either. We need good news stories."

Newman kept a cool tone. "Don't we all. All I'm saying, if the man at the top is pressing hard then more officers and resources are going the right way."

"So you're trying real hard." The contempt was ill-concealed. Rhode obviously felt his being on a restricted driving license resulting from a trifecta of speeding tickets, failing to wear a seat belt on too many occasions and refusing a Breathalyzer test was a cruel restriction of his natural justice. Most police officers tended to feel he should have taken his toothbrush to court. "How's that going to help? Public wants results. PDQ. Pretty damned quick."

Newman refused to bridle. He'd dealt with buffoons like this for years. Full of bluster but little kick. The opposite of Fotheringham who was sitting comfortably on the sideline. The AC wasn't going to engage in a scrap for anyone's benefit. "And they'll get it. I'm stating the obvious (for your benefit, blockhead) but the only person who doesn't want a quick result is whoever did it. I know how crucial this case is to various interests and you simply have to appreciate everything that can be done is being done." Newman was on message. He felt comfortable berating Mahoney: he was a subordinate. But he wasn't going to let a hick politician from the Midlands sully the force: a force he soon hoped to command. And for him this was a perfect case to boost his profile in the public eye and to solidify his prospects with the power-makers who would make the decision. He could show all care but held little responsibility. If it didn't go well, the shit would rain down on the Commissioner and the investigative team. If the squad came up tops he would claim his generous slice of the glory. Win, win.

"Well, I bloody well hope so. The economy needs this team to do well. Industries are keeling over. We need the bums on seats. Interstate bums with lots of cash. Happy team leads to a few wins. Wins generate publicity and the mainland fans fly in. With their money. And that's what we dearly need. Pronto."

Newman privately regarded the new club in the same vein as he did most sporting pursuits: a waste of energy. He paid lip service to the cause but his interests lay elsewhere: in the concert hall and art gallery. Fine wine, Verdi and a sophisticated woman punched his buttons: not lager, sport and a bunch of mates. The great unwashed could label him "un-Australian". Care factor zero. He didn't run into them when holidaying in Europe or tripping over to Melbourne Concert Hall. But what triggered his bemusement now was that the Minister for Sport so crudely equated sporting success to dollars. It was all just commerce. All major sports were now big business. An intractable bundle of television rights, advertising, gambling and public money ensured that. But to have it so baldly laid in front of him now was quite sobering. He knew his own motives for success in the case were hardly pure but to witness the rank commercialism first-hand was still a shock. At least he spared a genuine passing thought for the young man's family. He doubted it would raise a mention in this company.

Fotheringham had carefully held his counsel. It amused him to see two of his puppets stoushing, albeit verbally. If his various contacts were at each other's throats then they were divided and he could continue to conquer all. So far the conversation had secured this aim but time was pressing. He had a 9pm visit to pay to the partner of a judge who was away on circuit to the North West Coast. Sensual pleasures waited so the jousting needed to be halted. Time to address the real agenda.

"Bill, I think we are agreed a quick resolution to this case is vital. For many good reasons. And I believe AC Newman will do that for us."

Us?!

"I needed a brief meeting to check a couple of issues. Firstly, Bill, is the Premier onside for a fitting memorial service for Bradley Finch?"

Rhode was briefly taken aback by the direct mention of the victim. Soon recovered. "Yeah, yeah. All good. He'll give us all the bells and whistles we want. Can't do a state funeral but near as dammit. Plenty of media. Even do the eulogy, or part of it, himself. Money's there to fly AFL bigwigs in. Should get us plenty of coverage. Yeah, all good."

Newman was unsurprised that the poverty of language matched the paucity of emotional imagination. So the death was now a crucial link in the ongoing extravaganza of launching a sports team. His mouthful of Shiraz took on more notes of tannin as it slid down his throat.

Fotheringham didn't miss a beat. "OK, Keep Bruce Randall in the loop in all this. He's a safe pair of hands. Sproule will probably want some limelight but I'll make sure he's reasonably dignified. As much as he can be." A knowing smile to both of them. "We want to send off this young fella the right way."

Newman doubted the family would have much say in it. Fotheringham turned to him. "Mahoney's doing the case, right?"

"Yes, fell to him as head of the squad. He's got plenty of backing from the plain clothes department. All seem united to get the job done."

"Is he reliable?"

What a beautiful question, thought Newman. Can the squad rely upon him to conduct a scrupulous case? Can the public rely on him to give everything to apprehending the killer? Can the shadow makers rely on the DI to do what they may want?

"Yes. I have reservations about him. Can be very prickly. Doesn't respond well to direction from above. Not a great team man. Keeps a lot to himself. But the record is good. Cases get solved. And those cases hold up in court. So, yes he's reliable in that sense."

Fotheringham nodded. "Hasn't registered on my radar much. Not much of a joiner, as in outside organizations, as I recall. Overseas guy?"

"Not really. Trained here. I've got a memory of him at the Academy. Shipped off to England years ago for some reason. Returned a couple of years ago with a very strong recommendation. Since then he's established a good squad. As I say, I don't quite regard him that highly but the Commissioner trusts him."

"But can we?"

"We?"

"Don't be obtuse. Or cute."

Rhode suppressed a smile. He didn't want Fothers turning on him.

"We, as in the people who care for this state and make it run." He had leaned into Newman so the sharp whisper was clearly audible to the policeman. "Does this guy know enough to target the right suspects and leave well enough alone?"

Newman hedged his bets. "Possibly not."

"Well, he needs to be informed, as Bill would say, PDQ. I hear an innocent academic has been grilled recently. I'm telling you the heat's being applied in the wrong place."

"Are you referring to Cartwright?" How did Fotheringham know this?

"Maybe." Very cagey. "I'll just say you're not a million miles away there. This seems more of a low-life crime to me."

And you're a shit-hot criminologist now, are you? "Point taken. I'll do my best to guide the investigation along the right lines."

Fotheringham stood to leave. "Make sure your best is good enough. Evening, gentlemen. I'll leave you to a convivial drink."

Fat chance, they both thought.

CHAPTER 29

Tuesday 16th March 8pm

Forty-seven channels and nothing on. Was that the refrain in the Springsteen song? John Mahoney could not remember. Regardless, he did know there were far more channels accessible to him courtesy of his satellite TV box. Having resisted the lure for a substantial time, he finally acceded to the advertising offers so he could access Premier League Football. The record function had also proven to be a boon.

Tonight, among the myriad offerings, he opted for one of the property shows. A very chipper male presenter was doing his best to relocate a cashed-up couple from London into their dream rural bolt-hole in Devon but without much success. The sticking point wasn't so much the desirability of the houses but that Mr. and Mrs. Moneybags turned out to have wildly divergent ideas on what constituted their dream home. He wanted thatch; she wanted tile. He wanted outbuildings; she insisted on views. A degree of tension developed. They needed a counsellor more than a house hunter.

The emerging bitchiness suited Mahoney's mood. It had not been the best of times. In truth it had been perilously close to the worst. Mahoney switched the television off, poured himself a finger or three of whisky and sank into his favorite chair. Normally, he wasn't a great drinker of Scotch but every so often when he needed to mull things over he liked the fiery taste of a Highland Malt. On a holiday to Scotland five years ago, Mahoney had ventured over to the Isle of Arran. The distillery production, then just over a decade old, was unusual in that there was no peat in the malt. The local water was judged to be suitable enough by itself. Traditional connoisseurs may choke on their sporrans but for many this refreshing, sharply sweet brew was just the ticket.

As he sipped, the detective began to consider the direction in which he was heading. When pressed, he would readily admit his worst habit was to look at life from the vantage of a rear view mirror, a habit he was gradually learning to counteract. 'If' was a simple word laden with complex difficulties. 'If only' compounded the problematic mindset. You made mistakes, errors of judgment. Everyone did. The trick, easier said than done, was to glean any positives from experience and to move on.

No matter how much you turned things over in your mind, the past was not going to change. Not one jot. But you could learn to turn negative experiences to your advantage. Analyze a bad result and objectively assess how to improve from then on. As they said at AA, doing the same stuff over and over, expecting a different result, was insanity.

Over time, Mahoney had gradually changed the things it was in his power to change. Became better at listening to what people were really saying; acquired the skill of asking the questions that unlocked the reserve of others. The pity was, and didn't he know it only too well, he increasingly built barriers around his innermost feelings. If he were to be asked "Are you OK?" a few platitudes would be the best anyone could get.

The dialogue was unfailingly in his head. It wasn't so much he needed to get out more, although that wouldn't hurt. It was surely that he needed to get *out of his own mind more*. What were the chances of that? You would get better odds on England winning the Football World Cup. He bottled stuff up and kept the cork in nice and tight. Often enough, he'd counselled others on the advisability of controlling their emotions. Damage limitation. Think things through, he told them. Yet he knew his self-control was vice-like, constricting.

And look what had happened. He had drip fed the poison tree for two decades and finally he had spewed his bile over Newman. To what end? An own goal if ever there was one. He had succumbed to his rage over the long cherished grievance and belittled himself. Newman, being Newman, would brush it off. Some egos were impenetrable. Mahoney had felt temporarily better but then just a little bit impotent.

And his outburst may have adversely affected the case. Just when the squad needed allies in high places, Mahoney had given a superior the perfect excuse to doubt his judgment. For a person who could run the workshop 'Dealing with Difficult People', his stupidity really stuck in his craw. Perhaps there were other options? An alternative path to take. Forget his superannuation plan and get out. Try something else. Volunteer work. Travel writing. Don't think, do. Do something else. But what?

He got up, stretched, and went again to his excuse for a drinks cabinet. Another small one wouldn't hurt so he poured it. As he put the bottle back, he saw the Hawthorn Footy Club stubby holder. A former coach, a true legend in sports circles, had addressed a management conference of officers in the Protective Services. For practically every officer there from the Ambulance, Fire, Rescue and the Police Services, it had been the only highlight amidst the bureaucratic gobbledygook they had been expected to wade through.

The speaker's ideas on leadership were succinct but redolent with great anecdotal insights. One centered on the scenario of a young male driver who routinely raced off from a traffic light only to find himself having to wait impatiently at the very next one. And so on. The other driver took off at a moderate speed, maintained it and consequently cruised through a succession of intersections with minimal frustration and the output of significantly less energy. Better result and more in reserve. A story Mahoney routinely relayed to probationary constables.

But it was one of the stories that Mahoney now turned over in his mind. Quite simply, it involved a driver at a crossroad in the countryside in search of a previously unvisited destination. The signpost had been knocked and was skew-whiff in the soil. How could it help to chart the way? Simple. Turn it so one destination was correct. Which one? The pointer which indicated where you had just come from. With that going the right way, you could easily work out where you needed to go. Mahoney well knew how he had gotten to where he was now. He would dearly love to know just exactly where he was meant to be going. That wasn't too much to ask. Surely.

And his private life, such as it was. In this, he was guarded. On the rare occasions he went on a date, he was always asked if he played poker. Not a cards game person, he replied. Why do you ask? Because you have the right face for it and you give very little away. And they were right. As much as he tried to engage, he had a perfectly constructed retaining wall around his emotional core. Had the hurt and betrayal of decades ago been so powerful to stifle any attempts to fall for another person? Well, yes. His love life, though it could hardly be genuinely called that, was like a rugby scrum: set, touch, engage.

But he would never put any real oomph into it. He might look like he was trying but his heart was never really in it. Sure, he could involve himself, but whenever it came to anything serious being at stake, he would trot on to a different pasture. He assured himself he was not promiscuous but a series of fleeting relationships was hardly the mark of an emotionally intelligent and stable adult. He just found it easier to go to the cinema or whatever by himself. He had resigned himself to being a solo invitation to social gatherings. Went on holidays alone yet wished he had a special someone to share the experience with. And he was sick of it. Fed up.

Standing on the periphery observing the lives of others was useful for a detective but as a human it left you two-dimensional at best. Aside from his career and his cherished cultural life, he had what…not much. Paintings, albeit good ones, on the walls and shelves stuffed with books were signs of cultivation but he felt like an empty shell. He had begun to ghost through life. Being well read was fine. But so was Adolf Hitler apparently.

Investigations should be tidy and thorough but maybe his life needed to be just a bit messy. Some sense of the unpredictable. Take a chance here and there. Open up a touch. Maybe a lot. He knew the song. Dance like nobody's watching. Laugh often. Dive into life. To be able to have something on his tombstone other than Capable Detective. And then his thoughts returned inexorably to the case.

CHAPTER 30

Wednesday 17th March 7am

The query completely bewildered Kate. Bamboozled her in a number of ways. Should not have, but it did. "So what time for Mr. Buzzy this morning?" Part of it was that it came from someone in her own bed. It was a long, long time since there had been a conversation there. And as she was quite talkative, this indicated a lengthy period of abstinence. As things now stood, she was glad and relieved. Glad she had encountered this particular partner who stimulated her. And relieved she could enjoy the fulfilling pleasure they created together. Last night she was dog-tired but a tender foot rub from Rex led to further tender stroking and before long the bedroom pentathlon was in full swing.

Just before she drifted off to sleep, Rex had said he felt as if he had been kissed in a rare place by a fairy. Well, she felt fortunate too and slept six dreamless hours. She awoke feeling bright and alert and ready to wrestle him all morning. But the job called. Still, as she looked at the slumbering figure next to her, she knew there would be more times like this. Plenty more.

And then he awoke, kissed her, and asked the question. She turned crimson. Why was he asking about her vibrator? How on earth did he even know? What did she say last night? Her mind was racing.

"What's wrong? It's not that warm in here?"

"Nothing." Quick think. "I'm fine. It's just such a pleasant surprise to find you here this morning." Phew.

"Snap. I guess you have to resume the trail this morning. Mr. Buzzy the Beekeeper will be expecting you. Can't keep the big boss waiting."

Oh, thank the Lord for that. Her favorite toy was still to be introduced. Something else to look forward to next time they played. She smiled. "Definitely not. I wouldn't want him angry with me. May get disciplined by Internal Affairs." She winked at him and his eyebrows nearly took off.

A theatrically grave voice. "Mmm, yes. You'd be cuffed and mercilessly interrogated by whoever is on call. Almost certainly me, I'd say. I think a feather would be particularly effective in your case." He stroked her shoulder.

It was patently obvious the prospect excited him. His baton was very ready to be brought into action. So Kate gently flicked it and then whispered in his ear. "As soon as this case is done we'll book a weekend at Freycinet so we can verbal each other and conduct a series of probing interviews." That and a fulsome kiss on his lips left Rex moaning softly as she got out of bed to shower. Kate was genuinely unsure if this day could get any better.

*   *   *

As Kate entered DI Mahoney's office, she immediately realized her musings had been rhetorical. By the grave look on her boss's face, her day was not going to improve. If anything, it was about to become appreciably worse. He gestured for her to sit. Munro was already in the other visitors' chair looking hangdog. Another cock-up? Surely not.

Munro had been fully onside as far as she knew. What else? They had organized formal transcripts of yesterday's crucial interview. Notebooks were up to date. All in order. There were avenues to explore but the principal perpetrators were locked up. All good. So why was Mahoney looking agitated as he jabbed at his keyboard. With a final flourish, he finished slamming away and turned to face his subordinates.

"We've been butt-fucked." The tone was resigned. The volume moderate. The reaction was shock. Neither could imagine Mahoney employing such language nor could they contemplate him exhibiting any sign of defeat. This guy was Mr. Resilience and Mr. Composure in one. What on earth could have happened?

"Let me give you the abridged version. Last night I received a text. 'Well done on quick result. Brief me at 7am. CP.' So the Commissioner has heard and he wants a verbal report ASAP. So far, no problem. I don't know what you did last night but I took a couple of hours off." Kate sat extra still hoping Munro was not looking at her. "So I sat back and mentally reviewed our case." A slight smile creased his face. "I know, great relaxation. Anyway, I got to thinking that we may, no strike that, we do have further exploration to undertake."

He lifted his index finger. "First, the two guys we have next door in remand have no motive to harm this particular victim. They are motivated to commit a crime, but why Finch? Neither even knew who he was. I doubt they'd have agreed if they had. So, second, according to Coutts he was put up to it by this Colonel person. Now Coutts is a slimy piece of work but his claim is plausible. Tenuous, but plausible. If the calls were made from a public phone then tracing the caller is practically impossible. We can check Coutts' mobile but I doubt it would help us."

At this point Mahoney paused, looked in turn at each of his subordinates, then slowly and very deliberately raised a third finger. "And most damning of all….the meeting upstairs concluded half an hour ago. Present were myself, Assistant Commissioner Newman and the Commissioner. I updated them on the progress thus far and my ongoing suspicions. Not playing favorites but I'll ask Tim this one. Why does that worry me?"

Munro frowned. In for penny, in for a pound. "A few reasons, perhaps. How did the other two participants know so quickly? Why was it necessary for a top-level discussion for the case at this stage?" He hesitated here in a search for the most diplomatic phrasing. "Was the meeting a full stop instead of a comma?"

"Nicely put, Tim. Well, the first two are easy. A good result permeates to all floors of our building. This has been a high profile case with the Commissioner's involvement from the start." Mahoney hesitated as a very distasteful thought occurred to him and then continued. "Your final query. That is the most salient and in answering it I must insist on the cone of silence. You are both trusted and I'm sorry to have to ask but we are entering treacherous territory here. If either or both of you wish to leave now I would fully understand and you would duly receive commendations on your records."

Munro eased his buttocks off the chair then sat down heavily and smiled. Good answer. Kate nodded and remained firmly seated. Mahoney continued, "Right. You weren't here and we never had this conversation. Understood?"

"Crystal." Another smile.

"Yes, most definitely." Kate was resolute.

"The powers that be want this one put to bed and I'm not just referring to up there." Index finger pointed to the ceiling. "Over there is interested too." His hand gestured in the general direction of the Government quarter which housed Parliament and the Executive Offices. "The media shit storm will pass through now. We have the principal culprits. There'll be articles about violence in our idyllic city but the full wattage limelight will dim. They'll believe the Departmental media releases that Knapp and Coutts were acting independently; a random act of violence. Mugging gone wrong. Coutts' connection to Colonel whoever will be ignored. Easy to do as there's no evidence of collusion. It will be regarded as the delusional excuse of a desperate criminal. Case closed. Fish's arse." He clapped his palms together.

Kate spoke up. "But your, sorry our, feeling is the loose threads are un-ignorable."

Mahoney rotated his shoulders and leaned forward. "Absolutely. The whole case goes back to the victim. Why Finch? Nothing substantial links him to the other two unless we believe they were put up to it. If it was random they chose an unlikely mark. He was probably stronger than the both of them combined."

"And even though it is a shortcut it's hardly a place you could be sure of finding someone to do over."

"Exactly, Tim. From all we know it clearly looks like an arranged encounter. Somebody wanted Finch sorted out at the very least."

Kate tried to disguise her agitation. "So why do the big bosses want this one wrapped up so quickly, given there are obviously persons of interest we should be seeking and interviewing?"

Munro answered. "Partly for that reason, I guess. It's a quick fix. They all love the spotlight when its highlighting their, or more usually their officers', good work but this media frenzy is a bit of a blowtorch."

Mahoney nodded. "There is definitely that element to it."

"And?" prompted Kate.

"This is the tricky bit. The Rubicon for us." An encompassing hand gesture. "This morning's meeting covered just about everything including our visit to Cartwright. When I mentioned his name, Newman was unduly keen to know the academic's role in the case. I downplayed it a bit, to be fair, and then he piped up with quote 'It was only a small matter in the lecture theatre anyway' unquote." He let that nugget sink in.

A low whistle from Munro. "How did Big Bear react to that?"

"Well, he shuffled in his seat a bit but I ploughed on as if I hadn't noticed the gaffe. So Cartwright or somebody else close to him has been in the ears of the upper echelon. I say somebody close because, bugger me, two minutes later Dar Commissar puts his foot in it. As tactfully as he can, he suggests we wrap things up soonest. Parliament Square is pleased there's a result. Blah, blah. I can only presume, because he knows he's waffling, he lets slip that we can safely overlook any conspiracy figures people might dream up. He was just a bit too casual, deliberately downbeat. Now Ted Phillips retains my respect. It's a hell of a job he's got but when he starts to flannel then my nostrils really do start to twitch."

Kate was first in. "So we should delve deeper in your considered opinion?"

Before an answer was forthcoming, the phone trilled and Mahoney put it on speakerphone. "DI Mahoney here."

"John, it's Ted."

Mahoney picked up the receiver. "Yes, Sir." As the short conversation ensued, his expression became more drawn. At its conclusion he replaced the receiver and looked up. "Seems we won't need our spades after all as I've been given the wind-up signal in no uncertain terms. The official status of this investigation is that it is now closed. We are to prepare all material to present to the Crown Prosecution Service as soon as possible."

As it sank in, he held up his palms to his junior officers. "I have a fair idea what you're thinking and I agree but that was a clear directive to halt. Believe me, I'm frustrated too but we are duty-bound to follow this order. It is what I would expect of you and it is what is expected of me."

Kate sat silently but not so Munro. "But you wouldn't give such a bloody stupid order."

Mahoney breathed deeply and slowly exhaled. "That's as maybe. I've only surmised what is behind it. There may be more going on than we know."

"Too bloody right," snorted Munro.

"That's enough. Let's not eat our own. And don't dare quote Nuremberg and My Lai to me. There's a time and place to question orders and that is not now." The volume was up just a notch but the delivery was very measured. "I don't believe you would undermine me by flagrantly disobeying orders so you can hardly expect me to do so here. Ted Phillips has a long record of integrity and deserves our respect. It's unsatisfactory for us but the time to fight this battle is not right now."

Munro and Kendall sat chastened. Their boss leant forward. "However, just because a public declaration is being made doesn't preclude us from *finalizing* the case. Are you with me?" They were and there was a quick lightening of the mood. "Tim, you're in court soon?"

"Yep, preliminaries for the Calvert hearing. Should be done by midday at the latest."

"Good, we'll talk later. Kate, we're going for a coffee at Café Commandant. I feel like a short break from the confines of this building. A change of scene may give us some earthly idea of where to go from here."

CHAPTER 31

Wednesday 17ᵗʰ March 11am

"So that's how it is, is it? We sit on our hands and whistle. Terrific." Mahoney knew his best DC had fire in her belly for the job but up to this point she had been relatively unflappable. Now she was fuming. "These people, the faceless men, call the shots now, do they? Just who are they? I don't remember electing them. When were they appointed? We can't be that impotent, surely." She was fired up but briefly out of steam.

Sensing no immediate reaction from her superior, she slumped back in the couch and stared ruefully out the window. What she saw through the window of the cafe did precious little to lighten her mood. A cold southerly was shooting leaves up Elizabeth Street. The sky was clear and the sun was stoically trying to warm the streetscape but there was minimal encouragement for the stolid pedestrians beating their way up the footpath. A cold snap overnight had instantly taken the energy out of everyone's step. Even the students congregated at the bus stop opposite were none too cheerful this morning.

A distinct chill had fallen over the investigation. Mahoney sipped his latte. Rubbed his stubble. No shave this morning. Bugger it. At this point in proceedings he lacked the energy and perhaps the will to show a brave face to the world. He gazed at the Federation style post office and tried to conjure a response to what he truly hoped were answerable questions. Publicity banners flapped wildly in the wind.

So, so different from yesterday. In a number of ways. Was there more to this changeable climate? Any quick change in conditions was almost always met with the stock response: that's Tassie for you. Four seasons in one day. Usually quite happily. It was a wonder many a bride could fit on a ring after a week of having her fingers crossed for clement weather. Was this general attitude a sign of gritty stoicism or an apathetic acceptance of things? The old English 'mustn't grumble' approach. That could easily suggest an unwillingness to tackle problems. Just let things be. Fatalism. Perhaps that was what he was doing now.

Suddenly he thought of the old Red Lion pub. "Are you receiving me?" Kate was tapping his knee.

"Now that was a band. Out there, like Talking Heads."

"Who were?"

"XTC. That's some of the lyrics. The one decent cover a local band used to do."

"Back in the day." Kate teased.

"Yeah, in that foreign country. Back when I had your idealism, I guess."

Kate rolled her eyes. "I'm going to pretend that moment never happened. Doing the tired and wounded old stag is so not you. Earlier was bad. But so what, we pick ourselves up."

Mahoney considered carefully this young woman. Surely she was right. They were halfway up Mt Kilimanjaro and failing to get to the top was not an option. Well, not one he could truthfully live with. One path in the wood had proven a dead end. But there had to be others. "Yes, we dust ourselves off and start searching for other ways. Thank you, Kate. I never thought you'd be the boot up my pants my father used to be."

Kate blushed and lowered her eyes. When she looked up from the table her voice was softer. "When Gerard, my selfish unfaithful ex, buggered off last Winter, I couldn't see a way forward. Stuck here in Slowbart. But my Mum came down, mothered me for few weeks and then went back home. Told me I had resilience. That I'd be more than OK. She was right. I am, and on this team, I'm far more than OK. I'm flying. To be recruited to your squad has finally made all the crap disappear. I really don't want this to end. You know, with our tails between our legs. We'll find that link somewhere."

Mahoney had been hunched forward as she spoke. He sat bolt upright. The passing reference to infidelity had sparked something. "Yes, yes, we will. Kate, quick, think back. When you were back at the Kingston site, what sort of car did you say the manager was driving?"

"One of those flash Holden utes. Brand new model. Bright red. Looked too smooth to be a fair dinkum builder's car. Why?"

"I've seen it before. Where it shouldn't have been perhaps. Come on. We've got a house visit to do."

As they drove out of the State Cinema car park, Kate could sense the heightened energy of her passenger. The Beekeeper was excited by something. As she turned the Commodore from Strahan Street into Argyle Street, he was tapping the digits on his mobile and then held it to his ear. "Jerome, it's John Mahoney. Yes, well but flat chat as you can imagine. I'm hoping you can do me a small favor. Good, thank you. It's this. Remember the morning last week when I came by and there was a shiny new car at your place next to the convertible? Both with Tassie plates and we surmised they were locals on a romantic but not perhaps totally legitimate sojourn? Well, at least, I did. Can you tell me who those two cars belonged to? Can you quickly check for me while I hold? Righto, thanks."

Kate assumed the pause was for the call's recipient to check some sort of guest register. She concentrated on the traffic at the Federal Street intersection and held her curiosity at bay. "Gotcha, Larry Owen of Balwinnie Street, Lindisfarne and the lady was Jane Watson of Oceana Drive, Tranmere. Hers was the Mazda X5. Yes, I've got all that. Thanks again, Jerome. I'm in your debt. Hope to see you soon." He rang off. "Did you hear that?"

"What? The names."

"No, the satisfying clunk of some jigsaw pieces clicking into place."

"Um, I think so. Dots aren't quite joined up though."

"Get in the left lane. We're going over the river."

Kate indicated and eased into the Tasman Bridge traffic lane in front of Hobart's original university. "And?"

"A few links are emerging. This romantically inclined Larry Owen isn't just a randy chap getting it away down at Dover last week. He's also Cartwright's brother-in-law and the guy in charge of the building site at Osborne Esplanade. Has to be. It was all in the different reports on my desk but I allowed myself to be distracted and didn't follow up."

He turned obliquely to Kate as the car passed Government House. "We couldn't work out why the body was left down at Kingston. Well, I'd hazard a pretty good guess because it was established beforehand that was where it was going to go. Someone in the know set it up. Knapp and

Coutts didn't know but I think we're going to find out pretty soon who it was suggested that spot."

Kate drew a line. "Owen sorts things so there's a convenient place to put Finch. The delay with the cement for the foundations gave him the perfect opportunity and he hotfoots it out of town to avoid any immediate enquiries. And Cartwright put him up to it?"

"Quite probably. But that pig isn't going to squeal just yet."

"So we're off to get Owen?"

"Later. There's another link in the chain I want to test first. One that won't be quite as strong."

"Who, the woman?"

"Not just any woman. A grieving widow."

Another twenty minutes and they pulled up outside a McMansion with a jaw dropping view of the expansive river, Wrest Point Casino and the mountain behind. A vista of marketing dreams. They stepped out of the car to be buffeted by a boisterous wind. Exposed to the southerly wind, this new subdivision was still raw but most owners were making significant headway with landscaping. Timber sleepers supported terraced lawn spaces bordered with native plants. On the last stage, Mahoney had made two more calls and seemed satisfied with what he had learned.

They half jogged up the steps to the entrance of number 374. A tall woman in gym gear answered the door. She did not seem surprised to see them on her doorstep. "Hello officers, please come in. Thank you for coming again."

Again? Some police were expected but not these particular ones, Kate guessed. "Thank you, Mrs. Watson."

She led them into a Scandinavian interior not of blonde wood paneling but of clean lines and rigidly geometric furniture. Chrome and black leather chairs were configured precisely on a cobalt grey, polished concrete floor. Neat as a pin. Ascetic. Their hostess displayed about as much emotion as the room. If she was distressed it was being kept well in check. The detectives took the proffered chairs, declined coffee and introduced themselves to Jane Watson.

Mahoney offered his condolences before venturing into the conversation proper.

"Mrs. Watson, where were you last Friday?"

She looked taken aback. An eyebrow arched. "Friday. Well, I imagine I was dealing with the wash-up of the estate or something like that. I can't say definitely. The last week or so has been something of a blur. Why do you ask? Are these questions about my husband's death?" The jaw was tight and the lips slightly drawn in.

I'm beginning to think there's something fishy there, thought Mahoney. "Not at this stage, Mrs. Watson. There's no suggestion it was anything but a regrettable accident." Not that he was going to voice now anyway. "My colleague and I are conducting an entirely separate investigation." She relaxed ever so slightly. "Have you recently reported your car as stolen?"

"No, why on earth would I?" She paused and crossed her legs. "I'm sorry but what are you actually here for?"

"As I said, we're crossing a few t's in another investigation. An acquaintance of yours has been of some assistance to us and we're hoping you can corroborate some information." Kate suppressed a smile. Her boss was right. It was just that Owen was doing it unwittingly. She kept her eyes on Jane as Mahoney worked away. "A Mr. Larry Owen was at Taldana Retreat, near Dover, on that day and I'm wondering if you can confirm that."

She was good. Almost priceless. Her mind must be whirring as to how they knew that. What to divulge? Her eyes flickered to the view of the whitecaps on the water and back to the man who was most surely now her interrogator. "What I'm about to tell will doubtless not meet with your approval but I doubt that sanctimony genuinely helps anybody. He was there. So was I. We were playing together most of the day. Have been for months, if truth be told. My husband was barely interested so I got another builder in for some hands-on work. Do I shock you, Inspector?"

Well, just a bit, he thought. He secretly hoped they had shown some remorse following her husband's death. An intriguing tangent occurred again. Resisted pursuing it. There was the matter at hand. "No one is here to assess your sexual morality. It's impossible to be both a police officer and prurient. We simply wished to confirm that you were both there. And you have. Thank you." Smooth as silk. "By the way, when was this trip arranged?"

"Day before, I think. Larry said he'd had a brainwave. Told me there was some to be a delay on site because the concreters weren't available 'til the next week so he was giving his men a day off. He suggested a getaway. I packed a black negligee, in case you're concerned." She had struck a discordant note: in her desire to be unflappable she came across as callous. Into the damning silence that followed, she asked a question that should have occurred much earlier. "Why do you need to know where Larry and I were that day?"

"Well, it might be best if he explained that himself. Would you ask him to come out from his hidey-hole?" She narrowed her eyes at him but he simply waved towards the kitchen bench. "Two cups next to a full plunger of freshly brewed coffee and a pair of work boots by the kitchen tidy. Just call him. Don't muck us about."

"Alright. Larry?"

A tallish figure emerged through the pantry door and trudged sheepishly into the open lounge area. "Mr. Owen, I'm Detective Inspector Mahoney and this is Detective Constable Kendall. Mrs. Watson I think you already know."

"Very funny. Can't say I'm pleased to meet you."

"Fair enough. I presume you're up to speed on our conversation. If you'd just like to tell us now who prompted you to arrange for the site to be used, we can be on our way."

"And what if I don't like?" Standing his full height now.

"We'll start checking on your recent whereabouts with your wife, Mary." Check.

The cockiness departed as quickly as it had arrived. "She'll clean me out. Don't you dare. You pricks." Exasperation. His head was turned by Jane's voice.

"Tell them. I don't think there's much future in alienating your wife. Not for my sake, anyway." Owen looked like he had been smacked in the head with a large fish. No more of an affair by the sounds of it. Dismissal. Not a leg to stand on.

"James Cartwright." Checkmate. "I'm guessing you want me to come with you."

Kate spoke for the first time. "Yes, Mr. Owen. We will require a statement."

CHAPTER 32

Wednesday 17ᵗʰ March 5pm

If Cartwright was surprised to see him he certainly did not let on. Perhaps he expected Mahoney to call on him at his workplace as a matter of course. Regardless, the man who welcomed the detective into his spacious corner office was not displaying the slightest degree of tension. Mahoney immediately noted the similarities to the occupant's home library: not in size, obviously, but more so by its Spartan nature. There was a Blackwood desk just off center on the carpeted floor with ergonomic chairs either side of it. On the desk was a large ink blotter, a writing pad, Parker pen, and one of those ornate lamps with an emerald green shade that were all the rage in solicitors' offices. Apart from a rectangular window that overlooked the private school adjoining the UTAS campus, the walls were covered with bookshelves. Unlike the eclectic collection in his home, the books appeared to be solely to do with the lecturer's academic interest. The daylight was rapidly fading so the desk lamp was on. Cartwright remained seated at his desk where he had been doodling on the pad: some sort of letter was there.

He gestured to Mahoney to sit in the chair opposite him. "I was anticipating a visit, Inspector. I'm glad you are alone. It will be easier for me to speak frankly without your muscular sidekick. He unsettles me. I assume that's his role, but there's no necessity now. I am free to talk. Unburdened, shall we say?"

Mahoney simply nodded and sat down. He unbuttoned his jacket and looked straight into Cartwright's eyes.

"Jane Watson called a short time ago and apprised me of developments." He paused and rolled his eyes. "Sorry, that sounds pompous. I tend to get rather formal when I'm verbalizing my thoughts. Anyway, Larry told her to contact me and I'm aware of how the webs of deceit are unravelling. I'd appreciate a chance to talk with you before anything more formal occurs." He looked searchingly at Mahoney.

"Yes, Dr. Cartwright, I can do that."

There was a brief silence. A staccato series of shouts from the training session on the adjacent school's football oval came through the open window. Cartwright got up to shut it. Having sat down, he eased back into his chair. "Have you always lived here, Inspector?"

Mahoney saw no problem with this diversion. He had time to converse. They would surely get to where Cartwright, and he, wanted to go. "No, not at all. I went to England in the late '80s and stayed for just over a decade. It was a very worthwhile experience."

"Ever married?"

"Again, no. I was very close to it when I was young but it just didn't work out. If it had, perhaps I would never have left. House, children, Queensland holidays, school sport, shack, and retirement after forty years' service. It could all have been so different."

"Any regrets for that?" Cartwright was a dab hand at the open-ended questions but there was no harm in continuing. The academic was trying to establish some sort of camaraderie for whatever reason. Mahoney paused as he gauged his response.

"Recently, they've surfaced. In London it was impossible to be bored of life. And, initially, I was glad to be back here. My parents were still alive and Tassie offered a lifestyle I couldn't possibly afford in the UK. But of late, work, the job of detecting as it were, doesn't fill the gaps. You see your old friends getting such a kick out of watching their kids play that I wish I was in a nuclear family. Probably too late now. I feel a bit detached from life. Want to be a fuller participant. I'd settle for a happy relationship." He smiled at Cartwright. "How's that, Dr. Freud?"

His interlocutor also smiled. Held a hand to cup his ear. "Just catching a few of the echoes that are bouncing around this office. I hope I'm not being presumptuous but I think I know exactly how you feel. I feel it too. I don't want to die alone."

Mahoney, if with a close friend, would have said more but now was the moment for the detective to stay silent. They were at a tipping point.

"You see, Inspector, I can empathize with what you've described. It eats at me. I feel ... stuck, for want of a better word. Believe me, that's not how I felt when I was twenty-four. Do men always feel as if they're twenty-four forever?"

Some. Most. All of them. Mahoney could not be sure. That was the conundrum. Did some sort of emotional maturity require a male to leave irrepressible optimism behind or was it healthy to keep hold of that youthful vigor? At just that age the slamming shut of the door to his heart. Had England just been a sojourn into Never Never Land where he could start afresh because nobody knew who he was? Perhaps Cartwright should augment his furniture with a therapy couch.

Mahoney's pensiveness was interpreted as reticence by Cartwright. Unperturbed, he pressed on. He was on a roll. "God knows. Anyway, for me that was a crucial time. I'd done well here." His lifted arms airily waved at the walls and ceiling. "False modesty aside, I blitzed my undergraduate course. Just really took to academic study. The adolescent awkwardness, the stupid constraints at school, the banality of the suburbs just faded away. I found that the things I had begun to cherish were appreciated and valued. You must know what I mean... books, knowledge, whatever?"

Mahoney nodded. He could see it alright. Had felt it too.

"Then it was onto my Masters. The politics of Federalism. Loved it. I realized this could easily be my work, indefinitely. People were interested in me because I was smart. It didn't matter that I was hopeless at sport... or drinking beer. Was involved with a very attractive woman, studying law. I felt whole.

"Then in '86 I was offered a position at Columbus University in New York. Lecturer in Australian Politics and accommodation at a bargain rate in Manhattan. Had visions of being some sort of book-toting Crocodile Dundee. Alas, Anna didn't. She'd been offered an internship at a solid local firm. Couldn't see how going to America would be of any benefit. She stayed. I went. She's now a Magistrate in the line for the Judges' Bench and I'm maybe going to finish up in front of her. The wheel turns in interesting ways." He adjusted his spectacles ever so slightly. "And for a long time I was fulfilled. My course was popular. Plenty of invitations to conferences on the back of academic publications. I even had some articles make it to *The New Yorker*."

This begged an obvious question so Mahoney asked it. "That is impressive. Genuinely so. Then why are you here?"

"Family partly. Ego mainly. Larkin was wrong. My parents did not fuck me up. They were very supportive of me when I was younger. When I was little there would be different programs on TV about the Year 2000 and all the great gizmos we'd have. In the '70s, in my teens, it seemed far away. But Mum would always say, 'Your father and I will be old by then but you'll be thirty-eight and able to enjoy all these wonderful things'. Subconsciously I stored thirty-eight away as an age by which I'd better have achieved something.

"Well, guess what? In 2000 a fellowship opened up here and what with some Sydney Olympics-induced yearning for Oz, I returned. Spend more time with the folks. I'd learned to play golf in the States. Thought I'd play a regular round with my Dad. Mostly I wanted to be a big fish. So I accepted the offer and unfortunately found the pond was stagnant." He shuffled in his chair. "No one round here gives a stuff about scholastic reputation. Unless you're in business and making money, you may as well be emasculated in this town. Christ knows how teachers keep their heads up."

"I know just what you mean." Mahoney loved the vibrant artistic side to this town but he had to acknowledge the presence of a masculine business community that was anti-intellectual, greedy and downright boorish.

"Well, these people did take a bit of notice when my media work began to develop. I acquired something of a reputation. I was invited to lunch." The sardonic emphasis imbued the word with sarcasm. "Then charity functions and dinner parties. I was an interesting chap. Not a real man, mind you. Not a good bloke who you'd have a decent drinking session with but not a bad fella nonetheless." His eyebrows lifted in mock self-disgust. "Overall, although I began to seriously wish I lived somewhere else and had someone to live with, my life was pretty bearable."

"And somebody threatened it?"

"Yes, but not that seriously, really. The exposé wasn't going to be published in the paper. I could easily have ridden out the storm. But my sense of self-justification wouldn't let me. That young woman had played me. Good and proper. I guess I wanted to crush somebody. A classic bullying scenario. Felt useless myself so I wanted to demean another.

Damage someone. And that's why I got involved in all this. To vent my spleen. Not exactly the stuff of great tragedy. Hardly seems worth it, does it?"

No, it didn't, thought Mahoney. Sometimes, maybe even oftentimes, grand passion was not the motivator for crime. It could be as petty as this. The tragedy was that an innocent life had been swept away. That the why was less than a grand *crime passionnel* did not truly matter. What counted was a crucial link in the chain had been connected.

"Obviously I can't condone your motivation but you have at least provided a clear understanding of it. I trust you can bring the same clarity to a recollection of the part you played in what transpired last week."

"Yes, I can. I no longer wish to hide."

That's big of you, thought Mahoney. You've been sprung and you now want to be straight with the law. How admirable. He kept his growing contempt from his tone. "Then you can take me through it if you would."

"I was offered a way out of the embarrassing situation I'd helped to create. The price for keeping my name out of the paper was to exert some pressure myself."

"Upon your brother-in-law, Larry Owen?"

"Correct. Coincidentally, someone else needed a favor done that dovetailed quite neatly with one of the targets for my revenge."

"As you couldn't directly damage the young woman, Brad Finch was a sufficiently good target?"

Cartwright shifted uneasily. "That's right. Apparently he had put someone else's nose out of joint. I wasn't told who. Just what I could do to fulfil the obligation with which I was now saddled. The price was to persuade Larry to make part of his site available last Thursday evening. I was even provided with the silver bullet that would assure his acquiescence."

"His affair with Jane Watson?"

"Again correct. To be honest I didn't like doing it but my hand was forced."

Mahoney briefly wondered where the academic stored his spine. "And who forced it?"

"Rory Fotheringham."

"And he is?"

"A business consultant who finds solutions for people. He got the paper off my back in the blink of an eye. A force to be reckoned with."

Mahoney took a few moments to register this new material. Thorough checks of Cartwright's movements and communications had underscored the fact that he would have been very hard pressed to have anything to do with the implementation of the plan beyond what he had now admitted. "Can you verify what you are claiming, with regard to this man?"

"No, it's just my word. By the look on your face that is not anywhere near enough."

"Collusion is difficult enough to prove with verifiable records. A testimony based on a conversation you now recall is not going to fly. If I had the evidence to charge you for the homicide I would. As it turns out, you are an accessory to the crime and a relatively minor one at that. You are really not much use to me at all." He got up to leave. "I have important work to do this evening so you can leave it 'til tomorrow to present yourself at Police Headquarters to give the latest version of your statement. Don't get up. You can wallow in your guilt for a while longer."

CHAPTER 33

Thursday 18ᵗʰ March 9am

Back in his office the next morning Mahoney called in Munro and Kendall. Having talked them through the preceding day's discoveries, he brought up the sticking point. "Rory Fotheringham. Another link in our chain. From talking to contacts, I gather he's certainly a mover and shaker. I called him last night and the single admission I got was that he's heard of Finch's death and what a great pity it was. Beyond that he denied any knowledge of anything else I put to him regarding the investigation. Says he knows lots of people; it's the nature of his business. He didn't think that could be a crime. Very cagey man. No matter what angle I came at it from, he professed no knowledge beyond being acquainted with people. He may be a blind alley but you never know."

Before either officer could speak, the phone rang. "DI Mahoney here."

"Inspector, it's Amanda Pattison."

"Hello, I'm sorry. I meant to get back to you but it's been a bit frantic."

She was not fazed. "That's no problem. I don't need updates. I just found something that may help."

"Right, great. I'll just put you on speakerphone so my two colleagues can listen in."

"Sure. Can you hear me now?"

"Yes, go ahead?"

"OK. I've chanced upon the identity of the Felicity woman I saw at Brad's flat last Saturday."

"I remember. Go on."

"I was cleaning out some newspapers and started browsing, as you do. I came upon a double page spread of photos of the Devils' season launch on the social page. She was in the largest pic with the President of the club. Mr. Roger and Mrs. Felicity Sproule. I'd bet my first year's salary she and Brad were much more than nodding acquaintances from what I witnessed in her manner last week."

Mahoney was hooked. "OK, good. Thank you. We've made progress but this will nudge things along nicely. Can I ask you to keep this to yourself?"

"Of course. I understand, Inspector. Good luck."

"Thank you again. I'll be in touch." The call disconnected and Mahoney looked to his two subordinates. "Good old-fashioned jealousy. What do you think?"

"Just because it's textbook doesn't make it a cliché."

"Kate's right, Sir. Word is he doesn't take prisoners. Bit of a tough nut."

Mahoney nodded. "Righto. It's come out of left field but we can't ignore it. Our best course of action is to give him a wide berth and talk to the wife. You'll go together. That pairing should work for this one. Get your jackets while I work out how to play this. Then head off to see her. We could do with some luck."

*   *   *

Along Churchill Avenue to Sonning Crescent the strategy was rehearsed. Munro concentrated on the winding road while Kate enjoyed the scenic view of the established properties that rose up the hill from Nutgrove Beach. They discussed questions and body language. They knew, without being told, that the next hour was to be a telling one for this case and their careers. Number 2 was on the corner with an unimpeded view of the river by the virtue of the parkland opposite. Munro eased the car into a vacant spot in the set of spaces provided at the Alexander Battery installation. Originally created as defensive gun artillery to repel potential nineteenth century invaders, it now served as a municipal vantage point for locals and tourists alike.

The detectives got out and walked back across Churchill Avenue to the Sproule house. It was a house in the literal sense that people resided there but the property had been remodeled along the lines of the 'Look at me, I'm cashed up' school of architecture. It more resembled a boutique hotel on the Queensland Riviera than a home in Hobart. Kate thought it barely resembled a home in any sense of the definition. Two stories high with enormous picture windows to catch the view, and with columns. A temple to lucre, she decided.

As planned, Munro approached the double front doors but before he could reach the buzzer a voice to his left beckoned. "Hello there, you're early." Facing him was Felicity Sproule who was standing on a wooden deck just outside sliding glass doors. She was in a white bikini that clung to her dripping wet body. As Munro approached, she leant away to pick up a blue towel. "I was just having a quick dip."

She casually toweled her hair as he stood there. He looked levelly at her eyes. "My apologies, Mrs. Sproule. Must have mistimed the trip." They had not. She must have intended to meet him this way.

"Felicity, please. Would you like a drink or a swim?"

Both would be good. "No, thank you. Tempting though. We'd just like a quick chat and then we'll be off."

"We?" She wrapped the towel round her. On cue, Kate came through the wrought iron front gate and up the steps.

"Yes, DC Kendall wishes to speak with you. I'm just the driver today."

Felicity looked slightly flummoxed. She knew how to deal with young men but some women were a different matter altogether. The one approaching her now seemed to have dressed with the intention of camouflaging her figure entirely. Not butch exactly, but asexual.

"Good morning, Mrs. Sproule. Did DS Munro not mention I was coming?" Obviously not, by the expression on her face. "He doesn't always follow protocol, I'm afraid." Munro looked suitably chastised. Kate noticed he got the downcast look just right. Not too defeated but Mrs. Sproule was aware by now who was wearing the pants here.

She missed a beat but was back to her perky self pretty quickly. "In that case could you wait a sec while I get my robe?"

That was no problem at all and in the instant she was gone the two detectives occupied two of the trio of the deck chairs arranged on the patio. Their hostess returned and took the remaining seat. Clad in her toweling robe she sat demurely.

"I don't know how I can help but there must be a reason for your calling, I suppose."

Munro sat tight-lipped as Kate launched. "How long had you been shagging Brad Finch?"

Her eyes widened and she turned to Munro who was casually studying the roofline. She turned back to her inquisitor. "What sort of a question is that?" Her face had turned crimson.

"A simple one, actually. Please answer."

The death stare quickly subsided. "It wasn't like that. Not like the others. He was different. You wouldn't understand."

Kate softened her tone. "I might. Please tell us. How was he special?"

"He genuinely wanted me to come."

Munro blinked quickly but kept his gaze averted. Kate leaned forward. "Well, that puts him pretty high in any woman's estimation."

Felicity wiped an errant strand of hair from her cheek. Clasping her hands in her lap, she continued. "Sorry, that was blunt. He was able to make me feel good about myself. Like I wasn't just Roger Sproule's trophy wife. Like I was more than the ditzy piece to parade at social functions. He listened to me and let me know, in lots of ways, I was worth knowing. It didn't matter that he probably had others but when he was with me it was just me. Only me. Can you see that?"

Kate nodded. "Yes, I think so. Everybody does speak well of him."

"I'm not a rocket scientist but I do have a brain. Not that the pig I'm married to would care to admit it. He turns my stomach. And before you ask, it wasn't easy to leave. Roger took great delight in explaining how a very cleverly constructed family trust holds all of our assets. If I walk, I get to take my wardrobe. That's it."

Munro spoke. "Cunning bugger. Kind of leaves you with nowhere to go."

"Exactly. But I was going anyway. I told him about a fortnight ago. He could find another hostess with the mostest."

"How did he take that?" Kate realized they were verging on interesting terrain.

"Badly, to say the least. He didn't lay a finger on me but the next dinner guests will be served with new china. He was in such a rage. You'd have to be to call your wife a whore, among the other very choice terms.

It ran its course and then he walked out. Came back later that evening but he has barely spoken to me since. Went stone cold."

She was more confident now. More assertive. Kate could discern the strength beneath. "And Brad fits into this how?"

"I was going to be with him. Didn't care what else happened."

"Was your husband aware of this involvement?"

"Not really, no, I don't think so. He was his jovial bold as brass self at the Season Launch the other Friday but when he didn't know I was looking, he gave Brad a look that would stop a rhino. Not that Brad saw it. Nothing was said and nothing eventuated. Not then, at least." Munro had long ceased feigning disinterest. He was acutely aware now of his role. Sit quietly and allow his partner to continue the running. He could see this woman, despite superficial appearances, held deep emotions. A well of disappointment in how her life was turning that would now be tapped.

Again, Mahoney's assessment of how the currents would run and how to ride them to their advantage was proving to be true. Kate, as an empathetic female, would tap into Felicity Sproule's divided loyalties. As she proceeded to do now. "We've been able to establish that Brad's homicide occurred sometime on Thursday evening or the early hours of Friday morning. We're still unsure of exactly who was responsible." Some truth but not the whole truth. Kate opened her notebook and flicked through the pages as if checking for details. "Can you corroborate your husband's movements during that time?" Munro mentally applauded the choice of the verb.

Felicity re-crossed her legs and adjusted her robe. "His routine is to drink in the clubrooms with various football cronies while training is on. I presume he did that before he flitted in here about 8pm. He didn't want any food because he said he was off to Dr. Randall's for more footy talk. He came home late, about midnight, stayed in and then was up early on the Friday. He was a bit edgy and then he took a call on his mobile that sent him scurrying off into the city. He tried to make it all sound matter of fact but he didn't look too calm."

"Did he disclose to you what the call was about?"

"Of course not. I was pretty persona non-gratis by that stage. Just said he was off to see Rory. Rory Fotheringham.

"And he is?"

"A big hitter. His words, not mine. We know him quite well. He's one of those behind-the-scenes guys who make things tick round this town. He's usually so in control of things. But one night he'd had a few more than usual and he fancied his chances with me, I guess. Let me know how much leverage he had over various people; people I thought were pretty damned powerful. Hence the epithet. I suppose he thought the sexual overtones would play well." She looked at Munro. "They didn't."

Gears clicked into place in the heads of the two detectives. Munro spoke. "And after that, the rest of the weekend?"

"Full of beans. He even wanted to take me out for a special dinner on the Saturday night. Reckoned it was to celebrate sealing another government contract. I was still too anxious about Brad to think twice but I think now there might have been something else to it. Who's to know?"

Kate closed her notebook and slipped it into her carry bag. She stood, as did Munro. "Thank you, Mrs. Sproule, for your candor. I don't think we'll need to bother you again."

Felicity Sproule rose from her chair and smiled. "That's alright, Detective. If I helped in some way, good. Whoever did whatever they did to Brad will have no sympathy from me. If you need to contact me again, here's my mobile number."

She handed Kate an embossed card. "No use trying the home number. I'm flying to Bali in two hours. They'll be wearing ugg boots in hell before I'll stay with my very soon-to-be ex-husband again. Now, if you'll excuse me I'll need to quickly change. I'm all packed and ready." She reached into the pocket of her gown and then placed a mobile phone on the table. "This is Roger's. It might help you."

And so two rather more optimistic detectives departed.

CHAPTER 34

Thursday 18ᵗʰ March 2pm

"Brilliant. Just brilliant." Munro's voice contained no hint of irony. Something had excited him.

"What is? What's got you so chipper?"

"This phone, that's what. Kate, that Felicity Sproule has done us one huge favor." He waved the mobile in front of her. "If Dobosz is available we can use this to find out a lot of stuff; stuff Sproule wouldn't want anyone to know about."

"Really, how so?"

Munro reached for an internal line. "I'll get him over. He can explain it better than me." He tapped out the number; put the device on speakerphone and after precisely two rings:

"Sergeant Dobosz speaking. How can I help?" A nasal tone but not unfriendly voice.

"Snorkel, it's Tim. Need your propeller head skills. Can you come to the CIB incident room now? We think we've got a break in the murder case."

"Sure. Get me away from my computer screen. Be there in ten minutes."

"Cheers, cobber." Munro silenced the call. Extravagantly rubbed his hands together. "Wait till you see this guy. What he can't do with gadgets and computers you don't want to know."

Kate was bringing her case notes up to date when the focus of Munro's worship entered the incident room. To say his appearance was unprepossessing only hinted at her first reaction. Below his brown thatch of hair was a quite pleasant face. It was the garb that alarmed her. A thin black tie accompanied a brick red shirt under a thick woolen grey cardigan. The blue polyester trousers had a slight sheen and the zip-up brown vinyl shoes completed the eclectic ensemble. Obviously not a salesman. He had seemingly selected the most disastrous clothing items from the preceding four decades. He must have other strengths. Munro definitely thought so. He did the introduction to Kendall with genuine warmth.

"Hello, Detective Constable. How do you like the outfit? I noticed you trying not to look too hard."

Bugger, thought Kate. "Quite individual, Sergeant. Your own work?"

"No, my wife helped. Scoured her father's house. Worth it though. I'll walk away with the dozen wines. Me first, daylight second." He was beaming with pride. Kate looked a touch confused.

Munro chipped in. "Snork has won seven RIFF's in a row."

Kate was none the wiser.

Dobosz explained. "We wild ones in Forensic Accounting have an annual dress-up competition. Retro Insanity Fashion Friday. Final judging tomorrow. Raises money for charity and the winner collects a few wines as an incentive."

Kate nodded her comprehension.

"Geez, you don't reckon I normally dress like this, do you?"

Kate smiled while praying she did not blush.

"Anyway, let's get to your little gadget." They sat. Dobosz brought his attention to the mobile sitting squarely on Munro's desk. "I presume this is it?"

"Yes. It was given to Kate and me by the wife of a potential suspect. I thought it could be Aladdin's Cave and you're the man with the magic hands."

Dobosz did a quick parody of "twinkle twinkle little star" with his fingers, smiled and bent to his task. "Fingerprinted?"

"Yep, all done. It's yours to explore."

"Good. I'll think aloud so you know where I'm going. Firstly, an Apple iPhone like this is a gift from Job, pardon the pun. Not only is it a very nifty consumer product but it's a fantastic tool for us"

Kate chipped in. "How so? Why more than, say, a Blackberry?"

"Different purpose for a different market. Blackberry was created for and pitched at the business sector. So there's a particularly high level of security attached to that device. Hence the current fuss in some countries about the encryption capacity."

"In Iran and that?" Munro read the news.

"Yeah. Some national security organizations don't like it that individuals and businesses can keep stuff secret from their prying eyes. Good luck to 'em, I say. Anyway, the iPhone is different. It was introduced in 2007 as a consumer product so possibly, probably even, security was neglected. Or not given as strong a priority, shall we say. So a few of its features have inadvertently proved to be of help to the constabulary in different countries." As he spoke, his fingers tapped the flat screen of the phone in question. "Few consumers know the full capability of some functions so they're not fussed. I'm guessing your man Sproule isn't too worried about you having this."

"I'm unsure if he even knows we've got it," replied Kate. "Should he be?"

Dobosz sat up. "Oh yes. I reckon so." He nudged the phone toward the two officers. "He wouldn't be too keen for you to have access to all his deleted messages for the past six months since he bought the thing."

Kate looked at the man with total admiration. Then looked down again as Munro scrolled through a whole bevy of text messages both sent and received by the businessman.

"How did you do that?"

"Not hard really. The iPhone has a keyboard logging cache, ostensibly to correct spelling, that retains everything typed on the keyboard over the past few months. If you know how to access that little mine of information, then the delete button is somewhat redundant. And another thing, I can tell where he's been lately. So there's probably a record of numbers dialed as well even if he's cleared his call register." Munro was very relieved his man had come up trumps. "Is there one in particular you're looking for?"

"Absolutely," said Kate. "The last call received on the victim's mobile shows number withheld. And we've been having a hard time trying to weasel the information out of the phone company. Privacy issues for the caller, they told us. We need to know it obviously. The call was received at 9.17pm, not long before the assault. We've got an independent witness whose evidence suggests it was the call that set him off on the path to his death. If you can show it's from this handset then it saves some steps on the ladder, for sure."

Dobosz began to tap away again. "OK, should be possible. Let me sort out the text messages first."

Kate was on the verge of letting him beaver away at this but knew the real priority. They needed the number to be there for any of the other stuff to be worth combing through.

"No, that can wait. No offence but please check the numbers dialed first. The date we're looking for is…"

"The eleventh of March from about 6pm onwards. No problem." He winked at her, hopefully an indication of camaraderie not friskiness. "Just leave me to it for a few minutes."

Kate left the two men to ferret away for the vital information. She needed to check with the Office of Public Prosecution what the stipulations were for obtaining and using this sort of information. At her desk, she dialed the number for Graham Davis. As part of her training for this new job, she had been carefully briefed by him on the essential guidelines regarding the admissibility of evidence. The bane of prosecuting authorities the world over was the mishandling of material that could jeopardize a trial. Everything, literally every single thing, should be carefully catalogued and filed. There had to be a clearly identifiable path from the *locus in quo* to the courtroom. Thus far the whole squad could not be faulted, given the meticulous nature of the way the evidence trail was being assembled. All the i's and t's were dotted and crossed. The chain was secure for each link. The onus was on them now to ensure the same incorruptibility applied to the phone currently being examined.

Fortunately, Davis answered almost immediately. "Senior Crime Assistance. Graham Davis speaking."

"Graham, it's DC Kendall from Homicide. We met a fortnight ago. For the Case Management workshop."

"Yes, Kate. Hello. I hear you've landed on your feet in a murky swamp."

"Yes and no. It's a good team but a bit of a baptism by fire for sure. It's this case I'm calling you about. We've established a breakthrough but need to tread carefully with some evidence."

"Very well, shoot."

"OK. We have in our possession a mobile phone belonging to a potential suspect. According to an in-house expert, it could tie the suspect to the Finch killing." Kate was forcing herself to speak deliberately.

"Righto, a couple of questions. Was it obtained via a search warrant? Does it conclusively link the owner to the victim?"

"First one, no. The owner's wife offered it to us while we were interviewing her at their house about an hour ago. Second, we hope so. One of the guys is unpacking its secrets as we speak." She paused. Were they on shaky ground?

"Mmm. This is a curly one." The mannered voice was very evenly measured. "If this is your main connection we must be very clear in the way we handle it. How else is the phone owner implicated?"

"At the moment all the rest is circumstantial. Brad Finch was having casual sex with Felicity Sproule. She candidly admits that. There is another incident, via a third party, supporting that supposition. But not concrete. Mrs. Sproule cannot claim for certain that her husband knew but she firmly believes he must have. Intuition, gut instinct, whatever. Again, not all that firm. But she is convinced her husband was behind it all." Saying it aloud revealed how tenuous the theory was in terms of incontrovertible facts.

"If, always the big if, she testifies, can we be sure it will assist the prosecution and will her testimony be of any real value?"

Kate thought hard before replying. The phone cord was twisted in knots. "I think so. There's no love lost between her and Mr. Sproule. But you're right. She would only be testifying to feelings that she had about his behavior. And that's just her interpretation, isn't it? Not exactly cold hard evidence."

"Correct. She has the right to decline from even testifying at all, should she choose. If she does, can she verify anything else?"

"Yes, yes she can. Sproule's movements during the day in question. Well, at least on the night of the death and the next morning."

"Good. That's helpful. Better if it can be corroborated by independent witnesses." Kate jotted down a note to check for that as Davis continued. "Was Sproule directly involved in the crime or are you suggesting he used this phone to make arrangements?"

She felt more positive now. "The latter. That's why the phone is so important."

Munro called across the office. "Too right it is. We've got it."

Kate spoke into the phone. "Hang on a sec, Graham. This is relevant to us."

To Munro. "What? The number?"

Her colleague walked across holding the iPhone triumphantly. Held it up to her. "Yes. There it is. Finch's number. Sproule called him alright. At that time. Snork'll do the messages now. Good, eh?"

Kate caught his buoyancy. "Graham, did you catch that?"

"Crystal clear. So you've got Sproule making the last call Finch received. But how does that prove it led Finch to his death? Sorry to be pedantic but he could simply have been touching base."

This was what she imagined being in the witness stand was like. With the devil's advocate. Think it through, she told herself. "Granted." Another note on the pad. "So we need a witness who heard the content of the call. Another female can vouch it was the call that caused Finch to leave the Metz, but beyond that, not much. We have to find someone who witnessed the call being made at the other end."

"That would help. Well, more than help. The observation of Finch leaving is logical but still circumstantial. Is the phone good for anything else?"

"I hope we're not clutching at straws but apparently this model of phone stores messages sent even if the user thinks they've been deleted from the records. A quirk in the design. Our guy is accessing them now."

"That's better. You need to check that this Sproule chap is the registered owner and that he was also the user when the incriminating texts were sent. Can you get corroborating records from whoever received the messages?"

Another note. "Yes, we'll do that. And the call, too." Almost there. One more thing. "Graham, about how we obtained the phone. Is that legit?"

"According to the Evidence Act, you're fine. I've got it here in front of me. Section 135 clears you. Assuming you did not induce her to hand it over, it's perfectly acceptable to procure that phone. She gave it willingly?"

"Yep. We didn't ask at all. She'd answered our questions and as were leaving she gave it to us. All above board?"

"Then you're fine. Any half-decent defense counsel will seek to have it excluded from the trial but given what's in the statutes, it will simply be an ambit claim. No problem on that score. I hope it helps nail whoever did it. Anything else while I'm here?"

"No. Well, not just now. Thank you, Graham. You're a gem."

"Thank you, Constable Kendall. Just the job. Good luck with it." He rang off.

Kate turned to her colleagues. Holding tight on her elation, she said, "All clear. It's admissible and perfectly legit. Let's tell the boss. Where is he?"

"Right here." Nobody had seen him enter the room. "Tell me what, exactly?"

Their excitement was palpable. Munro spoke up. "Bona fide evidence. A cast iron link in the chain."

Mahoney sat down at a spare desk. "All right. Calm down. Tell me slow and steady."

So they did. Twenty minutes later, the DI was up to speed but still not smiling. All he said was, "Good work, very good work." But his face was actually set in anger. "For the love of God, have these people no shame? Talk about a moral compass that's out of whack." He stood. "OK. Write it up. Watertight. Kate, sit with Richard and catalogue everything in minute detail. Tim, go to training."

"What? Are you sure?"

"Yes, I'm serious. You are playing Saturday, aren't you?"

"Yes, but…"

"No buts. Just make sure you're back here showered and presentable at 9pm. We have a visit to make tonight. An unheralded one."

*   *   *

If asked, Mahoney would have said he was not best pleased. Not at all. The driver, seconded for this trip, was not going to ask anything much at all. He may be relatively new to the ranks but he knew when to keep his trap shut. Concentrated on the road ahead as his superior fumed. Constable Gibson had been minding his business in the cafeteria when a tap on the shoulder and a crooked finger from the DI beckoned him from his half-finished coffee. The conversation in the basement car park was perfunctory.

"Where to, Sir?"

"Down the Bay. I need you as a witness."

"Righto, Sir." Any further chat in the car was truncated by a series of phone conversations between the passenger and what seemed to be Forensics and then someone else entirely. Hard to tell in the busy traffic.

Just past the yacht clubs, he was directed to turn into Queechy Lane and pull up outside what was a handsome Federation house. In the front garden weeding a bed of daffodils was a portly middle-aged man who stood upon their approach. His large owl-eyed spectacles glimmered in the late afternoon sun. The smile was somewhat forced. "Good afternoon, this looks official." Some forced jocularity.

"No looks about it." Mahoney had walked onto the front path with Gibson remaining just outside the low brick fence. "I'm DI Mahoney. We've just spoken a few minutes ago. Thought I'd get down here as soon as practicable. This is Constable Gibson. He's here because I don't carry my own handcuffs." The remark caused the intended effect.

Randall's complexion turned ashen as he started to bluster. "What on earth do you mean? I'm blameless in all this. I wasn't really involved." As he looked anxiously from Mahoney to Gibson, it seemed to the latter he certainly sounded guilty.

The former knew it and pressed on. "Let's just unpack that claim, shall we? It is all a matter of degree but whether the charge is obstructing the course of an investigation or conspiracy to commit murder is up to you and depends on your level of co-operation in the next few minutes." Mahoney paused briefly to let that sink in. Then, in a low voice, "You'll be cuffed and whisked off to the station or you'll be tending your flower bed. Entirely up to you. But if I think you're dissembling then the embarrassment I can generate for you will be unbounded. Please do not discount that eventuality."

Gibson was a little unsure of the import of the warning but it was clear Randall knew the score. His arms now hung limply by his sides. "Alright, how can I assist you?"

"Do you want to have this discussion here or...?" Mahoney gestured to the balcony where an outdoor dining setting was placed.

"No, here is fine. Ask your questions. I'll tell you all I can."

About time, thought the Inspector. "When did you first hear that Brad Finch was dead?"

"On the Saturday morning. Last weekend."

"What were your movements on the Thursday evening immediately preceding that?"

"I was here. Dined at home. And stayed in for the entirety of the evening."

It was still like getting blood from a stone but at least he was talking.

"Did you receive any visitors?" There was a long pause as the man stared at his feet. "You are not under caution but you will be if the whole truth is not forthcoming pretty soon." Mahoney's voice had a very distinctive edge and the effect was immediate.

"Yes, one."

"Who?"

"Roger Sproule. The President of the Devils."

"Don't worry, Dr. Randall. We know just what his position is. That's why we're here." The look on the man's face betrayed his inner knowledge that he was in the dry corner of room with a floor that was freshly painted. No escape. Would he fight a rear-guard action or take the proffered hand? "And why was the President here exactly?"

"To discuss some ideas for functions during the season. Coterie Club, sponsorships etc."

The tooth was resisting extraction, still.

"And?" Mahoney's patience was sorely tested.

"Out of the blue, he says he wants to speak to Finch. I had the number and he used his mobile to call him. Put me on for some reason and I persuaded the lad to pop down from the Metz."

"Who suggested the short cut?"

"Roger. I had no idea what he was up to."

Too clever by half, thought Mahoney. Sproule would have thought Randall to be an impeccable alibi for his presence at the time of the assault and by using his mobile instead of the landline he would have control of the phone record.

Mice and men.

"When Finch didn't show what did you think?"

"That he'd found something more appealing to do."

"Did you really believe Finch wouldn't show after the rollicking he'd received from you the week before? Of course he'd front up. He was answerable to you, and Sproule, in a number of ways. He'd be a fool to go AWOL. You both knew that. That's how you knew he'd drop everything and come."

"Well, yes, I suppose I did but when he didn't arrive soon after the call, Roger was unperturbed. So we simply went on with the other business we had."

"And Sproule left when?"

"Just before midnight. Look, I swear I thought it was all legitimate." Desperation in his quavering voice.

Cut no ice with Mahoney. "Legitimate. Interesting word. At what stage of the investigation did you decide that the police did not have a legitimate right to this vital information? And don't dare say 'because we didn't ask'."

Randall was suitably hangdog. He took off his gardening gloves and held them bunched tight in his hands. "I'm sorry. I did think it was relevant but Roger cajoled me to hold my peace. Said it was most likely a random attack by thugs and we couldn't afford any adverse publicity for the club. Such a big season you see. And he's a very influential President."

"You mean he's directly, and indirectly, injecting a great deal of money into the enterprise that would be greatly missed without him."

"Yes, that is what I mean."

Mahoney could not hide his disgust. "The club has proven to be worth a lot more than one individual, wouldn't you say?"

Randall looked his accuser in the eye for the first time. "You are right to berate me. I've allowed myself to be corrupted by the supposed glory of getting the club up and running. Chasing success. A lot of dreams were wrapped up in this venture. But I was wrong to stand by in this instance and pretend it wasn't relevant."

"I'm not your judge but you must realize a young man's life has not only been lost but has also been cheapened by your behavior." Mahoney gestured towards the police car. "You will need to provide a statement at headquarters. Now would be a good time."

CHAPTER 35

Thursday 18ᵗʰ March 9pm

Roger Sproule was not sure how he should be feeling. As he sat in a leather recliner staring at the lights of Hobart, he was strangely moribund. His house felt very empty and the view of the Tasman Bridge above the dark river did not cheer him. The enormous picture window allowed him to see the expanse of the city that he had begun to dominate. But tonight he did not feel dominant. Anything but. He stared through the glass but saw little. How were things going so wrong?

A fortnight before, his affairs were in order. No, more than that. He was hurtling along the crest of a fantastic wave. When he saw photos in the paper of the big wave surfers at Shipstern Bluff defying all notions of self-preservation, he believed he could comprehend their exhilaration. Theirs was not drunken bravado. It was a yearning to test the limits. To break through the conventional restrictions of what people expected you to be able to do. What they allowed you to do. The exhilaration of barreling down the face of an avalanche of ocean was the reward. But the actual attempt was what intrigued Sproule. To have the balls to get out there in the first place, knowing that the attempt invited peril. To be prepared to defy the conventions of what was sensible behavior. If you got crunched, so what. At least you got in and had a go. Show all the pedestrian bastards anything was possible with a bit of ticker.

As he had done. Born in Triabunna on the East Coast, his future could easily have been nicely mapped out for him. Follow his old man into a job at the pulp mill. Play footy for the country league team. Get a boat to fish the waters around Maria Island. Marry a classmate from the District High School. Spend his weekends punting on the nags and pottering around the vegetable garden. Just like his dad. Nothing wrong with that. His parents were happy. They had brought up five children with nary a worry. No one went without the essentials and all had grown up in one piece. And all, bar one, still lived in Triabunna.

Except the youngest, Roger. The seminal moment came the year following high school. His girlfriend had moved to Hobart to continue her schooling at Elizabeth College. She was a real looker. They continued to see each other on weekends when she came home from the student hostel. Sproule had remained in Triabunna to start an apprenticeship as a mechanic. He wanted to play footy in the big smoke but no clubs came calling so he stayed put. Halfway through the year Sally won a modelling competition. She was off to Sydney and that was that. Suddenly Sproule's world seemed very small and constricting.

At seventeen he realized that he need not tread in the footsteps of everyone else. Although not very bookish he had retained the school texts from the year before. One novel had appealed to him. Some Yankee bloke who decided to pull himself up by the bootstraps. Sproule dug the paperback out and found 'the schedule'. He sat down and compiled his own. Apart from Technical College units for his apprenticeship, he enrolled in a Business Studies Course. Learned the basics of bookkeeping and the practices of the commercial world. Started putting money away. Did up an old bomb from scratch instead of blowing his cash on a flash car.

Another eye-opener came late the next year. He was drinking with some mates on a typical Friday night at the Blue Waters Hotel. The big landholder for the area, Harvey Maddox, was there with his son. The squire's boy was eighteen, the same age as Roger, but he was educated at boarding school in Hobart. Home for the weekend, James Maddox was still dressed in his school uniform as his father introduced him to a few of the fawning locals.

Roger could see here was a contemporary with his future laid out for him. A path without obstacles, thanks to the privileged largesse of his family. That much of the wealth was directly attributable to a generous grant of prime agricultural land to a fortunate ancestor over a hundred years before was conveniently overlooked. These guys carried on as if it was their innate superiority that merited their power and influence.

Tomorrow belonged to the private schoolboy. For the likes of him, Struggle Street would never be on the horizon.

Roger Sproule determined then and there that he would build a life for himself that put these people in the shade. He had a chip on his shoulder and he did not really give a stuff who knew it. So, for twenty years he beavered away. Before he had finished his apprenticeship he purchased a log truck. Stitched up a good contract with a logging company and the empire started. Next was the purchase of acreage with plenty of mature trees. Cleared that for a healthy profit and started plantation farming. A combination of tax breaks and subsidies made his venture a veritable cash cow. When the hardware shop in Triabunna fell on tough times he swooped. He turned it into the building supply depot just as the economy was shifting gear and sea changers were building on the East Coast.

He kept debt low and turnover high. Profits went to the acquisition of other supply depots throughout Southern Tasmania. The property boom was predicated on an appetite for refurbishment. His competitors could not match his prices or range so he swallowed them whole. His stores made hardware sexy. He was on a roll. With his commercial gains came social acumen. He knew success did not have a destination but his election to the board of the Colonial Club the year before last was a nice staging post though. Especially as it was James Maddox who nominated him. In modern Australian society nouveau riche was just a poncey French phrase. These guys respected power and Sproule's money afforded him plenty of that.

Over a series of lunches within the oak-paneled dining room, he had established a formidable array of contacts. The Fixer had been one of those. Another bloke who got stuff done. Two fists in velvet gloves, the pair of them. Together they worked away at the government for financial support for the AFL franchise. The best day of his forty years had been when the national executive formally agreed to the entry of the Devils into the 2010 competition. In terms of publicity and bonhomie it put all his other attainments and achievements in the shade. Roger Sproule was the toast of his home state.

Even his wife seemed genuinely pleased for him. Theirs was not the most loving of relationships. Admittedly, they had started well and the energy they shared was exciting. But eight years later and childless their shared experiences were dwindling. Owing to an adolescent bout

. of mumps, his testicles were about as fertile as the desert. He refused to adopt even though he knew his wife deeply desired a nurturing role. And a sperm donor was out of the question. If they could not have children that were a full genetic product of both parents then he was not interested.

So he and Felicity had gone on sharing a beautiful house and a pretty hectic social life but precious little else. They used to make love all the time. Now they had sex every now and then when Sproule was not meeting his myriad of commitments. His passion was power. He no longer really lusted for sex. He supposed Felicity continued to yearn for the physical enjoyment and he guessed she discreetly met her needs. He genuinely did not mind.

Or at least he had not minded until recently. At a recent fundraiser for the club, it became obvious to him that she must have a thing going with the gun recruit. Superficially, he doubted anyone could tell, but he could. The smile, the shared joke and the way they whispered something as he was leaving spoke volumes. There was no way he'd allow this to continue. No way was he having any players or supporters snickering behind his back. Finch might be the marquee player for the team but Roger Sproule was numero uno. He was the one who had created this Club. The young buck needed to be taken down a peg or two. So he hatched a plan and Rory Fotheringham provided the manpower.

But it had gone horrifically wrong. A potential champion was now food for worms. His wife gone. Her letter simply claimed she was tired of being an attachment: no mention of Finch. Perhaps she did not link him to it at all. He hoped so. But his guts would not calm. Thought about a drink but decided against it. He was wound up too tight and needed to think. Would any link shatter? Were his tracks covered? Where the bloody hell was his iPhone? All his contacts were on the damned thing. Including the unlisted mobile number of the Fixer. He needed to talk. Wanted to be assured it would be alright. A pair of headlights caught his attention. As they dimmed he caught sight of the tell-tale checked patchwork. Police. He went immediately to his front door.

"What the fuck is this? Who are you clowns?" Sproule was not laying out the welcome mat. Mahoney's decision to accord the man the respect of going to his house was not being reciprocated with any appreciation. So much for that.

The businessman was at his front door bellowing at them. Neighbors would soon be wondering. Munro had never witnessed a man turn purple quite so rapidly. Under the harsh porch light, an oversized knobbly beetroot was about to explode. Mahoney introduced himself and Munro and briefly explained the purpose of the visit.

"The fuck you are. Sneaking up to a bloke's house on a Thursday night. Gutless turds. Fuck off."

Discretion was hurled out the window. Mahoney tried. "Our intention is to speak to you privately. In your best interests. You are making a scene and it's not helping anyone."

Sproule's home phone started ringing. Perhaps a neighbor querying the noise. It was ignored. "I bet it was. Smart alec fucking copper." A pause in the tirade. The vein in his forehead subsided a touch. Sproule looked at them anew. "I bet you're here at the princely hour of ten pm coz you know my lawyer will be pissed to the eyeballs. Smart fuckers."

He was right but no one was going to officially admit that. "No, Mr. Sproule, we're here to ask for your co-operation as a matter of priority. We don't usually conduct business at this hour ourselves. If you want the spotlight we can provide it. Don't tell me you fancy a trip to the station?"

That Sproule stepped back and refrained from spluttering more abuse indicated that the inquiry had been rhetorical. "Alright, come inside if you have to. The nosey sticky beaks have seen enough."

Hardly their fault, thought Munro. They followed Sproule up an ostentatiously carved mahogany staircase that led to an atrium with various doors leading off it. They were led through the nearest door into a plush lounge room. Care was taken to negotiate the obstacle course of furniture. How many easy chairs did one room, admittedly fairly capacious, need? It resembled a reflexology lounge. On the coffee table near a lava lamp was a cut glass tumbler and an untouched bottle of Glenmorangie Scotch. Straight away their host poured himself a measure. Munro had rarely seen anyone drink liquor neat, apart from on television that is.

Sproule sprawled on the lounge. "You want one?"

The detectives declined and remained standing.

"What's this? Bad cop, prick cop." Sproule took a slug of his drink.

There would be little point in cautioning him now if he started knocking it back at this rate. Munro bit his lip. He knew anything he said at this point would be pouring oil onto the flame. Best leave it to the man in charge.

"You can regard us any way you like, Mr. Sproule. Believe me; it is neither here nor there to us. We've come to do our job, simple as that. Frankly, you being obstructive actually makes it a hell of a lot easier for us. So unless you want Sergeant Munro to cuff you while I call the divvy van I'd advise you to cut the tough remarks."

The flat delivery appeared to quell the noise. Sproule lurched forward in his chair and buried his head in his hands. A low guttural groan before he sat back again in the recliner. The drink pushed away.

"Alright. Fair enough. What do you want?"

Munro could not be sure if the businessman was on the level. They for sure were not there to discuss any company tax issues he might have. He spoke for the first time. "We want to get your reaction to some information that has been passed to us from another party.

"Who?" Not what.

"Rory Fotheringham."

Sproule looked as if Mike Tyson had belted his solar plexus. "No, no. He wouldn't say squat. Not Rory. I don't believe you." His eyes and voice suggested otherwise. The little men in his cortex must be digging feverishly.

Mahoney chipped in after a pause. "And Ronny Coutts."

"That prick. Couldn't trust him as far…"

He pulled his tongue in before it totally ran away from him. Looked from one officer to the other before dropping his head into his hands again. "Fuck."

Any fight had dissipated from the exasperated sigh. Tired and beaten.

Anything from now they should get on the record. "Roger Sproule, I'm arresting you in connection with the homicide of Bradley Finch." As Munro delivered the familiar spiel, Sproule glared out the window before rising from his chair.

In contrast to their entrance, Sproule was almost sedate throughout their departure. He did not gather anything nor did he turn off any lights. Just walked with his head bowed down the steps to the police car. As Munro got into the driver's side, Mahoney opened the rear door and gestured for the suspect to get in. He was not handcuffed so he did not touch his head to guide him. On television police officers did this regardless of a long history of people being able to get into a car unaided for the most of their lives. Munro could never fathom why this was necessary. Habit? Convention? Who knows? He did know that the planned leading jab had opened Sproule up beautifully for the blow Mahoney really wanted to land.

Their suspect now knew that they knew that he knew. Under interrogation, when faced with the evidence from his own mobile phone, he could hardly deny his role in proceedings. He may even cough up valuable information about the involvement of another but that could be an ambit hope.

*　　*　　*

Back at the station, Sproule was accommodated in the main interview room. The holding cells were beginning to fill with the detritus of Hobart's drinking houses. Besides, Mahoney wanted to press on immediately with the questioning. His feeling was that if Sproule slept on matters he may not be so forthcoming in the morning. Strike while the iron is hot.

He and Munro entered the room. At night the space was even less welcoming than during daylight hours. Sproule was seated with his head slumped over folded arms on the table. The two officers sat. Munro switched on the recording equipment and went through the customary preamble. Only when he finished did Sproule look up. His eyes were red-rimmed and watery. Munro fleetingly wondered if his boss would offer him one of the pair of pressed handkerchiefs he knew the Beekeeper always carried in his trouser pockets. ("One to wipe my own nose and the other to offer people who may need it. I would have thought that was obvious. Perfectly natural.") None was forthcoming. Sproule sat up straight and wiped his nose with the back of his hand. "I'll forego the offer of a solicitor. I can speak for myself."

Mahoney nodded. "Very well. Let's start in the middle. On the night Brad Finch met his end. Before you say anything, you need to know that we're not on a fishing trip. We would not be in this place if we didn't have reasonable grounds to suspect you so please carefully consider your answers."

The businessman shifted his weight on the chair. "Fair enough. Do your worst." His face had assumed a look of weary resignation.

"After training, Finch went to the Metz on Sandy Bay Road. A popular bar for some of the players. Presumably you knew this."

"Could have." A flicker of combativeness registered in Sproule's voice.

"Well, he did and for the rest of his evening to make sense I would safely say you did. You went to Dr. Randall's house for a meeting about club affairs?"

"So? Completely normal if I did. If I did." He was not giving up the ghost too easily.

"No if about it. Randall has made a statement to that fact and is himself facing a charge of obstructing an official inquiry. He could well be an accessory to a larger crime but that's another matter."

"What's the poor bugger supposed to have done then?"

"Either wittingly or unwittingly lured Finch to his death." Silence. "Using your phone."

"And you'll be proving that how?"

"His sworn statement for a start."

"Just his word? He could be saying anything."

"Quite so. Though he certainly seems credible to me. The sort of witness juries will believe." Before an indignant interruption, Mahoney pressed on. "But of course we don't just have his word for it. Your presence at his property has been verified by other means." The DI reached into his pocket and produced a plastic bag containing a mobile phone and placed it in front of him. "Do you recognize this item?"

"It's a phone." The sneer was back.

"Yes, thank you. In fact it's your phone. I appreciate many of these mobiles all look the same but it's definitely yours. And, as it was willingly given to us, it will be fully admissible as evidence in court." He let Sproule digest that for a moment. Could practically see the little men digging away.

"Bitch."

"You may well think that but I don't agree. Anyway, we'll get to your wife in due course. For now we'll concentrate on this little gadget." Mahoney tapped the iPhone. "These things are really quite amazing. Veritable computers they are. Precious few people even know the half of what they can do. For instance, there's a downloadable application that enables a caller to find by GPS the exact location of the person being contacted. That could put the cat among the pigeons in a few relationships. Few privacy issues there, I daresay. Anyway, back to this particular phone. It has the usual capacity to switch to 'number withheld' when making a call. So obviously the recipient doesn't know the number of the caller and the phone companies won't release that information for privacy reasons. Brad Finch's last call received was just such an example. So you see our problem. We can't determine the ID of whoever spoke to him for seventy-five seconds that night."

Sproule looked suitably unimpressed. "My heart bleeds for you."

"Well, we couldn't, that is, until we obtained your phone. A real mine of information it was. Bear with me here. I'll just walk you through it. There is no obvious record of a call sent to Finch at that time. Deleted almost certainly. So no cigar. But, and this is a beautiful but, we don't need it. This phone was used at that time to call Finch from Dr. Randall's house in Queechy Lane."

"Yeah, right." The bravado was still there.

"No sarcasm required, Mr. Sproule. I'll let Sergeant Munro explain. He's up on all the wizardry."

Munro assembled his thoughts. "First, the location. Whenever a mobile is turned on, it seeks the nearest phone tower, so to speak. It transmits a signal to that base station so it can be used as needs be. This very short 'ping' contains the digital fingerprint of the handset. With that information, you can determine where that phone is and at what time it's there."

Mahoney chipped in. "There's a whole lot of other stuff about identification codes and serial numbers. And triangulating the signal among phone towers to pinpoint a spot. But that can wait to the court case. Unless you want me to lay it all out."

Sproule did not. He was silently cursing himself. Bloody gadgets. It had seemed foolproof. Still, he was not going to lie down. "So, my phone was there. Go on."

Munro recommenced. "Assuming it was with you, and Dr. Randall confirms it was, then you were in Queechy Lane at the time of the call."

"What call?"

Mahoney recognized the stubbornness but decided the clutching at straws had gone on for long enough. "The call that's registered on his handset." He held up a hand as a stop signal. "Don't bother with the rebuttal. On your iPhone is another application that records everything that was tapped onto the keypad. Not only does it clearly record the number for Finch being tapped in but you also neglected to wipe the call duration record. A call to Finch's number was made from your phone that lasted seventy-five seconds. Hard to cover every detail, isn't it?"

No answer. Sproule had run out of objections. He stared through the two officers to the end of the road. "I'll take that as a yes. This very same keyboard device reveals the exact details of each and every text you sent to Rory Fotheringham." He produced from his other suit pocket two folded sheets of A4 paper. Flattened them out. "Would you like me to read aloud the transcripts?" The question lingered in the stillness. Finally a reaction. "No, no need. I know when I'm stuffed."

Munro knew how to react. Barely at all. An admission of defeat was not an admission of culpability. He knew Mahoney would want to keep the exchange going for a variety of reasons. A confession on tape was not essential but it would make a conviction that much easier to obtain. Also, his boss was a stickler for endeavoring to determine the victim's motivation for action. They thought they knew but external perceptions could simply be assumptions.

So, without hinting at any game plan other than the satisfaction of curiosity, Mahoney took up the conversation. "To be honest, that's a fair summation. But by helping us you could help yourself. As you are obviously aware, there are other people either charged or soon to be apprehended in this case. A straight version of your complicity will ensure you're not dragged down further." This variety of carrot offered less than it really promised or delivered. Still, it often worked because it sounded good. As now.

Sproule looked intently at the thumbs of his clasped hands as if viewing them for the first time. Perhaps he was trying to figure out what the pale crescent at the base of the nail was for. Munro tried to recall what they were called. Lunula? Lord knows. Whilst still in mediation mode, he spoke abruptly. "She was fucking him. That's it really. Because it was her and because it was him."

"Her?" Mahoney coaxed.

"You know, Felicity. The woman I married. My wife." His voice was without derision. Just matter of fact, if anything. "The wife I had to have." Mahoney pondered this Keatingesque remark. Was Sproule referring to her ripe sensuality? Did he need a partner to share his deeper imaginings? The truth was more banal. "A bloke in my position has to be married, really. Don't want folks calling you a shirt-lifter behind your back."

Or a Lothario to your face, thought Munro.

"You gotta have a wife to be respected. Goes with the territory. And she was a sparkler. Always looked good when we were out. Too good probably." He rested his chin on his palm. The brutal energy seemed to have morphed into reflective calm. "At different functions blokes'd be drooling. One snoozer at the club nearly tripped over his tongue. Shoulda seen the look his old battle-axe gave him. As they say, priceless." A half smile faded quickly. "Not much hope of me keeping a woman like that on the straight and narrow. Not with the time I put in elsewhere." Sproule sat up straight. Crossed his arms. Head slightly tilted as he looked past Mahoney. "Understandable, really."

"What's that?" Keep nudging him forward.

"Her. Flic. Getting some fun. Wearing the white shorts. Why did it have to be with that peacock?"

Munro was at a loss until he realized Sproule was referring to his wife playing away from home and to Finch. "What did you think your wife and Finch were up to?"

Sproule snorted. "Attending bleeding Mensa nights! What the fuck do ya reckon? Having a real good go at the horizontal folk dancing, you silly bugger. Christ almighty. The look she gave him at the Season Launch would have set your jocks on fire. Believe me, they were at it. Well and truly."

"And that was a problem?" Mahoney kept his voice in neutral.

"Apart from the obvious, yeah. You need to know this. I never strayed. Not once. Not even when I was on buying trips to Asia and the club hostesses are practically thrown in your lap. So I wasn't too keen on my wife's legs turning to butter with one of the players, if you catch my drift." Munro did and had to bite his lip. His boss maintained the customary deadpan. Maybe he suffers from Parkinson's, he thought. Regardless, Sproule barreled on. "And with the gun recruit of all people." His voice became belligerent. "Couldn't let that happen. Players find out. Supporters. Sponsors. Pretty soon half of bloody Hobart will know. Can't have that."

Mahoney measured a beat. "He needed a lesson taught?"

"Too bloody right." Any half-decent solicitor would have stepped right in and told Sproule to keep his mouth well and truly shut. Accepting involvement was bad enough but admitting to being of a mind to commit violence was very, very damning. "Some of these young blokes get it all dished up to 'em. Publicity, money, great training facilities. You name it they get the lot. Buggered if my missus was coming to him on a platter. Couldn't have that."

Mahoney could sense the bloody-minded determination that created the adult. Could also detect the rigid mindset that would only afford one solution. "Who helped you get this done?"

Sproule's gaze narrowed. "Me. Asked around for some likely types. Then set it up."

"Who did you ask? Fotheringham?"

Sproule's face was now a mask. "No, he's a business contact. Good man to know but he wasn't involved here. And you can look as skeptical as you like but that's it. Found the low-life Coutts all by myself. Stupid buffoon. Give him a seeing to, he was told. Didn't know they'd off the kid. Still, there you are. Whole thing's gone to shit now. Don't suppose they'll be backing me as President much longer."

It all goes back to you, thought Mahoney. Another alpha male who could not give a bit of ground. Saw their personal domain as just another battlefield. Right throughout history the collateral damage caused by such figures was not only regrettable but surely avoidable. They had the T-shirt: it's all about ME.

Munro could sense his superior wanted some evidence of further collaboration. A check of the phone revealed Fotheringham there as a contact and record of recent correspondence. But the messages were all from Sproule to the other man. They had nothing of any substance to actually tie the Fixer to the conspiracy. So Mahoney's gut feeling was just that, without any other corroboration from Sproule.

So they wrapped things up. It was a result. A good one, thought Munro, for the detectives at least. As he was rapidly learning, it would never be much of a result for the bereaved. And the fallout from this particular arrest would be enormous. But the squad did not deal the cards. They just tallied the correct score.

CHAPTER 36

Friday 19ᵗʰ March 9am

The team was assembled in the incident room. Word had rapidly spread regarding the successful interview with another suspect. A positive atmosphere permeated the space. Not quite euphoria but certainly a big step up from preceding days. Just as Mahoney prepared to address the squad, Assistant Commissioner Newman entered. No one could be sure why he had descended: to congratulate or cajole? Who could tell how the weather vane would go. He stood to the side of the group.

He gave a hint. "DI Mahoney, I understand there may have been a development."

"Yes sir, definite progress. I believe we have the perpetrators of the assault. A clear timeline of events from the last sighting of Finch on the Thursday to the discovery of the body. Forensic evidence to support the chronology for each step of the events that occurred. And the rationale behind the whole grisly business."

"Good, excellent. We can clear this up, and then I'll get the media liaison officer to draft another press release. An expeditious result." Newman shot his cuffs as he spoke. He seemed to be preening himself. A paternalistic gaze swept the room. "Well done, all of you." He turned to leave.

"Not quite yet, Sir." That stopped the peacock in his tracks.

"How so?" Instantly his bonhomie had evaporated. All eyes turned to Mahoney. This was not insubordination but it took a resolute man to confront a superior officer in such a situation.

"Well, we've established a connection between the two perpetrators and some other parties who may have had good reason to be rid of the deceased."

Munro considered dropping a paper clip to test the acoustics. Decided against it. "And this is necessary?"

Kendall thought that Newman must surely appreciate his query to be rhetorical but the man was either too proud or intransigent to avoid the stand-off. There must be something more to the dynamic between her two superior officers.

Mahoney, she noted, very deliberately stood facing Newman with his feet straight below his hips. Completely grounded. "Yes. The principal officers in this case firmly believe there is evidence of a conspiracy here. Coutts and Knapp were doing the bidding of others. I'm sure you'd agree we should thoroughly follow this course."

In other words, FYP.

To give him credit, Newman's only visible reaction to a psychological smashing was to blink a few times. He maintained eye contact with Mahoney. He was a survivor. "Of course. Carry on and keep me informed." A dignified retreat.

Just as the door clicked shut, Mahoney continued as if the preceding scene had never occurred. "Our current state of play: Coutts and Knapp admit to accosting Finch at the Bowls Club. They claim there was no *mens rea*. And I'm inclined to believe them. Coutts is a small-time thug, an opportunist, and Knapp, to all intents and purposes, was an unwilling participant. It was an attempt to intimidate that rapidly went pear-shaped. The plan, such as it was, was to bully Finch a bit, tie him up and dump him down at Kingston. Put the wind right up him."

A hand was raised at the back of the room – no doubt a constable trying to show some initiative. Mahoney waved it down. "I'll get to the why in a moment. Now, it seems Finch was no pushover. He resisted and in the confusion and panic one of his assailants clobbered him with a spade: our conclusion is it was Coutts, given the wound from Finch's fist was to Knapp's face. Regardless, Finch is killed. They've got a dead body. For some reason they think it's cleverer to not leave him there but to transfer his corpse to the building site at Kingston as per the original plan. And this is where it gets quite interesting." He gestured to the photo board.

"Where our other participants came into play. DC Kendall will explain." Munro nearly smiled. His boss's strategy was clever. Share the responsibility so his officers felt they were true contributors and shared the rewards. Kate was going to shine. She stepped forward.

"Right from the start Dr. James Cartwright was a person of interest. His quarrel with Finch at the university the week before indicated that. And his role in the piece of subterfuge created by a close friend of Finch, Amanda Pattison, implicates him further. He would have wanted to hurt the victim. However, it doesn't seem he sought a terminal revenge. He was livid but not so that his reaction was that extreme. Nonetheless, he was foolish enough to be lured into participation in this act of violence. Someone put him up to organizing the site at Kingston as a place the body could be dumped, as per the original scheme." She was assured in her presentation and it showed in her clear measured voice. "He was not party to the killing but his role as an accessory enabled us to connect some dots. So the question is there, as to who else might want to damage Brad Finch."

She picked up a fresh photograph of a very disgruntled face and stuck it to the board. "Roger Sproule." All in the room recognized it. A TV blitzkrieg of his hardware store advertisements ensured that. "Local business identity and cuckolded husband. His wife enjoyed the company of Brad Finch and he was not overjoyed to discover it, to say the least. He's downstairs now considering his options. Limited as they are. DS Munro has linked him to the events of that evening via phone records and Sproule has admitted to his role in luring Finch to the scene. More importantly, he has told the interviewing officers that he wanted rid of Finch so we have motive. We anticipate his lawyer will filibuster as per usual but there's plenty of strong evidence from other people that puts him right in the thick of things. There doesn't seem to be many prepared to risk their own necks for him. He wasn't anywhere near as well respected as he believed. He may yet have his Macbeth moment."

She returned to her seat maintaining a totally straight face. Not even meeting Munro's glance. It was the moment she truly arrived in the job but self-satisfaction could not even be considered. Do not give anybody an inch. She had learned the hard way.

*   *   *

Mahoney walked in through the side door of the Customs House Hotel. On the corner adjacent to the understated colonial elegance of Parliament House, the pub was in a prime position given that it also fronted on to Sullivan's Cove itself. Despite its location, it had been something of a sleeper until new management refurbished the interior and opened the whole place up. A brief flirtation with the dreaded pokies was now extinguished so tourists and locals could enjoy a relatively peaceful drink. What struck Mahoney as slightly odd was that the solitary drinker in attendance was standing at the bar. Although the public bar area was arrayed with a series of matt black plastic stools and a smattering of tables with bentwood chairs, the lone man stood bolt upright at the bar with a full pot of lager in front of him as he stared at the top shelf drink bottles. He blithely ignored the television above his head of lank greasy hair.

Mahoney stood beside the man. He too was unacknowledged but Mahoney could sense his presence had registered. "It's a bit early to start working your way along the spirits isn't it, Alan?" The delivery was light but no response was forthcoming. All that happened was the slow extension of the right arm towards the glass. Instead of picking it up, the forefinger drew a vertical line in the condensation on the outside of the glass. Then it was picked up but instead of necking it the man placed the amber liquid in front of Mahoney. The gnarly hand gripped the rail of the bar; gripped it so hard the knuckles whitened. After a minute or so, the tension was released and the man straightened up and started speaking to the empty space behind the bar. "That's where it would go. I'd begin at Dewar's and finish at the fancy cognacs. No problem. Stand and deliver. Give 'em to me. I can do it. No worries. Look, I'm still standing. The champ. Whole top shelf and still on my feet. Legend." The ironic celebratory tone shifted down a gear. "Weak as piss."

He turned to Mahoney. "You know what? Six months doing the steps. Going to meetings. Making the calls to my AA buddy. Walking the line. Doing really well." The voice was earnest and passionate now. "On the verge of being employable again. Job interview last week. Went all right." Mahoney nodded. Knew when not to speak. "And then my ex rings to tell me how happy she is with her new bloke and the kids would be better off with her at Easter. This snoozer has a beach house at Noosa and the kids would love it up there. What can I do? Refuse and assert my rights to access for the hols? Be the worst bloke in the world. So I agree.

I can't give 'em that." He started stabbing at his sternum. "I've pissed all my holiday money away. No house. No beach shack. No wife. No job. No ticker. So I decide to pop in to my old favorite for a cleanser. Just the one, mind. Before you walked in, I'd been contemplating that beer for a few minutes. Bit like a bloke at the top of a bungee jump. But did I have the courage not to leap into that abyss? Was seriously getting there and then you waltz in to remind me where it would lead." He turned and smiled at Mahoney. "I guess you'd call that community policing. Thanks. Still think you're a prick, but thanks."

"No problem. Saw you through the window looking a bit intense. Thought I could halve the problem. Sounds like the half you've got is enough to deal with."

"Yeah, right enough." He looked again to Mahoney. "Sorry, you're not really a prick. Tell you who is though. Bloody Daniel Weightman." Alan Massie shook his head at the very thought of him.

"He'd be the Mr. Sheen who's grabbed Mandy's attention?"

"Spot on. Shafted me in all sorts of ways that one." Mahoney knew the outline but let Massie color in the body of the story. As head of the Forestry Department, Weightman had let the word drop in a few places of influence that the chief executive of the Pines Timber Corporation was becoming unreliable. Liked a long lunch a bit too much and could not cope with the pressures of such an important position. Not at such a crucial time in negotiations of how best to manage the state's most bountiful natural resource. The whispering campaign leaked its way through to the Board of Directors. Massie did not help himself overly much. It was true his boisterous manner sometimes alienated people and the reduced economic circumstances provided the board with sufficient reason to forego his promised contract extension. It was no surprise to Alan when one of Weightman's cronies from the yacht club parachuted into the top job.

And that was when Alan Massie really started to give the booze a pretty decent nudge. Through the bottom of a glass, he watched his wife walk out with the children in tow. Once divorce proceedings had commenced a remarkably short time later, they had walked right back into the family home as Massie moved into what was to become a series of short term hotel stays. Having hit the wall, literally, during a session at the Theatre Royal Hotel, he had taken his broken hand across the road to the hospital for treatment and later his broken soul to the first

AA meeting he could find. Half a year on he thought he was doing well. Until that phone call. And now here he was with the police inspector.

Mahoney silently agreed with the assessment of Weightman. He had been introduced to the man at a symposium on maintaining harmony in the state's natural heritage areas. It soon transpired that the Department Head's idea of harmony was a blanket ban on all forms of protest. It looked bad for the state, you see. Affected jobs. The tired clichés trotted out by powerbrokers who found grass roots democracy an inconvenience. Mahoney wanted to teletransport the man back to 1970s Queensland but had to opt for thoroughly washing his hand that had been shaken by the malodorous bureaucrat. The officer of the law in him said, "Leave it, Alan. Actually doing harm to him would do you no good at all. Might feel satisfying but it would leave you a whole lot worse down the track."

Massie patted him on the shoulder. "I know. Don't worry. Besides, he's got Fothers on side. And you don't want him as your enemy. Could end up with a bit of my own four by two round the skull."

"Gets things done on the quiet, does he?" Mahoney now knew of the man and was interested.

"Yeah, you could say that. Where you off to anyway?"

"Public Prosecutions Office. Need to run a few things by the Chief. We've achieved a good result on a case. Pretty significant one but the trial process could present a few hurdles so I want to talk through a few of the potential issues. Make sure it's tight from our end at least." He wanted to tease out a thread of what Massie told him. "Fotheringham's a bit of a mover and shaker, then?" Tried to sound nonchalant.

Massie nodded. "Yep. You wouldn't know it but he's one of the wealthiest people in the state. And not just old money either. Fronts the wider world as a business consultant but he's got his fingers in lots of pies. Forestry plantations, farming, real estate development. You name it. He's in there somewhere. Milks the government for any subsidy that's available. Knows where the pressure points are. I'm damned sure he provided the impetus for Weightman to make his move. And why. Because guess what? Two months later, a very large contract using Forestry Department largesse between Pines Timber and Runneymede Plantations, Fotheringham's company, is signed. Did you hear about that one by the way?" Massie was warming to his conspiratorial theme.

"Err, no. Nothing really."

"Too right. Pens went to paper on New Year's Eve. Good timing if you don't want much publicity. Someone might pipe up in June when the Legislative Council Budget Committee meets but given Fotheringham's reach I doubt it. The guy's got leverage all right."

Mahoney was surprised he was not more aware of such intrigue. He acknowledged deals were done: that was the machinations of government. But he was chastened by his ignorance of some of the main players. He decided to rectify that. "Is he involved with the Devils footy club?" Did not like showing his hand that much to Massie but the man was not a loudmouth.

"This relates to your current case?" A light smile.

Mahoney nodded. "Not central, but there's the odd loose end."

Massie nodded. "Thought as much. Papers have been full of it. Yep, he's in there too. In a big way. Sproule's the puppet on show but Fothers pulls the strings. Admittedly, so I hear from the drums, he masterminded the whole push that turned the AFL Commissioners' minds around. His tentacles stretch across Bass Strait too, it would seem. But guess whose company won the bid for construction of the new stand at Bellerive Stadium?"

Mahoney nodded at the rhetorical question. "Doesn't seem to be much he doesn't do." He definitely wanted to have a good talk to this man who was starting to look like the central point of a few of the radii of the case. May not get anywhere but he itched to have a go at one of the faceless men that Kate had referred to at the cinema café. Even if it meant a few more eggshells would go. What the heck; no use shuffling along on your knees. He now knew where he would be going straight after the DPP's Office.

"Thanks, Alan. You've been very helpful. Cone of silence and all that."

"Don't fret, John. No fears there." They shook hands. "Seems the Samaritan is going to walk out the pub door with a fresh agenda."

"You could say that." Mahoney clapped the man on the shoulder and turned to leave.

"You'll be heading out with me?"

"Yep. I've stared it down. All good."

CHAPTER 37

Friday 19th March 1pm

Rory Fotheringham walked into the Salamanca Galleria Hotel as if he owned the place. Which he did. The freehold. The accommodation was operated by a national chain which specialized in boutique hotels. It catered to a niche market of discerning travelers who could afford life's luxuries regardless of where things were in the economic cycle. Once through the sliding glass doors he strode across the marble foyer to the stairwell. He preferred to ascend on foot to quicken his pulse for the assignation ahead. On the third level he walked fifteen meters to the double doors of the honeymoon suite and used his access card to let himself in. One of his favorite privileges of membership of that circle of people who never have to ask the price.

As the door swung quietly shut behind him, he detected the sound of a smooth buzzing. He snorted to himself. On the enormous bed lay a beautifully sculptured nude female. She was wearing an eye mask but she was certainly not sleeping. Her right hand held a pink rabbit on low vibration that was rhythmically caressing her breasts. "Perfect timing, Roar. I'm very ready for you."

"So am I. You can turn bunny off now. I have a better way to get you humming." At the end of the bed he quickly discarded his clothes and then knelt to address the wonder of her pubic topiary.

Half an hour later they lay sated on the rumpled sheets. "That was a delectable swansong, Rory. Thank you." The matter-of-fact tone surprised him as much as the content.

"What do you mean by that?"

Jane Watson slid the Cathay Pacific First Class eye mask off and turned her head on the pillow. Eyes like flint.

"Swansong, Rory. As in finale. I'm moving on. It's been fun. Great fun. All good things come to an end. You must know that."

He did. But it was he, the big hitter, who called the shots. There was no sentiment involved. That was never a factor in any of his dealings with people for any reason. And, truthfully, the pleasure was transitory and fitful. Mainly it was a means of exercising power: knowing that females wanted him. It was his ego that he enjoyed being stroked. And here was one of his concubines pulling the pin. Out of nowhere some long ago learned lines of Shakespeare passed his lips: "Therefore, I lie with her, and she with me, and in our faults by lies we flattered be".

Rich sardonic laughter was unexpected. "Oh, please Rory. Not the Bard. You'll be passing yourself off as Othello next." A sly smile. "And we both know, darling, that your true role is Iago."

Bitch. Clever bitch. Sassy, smart and ruthless. In some parallel universe they would make a formidable couple. But not here and now. The best he could hope for was a dignified retreat.

"Perhaps. Anyway, whatever you think is now pretty academic." He rolled off the bed and began to dress. "So, what's your future then?"

"A health and well-being retreat in Bali. I've negotiated a five-year lease on a run-down resort at Sanur. I've lined up a landscape designer to fix up the layout. It's at the end of the main beach; perfect location. Loads of cheap labor to refurbish the rooms to deluxe standard and build the treatment center. The existing restaurant, once upgraded, will double as the cooking school. Might even run writers' retreats in the off-season."

He didn't need to ask how this would be funded. By selling off the local properties, liquidating her bank shares and collecting on her husband's life insurance, there would be plenty of money to throw at the project. Particularly, once you factored in the favorable exchange rates. "Are you going solo? What do you know about this stuff?"

"You'd be surprised what you can learn over a few holidays if you keep your eyes and ears open. There's a lovely expat in Ubud called Janet de Neefe. Runs a couple of divine restaurants and a great cooking school. Even co-ordinates the October Literary Festival. I plied her for information and as I'm operating far enough away she was happy to oblige with lots of ideas from her business model. Seems you can literally hire an extended Balinese family and you instantly have a whole catering corps with a lifetime of local knowledge. And you don't have to pay much more than peanuts. Same goes for the beautiful girls who'll work in the health spa. Ditto for the yoga. Fit-out will cost the most but, as you can imagine, I've gleaned enough from close contacts in the trade to be on top of that. It should be a cash cow really."

"And is it just you in charge?"

She smiled. "I'll have a lovely deputy under me. I think you know Felicity Sproule." She absentmindedly stroked her flat stomach. "She and I get on ever so well. Hardly seems necessary to have men around really."

Now that she was rubbing it in, Rory actually felt better. She was trying to get under his skin but it wouldn't work. He knew manipulation backwards and had lifelong immunity. Not much could dent his armor. "All I would say to you, Jane, is be careful what you wish for."

"I suppose you have to be philosophical in some situations, Rory dear. Like now. But let's not bicker."

"Didn't realize I was. Just a bit of genuine advice, that's all." From his position at the end of the bed, he turned away to leave. Over his shoulder he said, "Leave the room pass at reception. Bon voyage." As he went down the corridor, he started dealing with the message bank on his phone.

CHAPTER 38

Friday 19ᵗʰ March 3pm

In his younger days playing club soccer, Mahoney never fully appreciated the concept of home and away matches. Many of their games were played at neutral venues operated by the Council; others were technically away games but as they were at grounds with much better surfaces then the pitch at his own club, Mahoney's team generally preferred them. Only when he started supporting Liverpool while living in England did he begin to comprehend the enormity of the task facing some teams when they ventured to away games in another stadium. Fewer supporters meant less vocal backing and that really did affect morale. For the Reds, playing home fixtures at the fortress of Anfield could be worth a couple of goals. Many clubs came not to attack but to survive. The venue was crucial.

Policing was much the same. Who did the interviewing and how the interchange was handled definitely contributed to the success or otherwise of an interrogator. But the place was paramount. A plethora of PhD studies factored in to the design and layout of modern police interview suites. All based on the latest psychological research. Mahoney was glad the funding lag in Tasmania meant their interview rooms would still be oddly familiar to PC Snow from *Z Cars*. No see-through windows here! A bit of discomfort never hurt and after a short stint in a holding cell, the starkness of the old-school interview space helped those new to the whole experience to "get a few things off their chest".

Similarly, talking to a witness at a place of their choosing was generally preferable as it helped them to relax and be more forthcoming. Of course, all such rules were flexible and could be jettisoned in different circumstances. But you could be pretty damned certain that the least desirable scenario was to have to go to a venue nominated by a person of interest to interview the aforesaid person at a time of choosing… in the presence of the best criminal solicitor in the state.

So here they were in Rory Fotheringham's office. He and Munro had been there for over half an hour being stonewalled by one of the best in the business. Giles Martinson looked like he'd walked straight out of the Temple Fields barristers' set. Such was his attire – 3-piece navy suit with a faint white pinstripe, crisp white shirt with cufflinks, claret and royal blue striped tie, black brogues, and an affectatious fob watch – that Mahoney was half surprised he was not sporting spats.

As the conversation ground on, it became clearer to Munro that the conclusion was inevitable: they could not lay a finger on this man. Sproule may well have unwittingly implicated Fotheringham in the botched scheme to fix the problem that was Brad Finch but, apart from this, there was no concrete evidence to link the two men. Aside from the obvious fact they would have obviously encountered each other in Hobart's small business community and Felicity Sproule's testimony, there was precious little to connect the two alpha males in any sort of criminal venture. The boys' club had clammed tighter than a crustacean's shell. One would be hard pressed to find any corroboration that they even knew each other.

And now Fotheringham was giving a passable imitation of a barnacle. Munro considered why they were here at all. The case was pretty much wrapped up. Perpetrators and conspirators alike were in custody and the Public Prosecution Service was already assembling a virtually watertight case to bring to court. And Fotheringham was clearly enjoying the show. Martinson was his unflappable best but he must be wondering why the Detective Inspector was persisting with what was palpably a fruitless line of enquiry. But Mahoney did persist. Munro could tell when his boss had the bit between his teeth and he was witnessing it now. Did he have something, anything, up his sleeve? Nothing that Munro was aware of. The only semblance of insight was that when he asked, on the way to Fotheringham's office what their aim was, Mahoney had simply smiled and with his fists made a shaking motion in front of his chest. Go figure, thought Munro.

The only glimmer of a fresh insight sparking was when Fotheringham was asked about his relationship with Felicity Sproule. He blithely admitted to having flirted with her on one occasion. "Had a few to drink so I tested the water. No harm in that, surely. Obviously, I wasn't in her target market."

Before Mahoney was able to tease out what exactly he meant by 'obviously', a quick warning cough from his legal eagle alerted him to the potential peril of his answer so he temporarily clammed up again. On a later run-through of the same material, the same arrogance betrayed him.

"Look, it hardly matters does it? She's flown the coop. Good luck to her. Selfish bitch. Bit of support for her provider wouldn't go astray." So a healthy misogynistic streak lay just underneath the controlled exterior.

Munro made one of his few allotted interjections. "How do you know Mrs. Sproule is not around, Sir?"

A slight hesitation with an accompanying shoulder shrug of false modesty. "Just have my finger on the pulse of things, I suppose."

As that very hand clasps the jugular, thought Mahoney. Right through the interview Fotheringham had played a mostly straight bat to any query his vigilant brief had allowed to be bowled to him. No tension was generated. No further slips emerged. Yet Mahoney kept to his appointed task without looking the slightest bit disheartened. If anything, he appeared to be relishing the subtle clash more than the expert lawyer and his smug client. After a time, Martinson said, "It would seem my client has helped you as much as he is capable, Inspector. Might I suggest he be permitted to resume his busy schedule?"

It could not be so busy if he could indulge an expensive power play in the middle of his afternoon, thought Munro.

"There would seem to be no discernible link between Mr. Fotheringham and the untimely death of Bradley Finch."

Mahoney stood so Munro followed suit.

"Well, we shall just have to agree to disagree there. At this point we shall not be seeking to interview your client again even though I believe he is more intimately linked to this than he is prepared to admit. We'll sort out how his wife's number wormed its way onto Finch's contact list another day."

Munro had never mentally measured a nanosecond before.

"What the fuck? You piece of scum" Rory Fotheringham was up and out of his chair, advancing on Mahoney. Martinson was startled.

"Rory, settle down. I implore you."

Munro tensed himself but Fotheringham halted two steps short of Mahoney.

Spittle flecked his lips as he pointed at Mahoney's chest. "You're just another bitter fucked-up public servant, aren't you?" The snarl brutalized the man's features. "Another nowhere bloke who squats to piss, I reckon. You and your poofy model offsider. Makes me sick. People who make things happen always get shit from losers who can't even put a foot on the ladder." The snarl morphed into a sneer. He was losing steam in the face of the stoic DI. Mahoney simply held his ground. Fotheringham waved an arm and turned back to his desk. "Piss ants, the lot of ya."

Mahoney turned to leave. Munro was delegated the farewell. "Thank you for your time, gentlemen. That was very interesting. A carbon copy of Roger Sproule's initial reaction to us. Another connection, you might say." He then gave the full 100 watt smile and followed his superior through the door.

Munro held his curiosity till they reached the car. "But her name wasn't on Brad Finch's mobile contact list, was it?"

Mahoney smiled as he repeated the earlier gesture. "No, I don't think so. But it certainly rattled his cage. We may never nail the smug bastard but now he's a lot less smug and shiny. And that meltdown will irritate him immensely. Almost as much, to be honest, as it satisfied me. Job done."

CHAPTER 39

Friday 19th March 6pm

Mahoney decided to play along. "Alright, Tim. I give in. Why are you waving your hands in front of your face like that?"

"Just clearing the moths away." A big grin.

"I can just as easily put my wallet away if you like. Your loss." Mock severity.

Munro played his role. "Oh no, Sir. Just kidding."

Kate chipped in. "Just a bit socially excited, Sir. And very relieved, to be honest."

"Fair enough, too. You have both worked bloody hard on this one, and very effectively. The truth of it is, there will be a next time, probably sooner rather than later, and I'll be glad to have you both on board. Until then, enjoy this one."

"Sounds good. I'm thirsty and I've got a leave pass. Our match was postponed till Sunday." Munro rubbed his hands together. "Hey Kate, is Captain Corruption swinging by this evening?" An exaggerated wink.

Kate smiled at the joshing. "If by that do you mean will my new man be making an entry?" She wiggled her eyebrows. "Well, that's my secret, my dear Timothy. But I can tell you he will be joining us soon for a drink."

"Good one. I'm always keen to see what's in fashion for dilettantes this year."

Kate mimed the action of a whip cracking. "Cut to the quick, Oscar. You are sharp tonight. Let me hold my sides in." Grinning all the while.

Mahoney interrupted the sparring. "If you can spare me from the Algonquin Circle for a sec, I've just spied an old colleague. Won't be long. The next few are on me." He sauntered off leaving a fifty dollar note on the dark oak bar. Called to his cobber, "Kevin, how's tricks?" Hand extended.

"John, not bad." Handshake happily reciprocated. Mahoney and soon-to-be-retired Sergeant Kevin Salmon began yarning away in the far corner of the Ocean Child Hotel. Adjacent to the Central Fire Station and a block from Police HQ, it was one of the inner-city pubs that managed to spurn pokies and avoid garish refurbishment. A pub for drinking, talking and the odd game of pool or darts.

Presently, Kate's new dandy appeared. Aside from the rainbow scarf, the most striking feature of his eclectic ensemble was the brown fedora hat atop his head. It appeared that he had shaved his raffish beard with geometrical precision. Reacting to Munro's smirk, he announced, "It's something called style. I don't anticipate everyone will understand." Turning to Kate. "Special K, greetings."

"Don't mind Tim, he's actually a big fan."

Munro rolled his eyes but stayed quiet.

"It seems you have the taste of success to savor. The Beekeeper looks especially chuffed. Mind you, he is with one of the all-time greats, Sockeye Salmon."

Kate glanced in the direction of her boss. "I don't think I've ever seen him laugh like that." There were tears running down Mahoney's cheeks.

Rex hazarded a guess. "Possibly the old chestnut about the body in West Hobart."

"Please explain." Kate asked.

"Well, the guts of it goes like this. Sockeye and the team are called out to check over a corpse that's been found in West Hobart in somebody's house. They give it a quick once over and the body's released to the morgue. End of the shift they're down at the pub and a call comes through from one of the attendants. Apparently there are three bullet holes in the corpse."

Munro was the first to react. "Strewth, what happened then?"

"That's just what I asked at the time." Rex put on a mock-squeaky voice in impersonation of the legend. "What do you reckon, you silly bugger. Finished our beers, took the body back and started taking photos, of course. You a screw loose or something?"

The group dissolved in mirth. It was going to be a good, good night.

*   *   *

What sort of eyes did Bette Davis have? Luminous? Sparkling? Come-to-bed?

He could not truly remember if Kim Carnes ever told him when he used to watch her video clip on *Countdown*. Presumably they were alluring. Or perhaps not. The hook line of the pop song stayed with him but he was unsure if he remembered or even understood the underlying point of the hit single. His old bunch of friends from decades hence, cadets and their girlfriends, had sung it lustily at boozy beach parties but it was now consigned to the past.

And it could comfortably stay there as far as he was concerned. Some memories were just that, snapshots of an era: of a time at the Training Academy when the teenage cadets were relishing the freedom of being out of home and earning money. Sure, the weeks were filled with study, training and a pretty Spartan physical regimen. But the weekends were... well, they were a different matter entirely.

By the summer at the end of the first twelve months of the two-year course, just about everybody was in proud possession of a driver's license and some sort of automobile. While most had borrowed to fund the purchase of a panel van or a sleekish saloon, trainee Mahoney had transferred his savings thus far for a Volkswagen camper van. It certainly did not zip down the highway like the late model cars of his classmates but it was a much better sleeping option for when they reached their favorite camping spots on the East Coast that long, hot summer.

He was seeing a senior high school student from Rosny College whose parents had no objection to her being taken away to surf, swim and whatever "young folks do these days". Lisa was intending to matriculate and go on to university to study commerce. She was smart, confident and keen on Mahoney. He was smart, keen on her and gaining in confidence as the training course progressed. Having learned that following others rendered him a sheep, he trod a slightly different path at the Academy.

Although very competent at high school, he wanted out of the religious education system. The police force provided that. All cadets were required to study some Higher School Certificate classes. Mahoney asked, and was allowed, to be admitted to the courses that would enable him to matriculate and thereby potentially go on to study law. It meant a greater sacrifice of time to hit the books and it probably was not going to enhance his prospects of promotion down the track. But he genuinely enjoyed the rigors of study and this amendment to his cadetship was the clincher that finally got the grudging agreement of his father to permit the sixteen year old to sign up. In an Australian history class at Rosny College he had met Lisa. As the vivacious blonde with a cute, slightly snub nose and a smattering of freckles on her cheeks did not see him as a plodding cadet but a likely boyfriend they hooked up.

That summer break from study and the Academy cemented their friendship. Unlike almost all of their friends, the partnership continued unabated into early adulthood. Both went to the local university campus to study their intended courses. She was full-time and consequently graduated ahead of her partner. When she started work at the Reserve Bank as a graduate economist, the pair decided to purchase an inner-city cottage and live together. They were busy, fairly solvent and very happy. Until the day that John Mahoney brutally discovered that love and trust may be golden virtues but they were not beyond being irreparably tainted.

That particular memory from the past was not one he could leave in a foreign country. The strategy of actually moving to another country did not really help him deal with it. It ate at his insides. It colored his view of emotions and for years it had kept his heart boarded up. The necessity of controlling such an internal rage had meant he became so controlling of his deeper emotions that he was hamstrung in any attempt to foster a relationship with any female who endeavored to be more than a passing interest.

But sitting here now on a comfortably padded chair in the upper level of Mures Waterfront Restaurant, he distinctly felt a shift in his attitude. The case was part of it. Of course it was. Confronting Newman was an exorcism of sorts. And his pursuit of an inconvenient truth was, any false modesty aside, indicative of a fresh resolution he had developed to his role. Dorothy's lion he was not. But was he a Tin Man? Perhaps no longer.

Not with the shining eyes of Susan Hart upon him. She had allowed him to ramble through a potted history of his time in England. A few questions here and there but mainly it was Mahoney doing the talking. He noticed no discomfort in revealing a side of himself very few people glimpsed. And he thought he was an adept listener. She was beautiful to his eyes and he felt he would gladly pursue her through any forest one could name. A door to his inner chamber was easing open and he did not mind the sensation. Not one little bit.

CHAPTER 40

Saturday 20ᵗʰ March 11am

The great and the good were in attendance. Mahoney wished he could avoid irony in applying that epithet to all who had come to pay their respects. He could not. He was not a cynical man but it was beyond skepticism to believe anywhere near this number of people would be attending the funeral if was held in Finch's hometown of Smithton. Or if the deceased had not been a star footballer. Mahoney had arrived early and sat quietly in one of the wooden pews to the side of the church alone with his thoughts. It would be an interesting exercise to ask people as they came in what they actually knew of Finch: beyond his record as a sportsman, that is.

Would they know his parents had already farewelled a daughter, Rosemary, to the grave? Four years older than Bradley, she had lost her life in a horrific car accident the night of her seventeenth birthday. Out with friends on a celebratory spree, she was in the passenger seat as the driver lost control overtaking a truck on a back road. The Falcon lost purchase on the gravel and slammed sideways into a eucalyptus tree at ninety kilometers an hour. When the Jaws of Life truck arrived to enable access to the warped chassis, three dead young people were what had been salvaged. Laughing one second, toast the next.

That had very probably cast a long shadow over Brad's own teenage years. Hadn't Amanda said the father was 'old-school' in the manner of his son's upbringing? Perhaps Mr. Finch had tightened the reins in the hope he wouldn't lose his only other child to youthful shenanigans.

The crucial role of the parents was enduring. Normally, Mahoney eschewed the biographies of sportspeople but recently he had read a compelling book on the recommendation of Sergeant Duigan. The subject of the autobiography was a recently retired Victorian footballer who was, sometimes grudgingly, admitted by supporters of every color to be a genuine champion of the code. The really intriguing aspect of the story, for Mahoney, had been the relationship between the father and son. Growing up, the player regularly received uncompromising feedback from his dad in the form of exhaustive letters. Even though they lived in a stable nuclear family under the one roof, the father believed these critiques would be digested most effectively in this unorthodox way.

Finch Snr must have exerted a similarly strong influence. You didn't walk out of a country town into the big league on the back of pure talent. You needed drive and determination and dedication: characteristics that had been instilled into Finch Jnr. The more the DI learned, the more he fervently wished the young man was still alive. To laugh, to prosper and to inspire people through his efforts on the field of play.

Mahoney genuinely admired those good enough to play top level sport. No time for the prima donnas who seemed to think they were the be-all and end-all of the English Premier League. No regard, whatsoever, for the waster from one club who thought setting off a load of fireworks in the bathroom of his luxury Manchester apartment would be a good laugh. But there was undiluted admiration for Steven Gerrard, the talismanic captain of his beloved Liverpool Football Club. Stevie G was the lynchpin of one of the great moments of football history.

Up there, in Mahoney's mind, with that Japanese Olympic gymnast who took gold at the Tokyo games. Going into the final apparatus, he needed a strong routine culminating in a steady landing. Which he did. That he did it having gone into the rings section with a fractured ankle turned the meritorious into miraculous.

For Mahoney, his great football moment came on a balmy evening in Istanbul in May 2005. By paying way above the odds for Champions League final ticket, he had transformed a package holiday into an abiding memory. At half-time, 3-0 down to AC Milan, it had seemed the night would be a bitter anticlimax. The interval transformed proceedings. There was singing of a kind he had never believed possible. Liverpool supporters, en masse, gave a rendition of "You'll Never Walk Alone" that reduced him to tears. Tears of joy that such spirit could find voice. Who could be afraid of the dark after hearing that? More significantly at the time, there was song elsewhere. As the Liverpool FC players trudged into their change room, they could hear, from along the corridor, opposition players engaging in a celebratory chant. No one should piss on a dead man. Especially, if there are signs of life.

And then the coach spoke. All Liverpudlians discovered what he said as, within weeks, commemorative posters of the inspiring speech appeared in every second pub on Merseyside. The bit that stuck with Mahoney was the coda: "Believe you can do it and we will. Give yourselves the chance to be heroes." The red shirts started the second half as if possessed. Gerrard was a Viking Berzerker. Pundits routinely opined about players who could assert their will upon a contest. When Stevie G rose to power a header into the Milan net, he appeared ten feet tall. As he ran back to position, he waved his arms upwards in such an emphatic manner even St Thomas would not have doubted one of the great comebacks was happening. A legend was forged. Liverpool FC triumphed.

Never before or after had John Mahoney witnessed anything like it. If only such euphoria could be bottled. It transformed Gerrard's career but it also lifted people's lives. Belief in the irrepressible spirit of humans could take many forms.

Alas, Finch's flame would never flicker again.

And here was the assembled throng to mourn his passing. From the beginning of the burial service, it had been glaringly obvious that very few attendees were in any way familiar with the routine of a full Anglican mass. The Cathedral had been made available probably on the condition that a proper air of solemnity be maintained. Mahoney could imagine the Dean refusing to give ground on the principle that this holy place would not be hosting a 'celebration of life' but would be quite prepared for a proper funeral mass to be conducted. St David's was the most prestigious church in the diocese and should be treated accordingly. Perhaps the Dean knew deep down that it was a convenient site to maximize exposure that drove the decision to hold the service there. Regardless, whoever organized the 'event' had not reckoned with the decorum demanded by the Cathedral. No cameras inside or even on the precinct at all.

The complete memorial service or none at all.

It proved to be a bit much for some of the players from the Devils, particularly the one in a flash new designer suit and dark glasses perched on his coiffured exuberance of hair. After about ten minutes he was staring around the stone walls looking for stimulation. A bit later he hazarded a wink at Amanda Pattison who was seated across the aisle. She shot him a look that could have frozen lava. He blushed and turned away, the moronic grin binned for now.

The congregation slowly acceded to the cadences of the traditional service. If there had been any intention for it to be hijacked by anybody looking to publicize the club or their political prospects then they received a rude shock as the Dean drew his homily to a close. "At the request of Mr. and Mrs. Finch there will be no eulogy given today. I have spoken of the goodness their son exhibited in his life. It is their preferred wish, and one that I fully respect, that their son be commemorated without fanfare. That he be remembered in our hearts for the good man he was."

And so, half-an-hour later, the time came for the six pall-bearers to carry the coffin down the long central aisle to the rear exit, and then into the waiting hearse. No favorite songs of the deceased. No pieces of memorabilia placed on the coffin. Old school and all the better for it, thought Mahoney as he too exited the cathedral with all the others.

Proceedings at the Hobart cemetery were conducted in exactly the same vein. Absolutely no fuss and not the slightest deviation from the official order of service. Mahoney stood a few meters back from the family as the Dean intoned the opening words, "Man that is born of woman, hath but a short time to live, and is full of misery. He cometh up, and is cut down like a flower; he fleeth as if it were a shadow, and never continueth in one stay". So not the happy-clappy version then. It was a sad occasion: a remorseful day. As it was meant to be. And it was fitting.

At the end, Finch's parents thanked the church officials and then abruptly left for their car. They looked devastated, as well they might. Two children lost in the beginning of their prime. Who could feel like making small talk in such a circumstance.

The remainder of the crowd stood around wondering what to do. Mahoney could see AC Newman in close conversation with Rory Fotheringham and the Minister for Sport, Bill Rhode. Stuff it, he thought, why not stir the pot a bit. He walked over.

"Gentlemen, a moving service, don't you think?"

"Who are you?" Rhode blurted out.

Newman smoothly announced, "This is Detective Inspector John Mahoney, the investigating officer on the homicide case."

Rhode's reputation for not standing on dignity surfaced quickly. "So you're to blame for this mess?"

Mahoney had expected some niggle but not from this quarter. "What do you mean by that? I thought it was a fine memorial to the young man."

"Piss off. You know what I'm getting at. Dragging all and sundry into your little witch-hunt. You've scuppered a few good men with your vigilante shit."

"*A Few Good Men*. Good film. Didn't the mouthy one in that show himself as the most evil prick of the lot. Is this a hint I should be looking at you as well?"

Rhode looked daggers. He turned to Newman. "Tell your mutt to heel. He's pissing down my leg."

"Shut up, Bill," Fotheringham said in a voice short on volume but high on menace. "DI Mahoney did his job. We don't necessarily like where it took him but that's as it is."

Newman suddenly needed to speak to Commissioner Phillips and slid off. Rhode looked like he'd been pistol-whipped. "What are you sticking up for him for? Bloody filth."

Fotheringham took the politician's arm just above the elbow. The grip made Rhode wince. "Listen to me very carefully. I can see you're tetchy. Two hours without a drink is a long time for you. I understand that. But I wouldn't be alienating this guy if I was you." The grip released. "Now shuffle off and badger someone else. The adults need to talk." There was nowhere to go here so Rhode followed the instruction.

If this little scene was intended as a show of strength, it didn't do much for the detective. "You don't need to belittle people on my account."

"I didn't. Damage limitation. Don't need a loose cannon going off right now. His nose is out of joint because none of the pollies or footy people got to speak today. He'd promised some good PR time to a few people. The Finches pulled the rug on that by insisting on a fair dinkum service without the gloss."

"You knew that was their intention?"

"Yep."

"And you didn't share that information?"

"Nope"

The mushroom strategy. Keep them in the dark and feed them fertilizer. Mahoney mentally tipped his hat to the Fixer. A complete and utter bastard but a very effective one. "I hear you're stepping into the President's chair now Roger Sproule is unable to carry out his duties."

"An interim measure. I've no interest in that role beyond the time it takes to find a suitable replacement. Won't be easy seeing as Doc Randall has also withdrawn from the executive. We'll find someone."

"I'm sure you will. A few casualties but I somehow doubt it is a mortal blow for the club."

Fotheringham cricked his neck. "No, it won't be. Nor will the absence of Finch, to be honest. The club is bigger than that." He looked away to the burial plot. "Life can be very random. Being emotional about it strips you of the little control we have of our own destiny. Cop the worst on the chin and move on, is what I say."

Easy to say if you're standing above ground. "Very stoic."

"Not really."

"How do you mean?"

"That's not exactly what the original Stoics believed. They believed passion should be rigidly subdued right enough. But they also held that the highest good was virtue. I doubt you believe that of me, Inspector."

"I stand corrected. Yes, that Roman philosophy has been corrupted by modern usage. Not as much as our view of anarchists but still you're right. In both respects."

Fotheringham smiled. "My pedantry and that virtue, for me, is just something you make of necessity."

"That's about it, yeah. Though I would say there's more passion surging in you than you let on."

"And you'd be right. Can we walk for a bit? There's a short trail over to Cornelian Bay. Do you have time?"

"I do. And you? What about the wake?"

"Cancelled. The Finches didn't want to know. Reckoned it would just be full of cameras and pissed hangers on. They're driving straight home to Ulverstone. Can't blame them really."

"Ah, I see."

They had reached a wooden bench placed on the riverside promontory overlooking the water. "Sit for a bit?"

"Sure." Doubtful that this man needed to get some guilt off his chest.

"I want a brief period not surrounded by babbling fools. And you're not one of them. Saw that in my office."

"And I saw raw emotion erupt for a moment."

"Touché. I do have emotions. Everyone does. But I'm not a slave to mine. If they surface, on rare occasions, they're tucked away pretty quickly. Yesterday's done and dusted. Move on. Don't make the mistake again, then move on. Regrets are a waste. You can never, ever, repeat the past. That was Roger's problem."

What did this man know? "How so? Seems he was a doer to me."

"Yeah, he dragged himself out of nowhere. I don't reckon he ever got over his first romantic crush. A girl left him when he was younger. Went off to Sydney to be a model. Took up with a rugby international rep who worked in finance. Private school background, flash car, apartment on the beach at Manly, the works. Seems to me all Roger accomplished, and it was a fair bit, was designed to ensure that wouldn't happen to him again."

So this was the original chip on the shoulder, thought Mahoney. "And you think that when it did occur the wheels came off?"

"Yep. Couldn't handle his wife giving her heart to a younger man. Ego, self-esteem, arrogance, call it what you like. Passion overrode his mental faculties. In the end, he couldn't see that what he was needed to be divorced from how others saw him."

"And you can do that?"

"Easy. The bit of me I let others see is the bit that makes sure they tow the line. Beyond that I don't care if there's no love lost. My satisfaction comes from turning the wheels that get things done." His arm stretched up towards the Queen's Domain. "Things like that stadium. That stuff doesn't happen without the sort of dealing most people would shy away from. It's a greater good."

"And that justifies any means?"

"Good try. I know you suspect me of orchestrating things behind the scenes. As you've discovered, there is no provable link from any of that train wreck to me." Fotheringham stood and walked off a couple of paces. Turned. "Now whether that's because I'm innocent of any wrongdoing or untouchable, I'll have to leave for you to run over in your busy mind."

Mahoney lifted himself off the bench. "Yes, leave it with me. All it needs is one dogged cop who won't let it go. And that's me, I'm afraid. So despite Newman's, or whoever's, best efforts, I reckon we'll be seeing each other again one day."

CHAPTER 41

Tuesday 23rd March 10am

The two detectives waited patiently for their coffees in the outdoor seating area of T42. Named for the latitudinal line that ran across the island state, it was their favorite café bar on the waterfront. Not even the starkly hewn monstrosity at the northern end of Hunter Street could totally ruin the aspect from this spot on a sunny day. The apartment hotel was truly a blight on the landscape. Mahoney surmised that the designer had been told to completely ignore the architectural heritage of the remainder of a street which encompassed the sympathetic development of a former jam factory into an award winning hotel and the UTAS School of Art.

That must surely have been the case. Otherwise how would anybody have thought a seven-story toilet block was appropriate? Perhaps the architect had not visited the site. Apparently, that was the case with the equally hideous Grand Chancellor Hotel adjacent to it on Davey Street. What must visitors approaching the city through this gateway think? That Oedipus had sketched the plans? Mahoney was pragmatic regarding development of the waterfront precinct: investment was essential in such a moderately sized economy but why did it have to be so jarring to the naked eye.

Lattes now in front of them, the waitress back inside the restaurant and the surrounding tables empty, Kate was eager to discover why her superior had convened this informal meeting. To all intents and purposes the Finch case was wrapped up and in the capable hands of the Public Prosecutor. Roger Sproule would certainly be serving a custodial sentence as would Ronny Coutts. How Cartwright, Owen and Knapp would go after their turn in the courtroom was more problematic but essentially real justice would be served on the main perpetrators of the crime. The ones they could construct a verifiable case against at least.

"Thanks for the coffee. And I'm glad to be out of the office but why are we really here?" Kate was curious. She knew the Beekeeper had been working the phones the day before and using up more than his fair share of the midnight oil.

Mahoney stirred in a carefully measured spoonful of sugar and took out his notepad and pencil, placing them on the table. "There's a strand from the homicide that is still dangling in the wind. And you know I'm not one for untidiness." She smiled at the acknowledgement.

Kate asked, "But the impression I got from Tim was that Fotheringham would remain out of our reach. Not so much because of the influence but because his tracks were covered."

Mahoney nodded. "Regrettably that's correct. Despite our best efforts, anything we suspect him of is, at the absolute best, circumstantial. No, that is probably a dead end. I'm thinking outside the square of the main case. Do you remember the visit to Jane Watson at Tranmere?"

Kate could not but recall it. Flint would be softer. "Yes, to the black widow, so to speak."

"That is quite apt. The person I thought she may be exhibiting more grief for was her husband, Max Watson. Do you know at all how he died?" She shrugged. Could hardly be blamed for it not registering a blip on her radar. "That's understandable, given nobody considered his death to be suspicious at the time."

Kate drew in. "But now you think it might be, given her involvement, sort of, in the Finch investigation?"

"You're partly right. I'm suspicious but not because of her link to Larry Owen: that is a tangent. It's because she struck me as so completely callous when we spoke to her. A few things nagged at me, once I got to thinking about them. Bit of background first: in a nutshell, he was a builder working on a new construction at Acton. One morning, while doing some excavating by himself he was bitten by jack jumpers. The resultant anaphylactic shock was fatal. A tragic accident, seemingly."

"Seemingly? Pretty hard to plant jack jumpers in a particular spot." Kate hoped her disbelief did not register in her voice. He must have more.

Mahoney was undeterred. "And you'd be right. Fiendishly difficult. But hear me out." He took a sip and continued. "What I'm suggesting is again a complete hypothetical but an intriguing one. Autopsy notes suggest nothing unusual in the circumstances of the death apart from the very fact that it is unusual. Do you know why?"

Kate thought she did. "Like on QI last night. You know the Stephen Fry thing. The TV panel show." He did. It was hard to avoid the ubiquitous host these days. "There was a question about poisonous spiders in Australia. Apparently deaths are few and far between now due to advances in serums. So I guess the same is true for other insect bites. At risk people have epi-pens. My cousin does. She has one at home and one at her school."

"Yes, exactly. When I read about the death in the paper weeks ago, I thought it odd that the poor man hadn't tried to use one. So there's one thing. And once I spoke to various people who attended the scene a few other oddities surfaced." He opened his pad revealing a neat sketch of a house site. "This is an approximation of the site where Watson was working that day."

He pointed to the page. "The body was discovered next to his vehicle by a bloke delivering a load of tiles. Given the amount of freshly dug earth near the bobcat, presumably he'd been excavating. Most likely for a pool. That's what the plans show. One of the police officers had a look-see a bit later and found a good-sized nest of the venomous little critters. So one can safely assume that's where he was bitten."

"So he races to the utility to get his epi-pen. But it's not there. He's forgotten it or whatever and he tries to phone for help."

"That's the logical conclusion. He was unlucky that his battery was drained. Help probably wouldn't have arrived in time anyway. He had quite a few bites on his forearms. And that would normally be it."

"But?"

"Someone tried to be a bit too neat. Bit too calculating. Are you with me?"

Kate was now very interested. "Yes, Jane Watson. But how?"

The waitress re-emerged and Mahoney ordered two more of the same and requested a carafe of water. Kate took the opportunity to use the toilet. Upon her return, the requested drinks were in place.

"Thank you." She sipped some water. "Jane Watson?"

"Right. You'll need the sequence of events a bit clearer. The delivery guy discovers the body. Calls for the ambulance and our boys. They both arrive within twenty minutes. The paramedics determine they're too late: nothing they can possibly do. The attending officer calls it in to make sure everyone is covered. The medical examiner eventually gets there as does Mrs. Watson. Her name was listed as next of kin on the emergency card in his wallet. So far all as per normal. Agreed?"

Kate nodded. "Perfectly. A death in slightly unusual circumstances so all concerned stick to procedure. As you say quite normal. What's the sting?"

"Sweet Lady Jane, to corrupt Mick and the boys. Here's what the ambulance officer and Senior Constable Douglas both agree on." He proceeded to tick off on his fingers. "One: she gets from Tranmere to Acton in police pursuit time. Two: at the body she does the full final act of a tragedy anguish. Three: she has to take a fair while to compose herself before she can even speak. Now, does that match with the woman we met at Oceana Drive?"

"Not in the slightest. She must have been whacking it on. Sounds like a parody of despair. So that's spooky. What else?"

"Something she didn't have to do at all, when you think about it. The ambo guy remembers her going off to the far side of the building to have a few quiet moments. Fair enough. Then she comes back around, wanting one of the police officers. Says she's perplexed. Shows him the electricity meter box. Right there is an epi-pen. This is where he knew it would be, she says. Why didn't he just come and get it. It would have saved him. Cue more tears. And why indeed didn't he grab it?"

Kate waited for a few suits to pass by on their way to a stylish new restaurant at the end of the quay. "Because it wasn't there. She'd just replaced it."

"Most likely. And that's what's odd."

"How so? Because it throws up other questions?"

"Yes, I think that's the problem. She need not have alerted anybody to the hidey-hole. She could simply have said that her husband usually carried one with him and he must have forgotten or something. Play dumb. But she can't. She's shrewd so she believes she has to play cunning. I'd bet that there was usually an epi-pen in that meter box. A fairly secure spot that's readily accessible. You'd always know it's there no matter what car you bring etc. One day she takes it away hoping for just such an eventuality as occurred. If it's ever noted as missing by her husband he'd hardly think to ask her, just assume it's been nicked."

"Would others know it's there or should be there?"

"Possibly, but that still doesn't impinge on her method. All she has to do is plead ignorance of what he did to ensure his safety on site and that would be credible. But, and it's a great but, she wants to have a clever finish so she surreptitiously replaces the epi-pen. Too clever by half. In seeking to muddy the waters, she overplays her hand and casts suspicion where it need not have been. If she'd acted in character, i.e. calmly, at the scene and not 'found' the epi-pen, nobody would think to question the death. Unusual, yes, suspicious, no."

"So her plan comes to pass as she'd hoped. With the element of random luck, there doesn't seem much we can prove."

Mahoney leaned back in his chair. "That's what I told her."

Kate was momentarily taken aback. "When was this? You've interviewed her?"

"Not formally. I worked through the possible scenario last night and this morning we met at the Acton site."

"You and the Watson woman? No one else?"

"That's right. Man versus Amazon. There's no point in bringing her in because a juggernaut could fit through the holes in any case we could construct. I just wanted to let her know we knew." He paused to finish his glass of water. "And to let her know exactly what I thought of her. In no uncertain terms."

"So without another officer you don't have to worry about one of us feeling obliged to lie about you calling her a scheming bitch." Kate smiled at her superior. There was a wide streak of passion beneath his cool exterior after all. "How did she take it? Bit like Fotheringham?"

"No, true to former type. Played a cool hand but she was not happy to face her duplicity."

EPILOGUE

Friday 26th March

And so here he was, standing on the old wooden jetty at Gordon. The wharf was shaped like an elongated capital block T and, on a fine day, plenty of recreational anglers would perch on the grey railings while every so often pleasure craft tied up for a time to allow people to disembark or embark.

Today Mahoney was relieved to be the only presence on the baulking, weathered frame. The soft-dying day suited his present mood. The high banks of light grey clouds that loomed overhead were turning the body of water in front of him a steely hue. Behind him, the mellow sun was retreating behind the thickly wooded hills. He gazed out upon the D'Entrecasteaux Channel to the green patchwork quilt of paddocks on Bruny Island. Like the East Coast, the nomenclature of this area was testimony to the remarkable vagaries of history. Captain Bruni D'Entrecasteaux had sailed into this body of water and then up the East Coast of Van Diemen's Land.

Dutch mariners led by Abel Tasman were the first Europeans to hit the island in the seventeenth century. Seeking warmth and valuable spices, they showed little subsequent interest: too cold, too bleak and too far south. In the latter half of the next century the two superpowers either side of the English Channel had jostled for control of Terra Australis. Playing out a smaller version of the larger theatre of conflict in the Old World, Captain James Cook, on his third antipodean voyage of discovery, had landed at Adventure Bay on the eastern side of Bruny Island.

Mahoney wondered if Cook or D'Entrecasteaux or Tasman felt anything like the sense of wonder ascribed to the Dutch sailors who encountered the New World of the Americas for the first time. Not too much would be dissimilar if they cruised the sound now. Sixty kilometers from Hobart, there was some signs of habitation and domestication of the environment but mostly what one saw from the water was swathes of eucalyptus trees interspersed with patches of green fields. With a bright sun on a clear day, the reflection of the landscape on the water was so clear as to seem almost real. A parallel landscape.

So much akin to Mahoney's experience. The world the majority of people witnessed was seemingly characterized by regularity, order and fairness or at least a show of it. But the reflection the detectives worked in was a chimera: it disguised dark cold depths where accountability, integrity and compassion were treated as punchlines for a series of sardonic jokes. Mahoney acknowledged the inevitable existence of the parallel world: he dealt with the corruption, violence and deception almost every day. He could not change it.

If history demonstrated anything, it was that the human condition tended just as much toward dysfunctional dystopia as any Arcadian utopia. But he would not ever begin to believe that that should be the natural order of things. This just required him to wade in the mucky shallows and murky depths of his society but that had to be done to ensure many people could enjoy some cleanliness in a normal world.

He had decided to press on as a detective. He was drawn to the battle. And, moreover, he was relishing life. There were prospects.

Now he was in the present it was time to experience a "season of mists and mellow fruitfulness".

ABOUT THE AUTHOR

SJBrown (Stephen John Brown) resides in Tasmania where the D.I. Mahoney series is set. His passion for crime fiction determined his choice of the police procedural format as a means of exploring the challenges of modern life. A former teacher and sports coach, he drew on his travel experiences and observations of Australian society for the writing of HIGH BEAM. The sequel to this debut novel, DEAD WOOD, is to be published in early 2015. Negotiations for the production of a TV series set in the Apple Isle have commenced.